VENGEANCE STREET

LOUISE SHARLAND

BLOODHOUND
— B O O K S —

www.bloodhoundbooks.com

Print ISBN: 978-1-917214-04-9

For my family, and all those who advocate for the less fortunate in our society

Beloved, never avenge yourselves, but leave it to the wrath of God, for it is written, "Vengeance is mine."
Romans 12:19

1

It has not taken long for you to find the three lads huddled behind the bus shelter, passing the joint between them. You inch closer, pretending to be reading the bus timetable, but really you're focusing your attention on the tallest of the three. He's well built, with shiny, slicked-back hair, and a tattoo of a crucifix that edges past his wrist and onto the back of his hand. They're all dressed for a night out: crisp white shirts, black jeans, and leather trainers with designer logos that reflect the headlights of oncoming cars. You check your watch. *Still early.* From experience, you know it will be another hour or so, another trip to the off license for some cheap rum and a bottle of Diet Coke.

It's nearly ten by the time they finally stumble their way to the harbourfront. It's a bank holiday weekend, and the crowds are out in droves, the queue outside The Dolphin winding its way past the chip shop two doors down. By the time you make it inside they've already finished their first round and are ordering a second. You settle yourself in a far corner, and you watch.

For the next two hours the lads ricochet between mellow and hyper, jostling the Chinese students who are quietly introducing themselves to a pint of scrumpy, or eyeing up the locals who have made it in for 2-for-1 ladies' night. You're about to leave, when you notice a small blonde with dark slashes for eyebrows struggling on her way to the bar. The shiny-haired boy marks her approach with a grin, downs his shot, and signals to the bartender for two more. He gives his mates the nod, and they clear off, leaving him to it. The girl smiles shyly as he pulls up a bar stool and helps her on, all the time giving her a greedy once-over. It's as if you're watching one of those wildlife programmes where they film the shark circling the sea lion. No matter what the outcome, human intervention is forbidden. *Nature, after all, must be allowed to take its course.*

A while later, outside, the breeze feels cool against your back as you follow them into the darkness. Streetlights glimmer in the harbour, opposite the cobblestoned alley where the boy has led her, where there are no cameras. Her back is against the wall, and he is pushing up against her. She puts both hands on his shoulders.

'Got a condom?'

'You kiddin' me?'

'Won't do it without no condom.'

'It'll be fine, I promise.' His voice is soft, persuasive, but there's an edge to it now. He slips one hand between her thighs, and begins pulling up her (fake leather) miniskirt with the other.

'Don't!'

'What do you mean, don't?'

'Stop it!' She sounds frightened, like a little girl.

'Come on, baby, don't fight.' She tears at his designer shirt. A button pops and spirals to the ground, bouncing off the uneven stone. 'This shirt cost me a hundred quid!' He gives her a shake, and then slams her against the wall, her head hitting the bricks with a soft thud.

'Get off me!' she screams, and in a moment of inspired desperation she stabs her stiletto heel into the toe of his trainer. You see him stumble, and to your surprise watch as she pushes him away so ferociously that he topples backwards onto the pavement.

Good girl.

Kicking off her heels the girl runs barefoot into the night, her cries echoing the squawks of the ever-present seagulls.

You hear footsteps and slip into a dark alcove just as two long shadows appear.

'Like a girl wif spirit,' says one.

'Don't take no shite,' says the other.

'What'd the message say?'

The larger of the two – bald, six feet plus, and at least twenty stone – checks his phone for the text message you sent only minutes before. 'Says to make it tidy, not like last time.'

The other – short and tight, ready for a fight – laughs. 'Reckon we can do that, don't you?'

Ahead of them a shaky silhouette struggles to his feet. The two shadows move towards him.

'Like to pick on helpless girls?' one of them says.

'Make you feel like a man?' says the other.

'Piss off,' the boy replies, dusting dirt off his skinny jeans.

'That's no way to talk to your elders,' says one.

'Your betters,' says the other.

'Why don't you just mind your own fucking business?' replies the boy, squaring up.

The first punch sends him flying. His jaw smashes onto the cobbles, teeth shatter. There is a kick in the chest, then another, the sound of splintering ribs, and red foam on his lips.

'That'll do,' says the small one. 'Don't want no first degree on my sheet.'

The larger one hitches his trousers up past his belly button. 'Me neither. Fancy a pint?'

You wait until they're gone, and slowly make your way out of the darkness. The boy has tried to crawl his way towards the light, but has only made it as far as a small inlet used by fishing boats to unload cargo. He's collapsed into a tangle of nets, his shallow breathing overlapping with the soft slap of water against stone. He looks up, his eyes unfocused and unsure. Small mewing noises are coming from his bloody and ruined mouth. His eyes widen in recognition. He tries to speak, mouths something desperate, indecipherable. You lean in closer.

'Like the water?' you whisper, before slowly tipping him into the harbour.

2

The high-risk interview room has a particular smell. A mixture of sweat, stale air, and used fat from the tapas bar across the street. I keep a bottle of Neal's Yard breath spray, Mint & Lemon, in my back pocket, and I often give it a little spritz just before I start the interview.

'What's that smell?'

I'm waiting for my first client of the morning – Michael Fellows, a convicted rapist – to take his seat. 'Good morning, Michael. My name is Grace Midwinter. I'm your new probation officer. Please sit down.'

'What's that fucking smell?'

I decide to take a few minutes to let the silence do its job. The trick is not to give them the opportunity to get a handle on you. Reacting too quickly; a raised eyebrow, a tightening of the voice, is always a mistake. It makes them think they can work you, push your buttons. The trick is to remain neutral, calm, and when necessary, absolutely silent. I wait until he's seated, and I've counted ten ticks from the clock on the wall above his head, before continuing.

'Let's get to it shall we?' I glance at the notepad on the desk in front of me. 'As you were convicted of a serious sexual assault, it's my job to gain a clearer understanding of your current level of sexual preoccupation before we can put together a realistic risk management plan.' He yawns indifferently. 'This may involve asking you a few rather difficult questions.' I glance up and am struck by how handsome he is: strong jawline, high cheekbones, movie star looks. 'So, Michael,' I hold eye contact, 'how many times a day do you masturbate?'

That's got his attention.

He doesn't answer. I give a tiny huff of frustration. I still have two drug dealers and an arsonist to deal with before lunchtime. I scan my scribbles taken from his electronic case file five minutes before. I take in the sketchy case notes, and unsigned consent to share information forms. *What was his last PO thinking?* I clear my throat.

'Did your previous probation officer tell you the reason for these questions?' He gives me an inscrutable shrug. 'Well then, let me try and explain it to you.' I'm conscious he is only booked in for a half hour slot, and so far it has been very slow going. 'A lot of what we do in probation services is based around reducing the risk of re-offending. That's why I'm asking you these questions about how you spend your time, where you go, what you're thinking and doing, particularly regarding... inappropriate sexual fantasies.' A slight smirk plays at the corner of his mouth, and I find my patience fading like shadows in sunlight. 'In your case this could be viewed as a significant risk.' I don't need to say much more. Michael knows from experience how one wrong step will result in an immediate recall to prison.

I hear a loud grumbling noise and realise it's his stomach. It sounds like he missed breakfast, and lunch at the bail hostel is always an uncertain thing. I reach into my briefcase and bring out the sandwich, crisps, and Diet Coke I bought myself for lunch less than an hour ago. 'You look starved. When was the last time you had anything to eat?' His eyes meet mine finally, and for the first time I see the true extent of his uncertainty and fear. I slide the food towards him. 'Go on.'

I return my attention to my notes. 'As I understand it, one of the actions you agreed with your previous PO was to attend AA meetings. How's that been going?'

'Okay,' he says, through a mouthful of ham and cheese.

'I also see that you're interested in taking part in the restorative justice programme.'

He takes a sip of his drink.

'While I was inside, you know, I got to thinking.' There's a lot of time to think when you spend twenty hours in a ten-by-twenty-foot room. 'What happened with Chantal. I want to try and do something about it.'

'That's good, Michael.' I could dash his hopes by telling him that the programme is primarily aimed at bringing low-level offenders together with their victims to try and explore what has happened, its impact, and what they need to move forward. Rape is a far more complex issue. 'You know that for it to work she'll need to agree as well.'

'I know.'

'And probably her family, too. From what I hear they made quite a scene at your trial.'

'Don't matter,' he says. 'I deserved it.'

'It'll take a while.'

'I'll wait as long as it takes.' He looks at me with such sincerity that I just about believe him, but this isn't his first offence, and it might not be his last. 'I know I can't make up for what I've done,' he continues, 'but at least I can try and take some responsibility.'

I sit back and study him closely. *Is he shitting me?*

'I'm really pleased to hear that, Michael.' If he's genuinely committed to his rehabilitation this early in the process, I may have a very successful outcome indeed. If not, he'll be back inside before you can say *prison transport*. 'I'll see what I can do to support you with this.'

He gives me a broad, open smile that I reckon will just about make my day.

'And how are things with your move-on from the bail hostel?' No point in softly, softly; it does them no favours. 'You know you won't be able to move back in with your mum and stepsister, don't you?'

'Don't need to,' he says, gulping down the last of the drink. 'I'll be moving in with my new missus.'

My eyes travel to my notepad. Was there anything in his case notes about permission to cohabitate?

'You can't just move in with anyone,' I remind him gently. 'You have to get permission.'

'From you?'

I nod. 'But I'm pretty reasonable.'

'Not what I heard.' His tone is light, playful.

I smile in response. Being hard-nosed has its moments, but compassion works too.

'I've got a few ideas of how we can support you with what is already excellent progress on your part.' Michael looks pleased. 'Along with your resettlement courses, maybe some practical skills training.'

His expression is genuine, open. The mood in the room has eased, softened. Now we're really going to get somewhere.

3

I'm just making my way back from lunch when I hear the ping of an incoming text. It's from my line manager, Senior Probation Officer Simon Ellison.

> Urgent comms meeting. Briefing room pm.
> Don't be late!

'Dammit,' I mutter. It's two minutes to. I take the back stairs two at a time and find myself racing towards the briefing room. Stealing my way through a set of squeaky fire doors I manage to secure a seat in the back corner. The tension in the room is palpable. Unscheduled communications meetings mean something is up. *Is it more funding cuts, job losses, the death of a colleague?*

'Good morning, everyone,' says Simon. He's medium height, with nondescript features, and sandy-coloured hair that has the tendency to flop into his eyes. 'Apologies for the short notice, but the Police Protection Unit has requested this meeting to update staff regarding a recent situation.' The Police Protection Unit, or PPU, is normally comprised of one or two constables seconded to probation services. They have links to the

Immediate Response or Management of Sexual or Violent Offenders Team, and step in when things get nasty. 'However,' continues Simon, his tone putting my nerves on edge. 'Due to the serious nature of the situation a member of Plymouth CID will be leading the briefing. I'm delighted to say that one of our very own, a former PPU officer himself, has joined us today.' I feel my stomach lurch. I have a feeling I know what's coming next. 'Let's give a big welcome home to our very own Detective Inspector Alex Treglann.'

A few of my colleagues applaud jokingly, but I gently ease my chair further back into the corner. DI Treglann takes centre stage, slips off his jacket and lays it over the back of his chair. He is tall and slim, in a long-limbed way. His dark hair is close cropped with a few distinguished flecks of grey. He has intense brown eyes. His gaze catches mine, and for a furious moment I think I might blush.

'Thank you.' His expression is grim. 'It is great to be back at Tamar House, and to see so many familiar faces. Unfortunately, a visit from CID usually means a serious crime has taken place.' He picks up a remote control from the desk, and the whiteboard behind him glows into life. 'As you're all probably aware, there've been a number of assaults in the city over recent months.' On the screen in front of us are the photos of two young men. Both have been badly beaten. 'To your left, we have Robert Lawson, found unconscious on the morning of 9 February. He has had dealings with the police for a history of domestic violence and common assault, as well as a number of minor possession charges.' He clicks the remote to highlight the second image. 'Victim number two, Darren Murphy. Released from Dartmoor Prison in March of this year for aggravated assault. He attacked a shop assistant, who had caught him lifting some cut-price brandy. Fractured her jaw.' There's a slight murmur of disapproval from the group, but he continues undaunted. 'Sometime during the early hours of 15 April, he was beaten up and locked inside a skip on Union Street for nearly twenty-four hours. CCTV was out of order that night.' Treglann pauses and surveys the room. 'I know what you're all thinking, but these were still serious crimes. Murphy is lucky to be alive. Lawson lost the sight in his left eye. This brings me to our current situation.' He clicks the remote once again. The arrest photo of a young man glowers at us from the screen. 'Nicky White.' There is a collective groan. Twenty-two-year-old Nicky White is the youngest member of a notorious Plymouth crime family. Treglann raises his hand for silence. 'I know you've probably all had the pleasure of working with a member of the White family at one time or another, particularly his mum Cath, but let's stay focused, shall we? Our friend Nicky was out with some mates on Saturday night. He and the lads did their usual pub crawl and ended up at The Dolphin.' He clicks the remote, and an electronic map of the harbourside area of Plymouth comes into view. 'From witness reports it appears that sometime after 1am, White left the pub with a young woman, and never returned.'

'Sorry to interrupt, Alex,' says Simon. 'Couldn't it be that he's sleeping it off somewhere?'

Treglann scrutinises the senior probation officer. 'I wish that were the case, Simon, but unfortunately Nicky's body was discovered at 5 o'clock. this morning floating face down in Sutton Harbour.' He pauses to let the news sink in. 'Cause of death has not been confirmed, but it appears that he was badly beaten.' There is a sudden silence in the room. 'I'm sure you all know what this means. Every member and associate of the White family will be out for blood. There's already been considerable tension between the Whites and other local crime families for months. We're also looking into intelligence, which suggests the family may have been trying to diversify their drug dealing patch into the Stonehouse area of the city.'

'So, a drugs war?' comes a voice from the other side of the room.

'Possibly, but at the moment there's very little to go on. That's why I'm asking you all to consider your guys – their previous form, present status – particularly whether they have any links with the White family. It might even be prudent to call some of them in for interview.' Alex, normally so composed, seems edgy. 'I'm sure you're aware that this is all highly confidential. We'll be making a public statement shortly, but under no circumstances should any of you speak to the press. Thank you.' He gives a quick nod, throws on his jacket, and makes his way to the exit.

I deliberately take my time leaving the meeting room, so I'm surprised to see him waiting for me in the corridor.

'Grace.'

'Alex.' I feel my heart race, for all the wrong reasons. 'How are you?'

He runs his hand across the back of his neck. 'How do you think?'

Colleagues are starting to emerge from a meeting room next door. Alex takes me by the arm and leads me into the empty video conferencing suite opposite.

'Don't you want them to see us together?'

'We've been divorced for more than a year,' he snaps. 'I doubt anyone thinks there's anything going on between us.'

'It was just a joke.' I don't want a row, especially not here. 'Seriously, are you okay? You look awful.'

'Thanks.' He gives a wry grin that reminds me of our daughter, of Jodie. His mobile buzzes, and his expression darkens as he reads the message aloud. 'Initial report suggests cause of Nicky White's death as drowning.'

'But you said he was beaten up.'

'Badly,' he replies, 'but alive when he entered the water. According to the forensic evidence at the scene, it also looks like someone put him there.'

'Jesus.' I automatically scan my mental list of ex-offenders for any who would be capable of such brutality. Something obvious comes to mind. 'They're connected, aren't they?'

'What?'

'The attacks. Lawson, Murphy and now White? Three serious assaults in six months on ex-offenders with a history of violence and sexual offending.'

Alex gives me a look.

'Why don't you leave the detective work to me, Grace?'

'But it can't be a coincidence, can it?'

'We're exploring every angle.' It's clear that's all I'm going to get from him. 'Do you have anything for me?'

'Not really. Nicky was one of my guys at the beginning of the year, but after the workload restructure in February, he was handed over to someone else.'

'Good,' says Alex, and under his breath he adds, 'the less you had to do with that little scrote, the better.' Seeing my surprised look, he quickly changes the subject. 'So, how *is* the happy couple? Is Magnus finding my bed comfortable?'

I rein in my temper, knowing full well that he's trying to goad me.

'His name is *Marcus,* as you very well know, and what business is it of yours how he finds my bed?'

Alex gives me a sheepish look that a few years ago would have won me over. Now, I find it irritating.

'How are things with you and Denise?'

'We're not together anymore.'

'What?'

'Broke up a few months ago. Didn't Jodie tell you?' He

lowers his eyes. 'We were never really right for each other. Not like you and me.'

'It's been a while since there was a you and me, Alex.' The silence stretches out between us, and I find myself grappling to fill the space. 'Is there anything I can do?'

'Oh yeah,' he replies, bitterness clouding his voice. 'You could invite me over to dinner. I could sit at my old dining room table, in my old house, and enjoy a fabulous meal with you, my daughter, and your new boyfriend. That would really cheer me up.'

'For Christ's sake!' I push past him towards the door.

'Grace, wait.' He places his hand firmly on the door, holding it shut.

'You're the one who cheated,' I say, anger overtaking reason. 'You're the one who sacrificed our marriage, our daughter and our life together so that you could screw some twenty-four-year-old.' I've got to get out, before I say something worse. 'Let me out.'

'Grace, I'm sorry.'

'Too late, Alex.' Pushing his hand away, I yank open the door, and stride into the corridor. 'Too bloody late.'

I head towards the toilets, hoping that I won't come across any of my colleagues. I know Alex's affair, and our subsequent breakup, was once a source of office gossip; all those friendly *'How are things?'* and *'How are you coping?'* tinged with the notable aroma of schadenfreude.

I run cold water across the inside of my wrists and pat it on my blazing cheeks. My reflection is alien, ghostlike, my dark hair contrasting starkly with the pale tiles on the wall behind me.

'Why does this have to be so hard?' I mutter to the spectre in the mirror. It was his actions that ended our marriage. Not that things had been going particularly well between us before Denise came on the scene. But I have my limits, and a discovered text with adult content had sent me straight to the solicitors.

I stop by the water cooler at the far end of the office to fill my drinks bottle. Behind me are stationed two PPU constables.

'Useless nonce that Nicky White,' comes a familiar voice. I know at once that the inappropriate comment has come from Ryan Denzies, a PPU officer with more muscles than brains.

'You can't say that, Ryan,' hisses his partner Sian, who's young, bright and has a first-class degree in Psychology.

'Give us a break, Sian. He's got a string of offences as long as my arm. The way he treated the girls he was running.' Ryan makes a sound like he's sucking air through his teeth. 'Beat 'em, got 'em hooked on gear. Some of them underage, too. Better off dead, I reckon, and I'm not the only blue who thinks that.' There is a pause, and I try my best to disappear into the wall of information leaflets beside me. 'You know what they say, don't you? "A bullet only costs fifty pence."'

'Jesus!'

'I'm just saying.'

'Well keep that inappropriate shit to yourself,' says Sian, 'because if you don't it could cost us both our jobs.' Her tone has shifted from good-natured to condemning, and I find myself giving her a tiny internal cheer of approval.

'Don't have a hissy, mate,' snarls Ryan, 'your time of the month, or summit?'

'Fuck off, Ryan.'

I flick the lid shut on my flask with a loud click, and turn to see both officers looking up at me.

'I would suggest you listen to the advice your colleague is

offering, Ryan. Equality, diversity and inclusion guidelines, and all.'

'Yeah, right,' he says. His neck has gone very red. 'It was just a joke.'

I give him a sceptical look, turn, and begin walking back to my desk. 'It's only a joke depending on who hears it, *mate.*'

4

It's after seven by the time I make it home. My schnauzer Bismarck stares accusingly at me through the front window as I struggle with my front door key, a bag of groceries, and a briefcase containing my laptop.

'Bloody Simon,' I mutter. I was just leaving the office, tiptoeing past his half open door earlier, when I heard him call, 'Grace, is that you? Can you pop in for a mo?'

I recognised his tone of false friendliness and gave a great inward sigh. With key staff currently off with long term illness or stress, someone was going to have to take on the outstanding caseloads.

I drop my cargo on the kitchen table and make my way into the lounge. 'Sorry, Bizzy,' I say, not daring to meet those sad, reproachful eyes. From upstairs comes the monotonous boom of heavy bass music.

'Jodie,' I call. When there's no response, I trudge upstairs to my daughter's bedroom. As I enter, I see Jodie, headphones on, scrolling through an online shopping site at dizzying speed. On the bed next to her is an abandoned sketchpad. A box of pastel crayons has been tipped onto the bed, speckling her white cotton sheets with confetti dots of colour. I lift one headphone from her ear.

'Honey?'

She gives me a disinterested glance.

'Oh hi, Mum.' She slips off her headphones, and lets them settle around her neck. 'I'm just catching up on coursework.'

'Have you had any tea?' She shakes her head. On the table next to her is an empty tube of Pringles. 'I texted you and said there was lasagne in the fridge.'

'I'll have some later.'

'And your meds?'

'I'll take them in a minute.'

I close my eyes, and count to three. 'I don't suppose you took Bizzy for a walk?'

'I told you I had coursework.'

I study the laptop screen. 'That doesn't look like coursework, to me.'

'Gimme me a break.' Her tone is typical teenager; a mixture of surliness and incredulity that her actions should ever be questioned.

'I thought you said you've got mocks coming up?'

'I'm on it. I was in the library with Matilda till five o'clock.'

The school library closes at four, but I'm too tired to argue. I reach forward, and gently fold down the laptop lid.

'Here's the score, Jodie. I'm going to take Bizzy for a walk, something incidentally you promised to do when you got home, then I'm going to catch up on some work. I would suggest that you stick that lasagne in the microwave and get on with revising for your other subjects.' From the look on her face, I might as well have been talking to her computer. 'Jodie!'

'Yes, Mum, of course, Mum.' But she has already lifted the lid of the laptop, and is gazing spellbound at the screen.

I head back downstairs and am just reaching for the dog lead when I feel a warm, wet nose rub up against my thigh.

'Sit,' I say, and wait for the dog to obey before slipping on his harness. 'Well at least *someone* does what they're told.'

It's getting dark, so I steer clear of Victoria Park and its memorial benches populated with rough sleepers and junkies, and instead lead Bismarck east along the incongruously named Paradise Place. An eclectic mix of upmarket semis nestled alongside dingy council flats, it exemplifies the diverse and increasingly divergent nature of the town. Crumbling Victorian terraces are being renovated and flipped for a tidy profit at a rate of knots, while a few miles down the road in the North Prospect, a huge social housing rejuvenation project is transforming decrepit post war council houses into investment opportunities for ambitious millennials. You can easily step out of your five-bedroom mini mansion and cross the street to where a slum landlord is exploiting benefit recipients five to the dozen.

Puffing slightly, I make my way up a steep slope past the local community college, opposite which sits Balliol House – an approved premises, or bail hostel, which houses newly released Category A and B ex-offenders, Michael Fellows being one of them. To unsuspecting eyes it's a charming, white-washed Georgian townhouse, but if you look closer, you'll discover CCTV cameras, security staff with panic alarms clipped to their belts, and razor wire discreetly embedded in the fencing that surrounds the internal courtyard.

Crossing at the lights, I follow a tree-lined route that makes a large loop behind the nearby Girls' Grammar School, down Exmouth Lane with its assembly line of care homes and B&B's, and then back again to Penzance Street. As I approach my house, I feel an odd sensation of being watched. I glance around, peering into shuttered windows and the darkened alleyway across the street. Sensing my unease, Bismarck gives a low, steady growl.

'It's nothing, Bizzy,' I say, but still hurry across the street, let myself in, and lock the door behind me.

Once back inside, I get Bizzy settled, grab a quick shower, and reheat the lasagne that Jodie hasn't bothered to eat. Making my way into the lounge, I settle down with a glass of Merlot and my laptop. I log in and click on the electronic case files that Simon has forced on me, I mean *asked if I could help with*. The first is straightforward. GBH, prolific offender, drug related. I make a mental note to contact drug and alcohol services in the morning, as well as child services. If he's using again, it's pretty certain his missus is too. I close the file and open up the second. Inside is a risk management form, which will provide all the key intelligence on the offender, including notes from his previous probation officer. I've seen hundreds in my fifteen-year career and am now adept at speed reading through most of them. In the bottom right-hand corner, someone has typed the letters *DV*. I feel my heart rate quicken. For most of my career, I have specialised in domestic violence and sexual assault cases. Once upon a time, my work with violent offenders was commended as far north as Bristol. There had even been talk of my heading up a specialist unit in Exeter.

'It was all going so smoothly,' I whisper. My cursor hovers for a moment before I click to open the file. I take a sip of wine and begin to read.

Perpetrator: *Mr William (Billy) Vale*
   Age: 24 years old.
   Ethnicity: White British
   Place of residence: Flat 4, 15 Cumerside Avenue, Stonehouse, Plymouth
   Overview of Index Office:

On the evening of 7 January, Mr Vale, after having a verbal altercation with his girlfriend Nicole, struck her in the face, incapacitating her. He then dragged her into the bedroom where he tied her to the bedposts with her tights and proceeded to burn her breasts with the straightening irons he had bought her for Christmas.

I try to shake my feelings of revulsion and frustration at the received sentence of six years' imprisonment, knowing he would have only served half. I consider opening the risk predictor form, where I can access more detailed information on what level of risk the ex-offender poses, all of which has been calculated and presented on a hazard score of one to ten. There was a training session only a few months ago, in which a baby-faced facilitator insisted his software programme could provide an accurate prediction of recidivism within a margin of 1.5%. I can still remember his look of incredulity when the room erupted into gales of laughter.

'Of course, it's all down to a simple algorithm.'

Bismarck looks up in puzzlement, from where he has been dozing. Stifling a yawn, I scan the last bits of information to discover why the unpalatable Mr Vale has been called back into probation, and why I will be interviewing him first thing tomorrow morning.

Incident that instigated recall to probation services:

26 May 19:00 hours.

Ms Baines returned to her flat on Sedgemoor Street after her shift at the Sunnyvale Care Home on Nepean Avenue, to discover four Post-it notes had been placed on her front door by Mr Vale. These notes included pleas for forgiveness and requests to have access to his four-year-old daughter. In these notes, Mr Vale was "seeking to make amends." Ms Baines was understandably distressed. This matter is currently being investigated by her legal team with a view to putting in place a further restraining order.

'Not very bright is our Billy,' I mutter, too tired to put my unconscious bias training into practice. I rest my head on the back of the settee. My eyes flicker shut.

5

Somewhere I hear a sound, a soft thud. I jolt awake. The living room is bathed in the salmon-coloured glow of dusk. My notes lay scattered across the floor, and my neck aches. I check my watch. Nine thirty. I've been asleep for nearly an hour.

'Bizzy?' The dog, clearly agitated, gives a yelp, races into the room, and circles the carpet at my feet. 'What is it?' He barks, runs forwards, and then jumps up, his front paws on the windowsill. Even from this distance, I can see his raised hackles. In my first year as a probation officer, I was followed home by a client. I woke up at two in the morning to find him sitting on my front step, off his face on ketamine, and proclaiming his undying love. That's when I got my first terrier, a bitch called Bella. Unfortunately, she was more likely to lick an intruder to death than attack one, but my love for dogs was firmly established.

I get up and walk towards the window. 'What is it, boy?' I push aside the venetian blinds. A silhouette stands at the front gate. My mind is numb, I'm confused. I watch, helpless, as it turns and begins to walk away.

'Jodie!' I yell, knocking on the window. 'Jodie. Where are you going?'

My sluggish brain kicks into life with a surge of adrenalin. I hurry towards the front door, slip on my trainers, grab the dog lead and harness, and my house keys from the hall table. With trembling fingers, I pull open the door. The night is warm and claggy. A thin layer of mist floats just below streetlight level. I look right to where the road ends, the small turning circle cluttered with parked cars. I see my daughter's slim dark profile disappear down a back alleyway.

'Jodie,' I call. 'Jodie!' But she has her headphones on and can't hear me. The dog yelps in excitement, as I hurriedly slip on his harness, and we make our way into the night. The alleyway is dark and littered with green recycling bins. I step around an abandoned BMX bike, its front wheel warped and twisted. Ahead, I see Jodie turning past a row of garages.

'If she's going to meet that boy again, I will bloody kill her.' Bismarck gives a growl of agreement, and I quiet him with a gentle hush. I quicken my pace just in time to see her cross the road and head into the park. *What the hell is she thinking?* I reach into my pocket and, clenching my keyring, slide the individual keys between each finger. Ahead of me, Jodie is picking up pace. The dog stops to sniff at a tree stump, and I give the lead a gentle tug. She passes the Victorian bandstand, turns right, and heads towards Paradise Place. I follow, dipping in and out of the shadows like a stalker. I pass the bail hostel and keep my head down in the hope of avoiding any of my clients returning in time for curfew. Ahead of me I see a couple arguing, their postures confrontational. I side-step around them and follow Jodie's disappearing figure down a poorly lit path.

Where is she going?

My question is answered as Jodie vaults over a low stone wall, crosses an empty car park, and pulls open the back door of a building. I find myself racing alongside the wall – my vaulting days are long gone – until I find the pedestrian entrance to the car park. Next to me, Bismarck growls.

'Quiet,' I whisper. I gently ease open the back door. 'I'm not quite sure what we're in for.'

Ahead of me is a narrow corridor. To my left, a half-opened doorway presents an empty office. As I make my way forward, I can see the bright fluorescent glow of a large communal kitchen. Coffee cups are tidily stacked on a draining board next to the sink, and a row of tea towels, carefully folded, is laid across an oven door handle. I enter the room with a mixture of curiosity and dread. Jodie, her back to me, is sitting at a table in the far corner. Opposite her sits a man. He's wearing a purple fleece, and his hair is dishevelled as if he has just gotten out of bed. He's leaning forward, listening intently as she speaks.

'Jodie?'

My daughter starts, turns, and takes in the situation.

'Mum? What are you doing here?'

I slowly make my way forwards, Bismarck pulling at the lead. 'I heard the front door close.' My words sound as sleepy as my brain feels.

Jodie's face is closed, furious. 'Did you follow me?'

'You left the house without telling me.'

'You thought I was sneaking out, didn't you?'

'For God's sake, Jodie!'

The man sitting across from Jodie clears his throat. 'Why don't you have a seat, and we can talk about this calmly?'

I take him in. He's in his early forties, with frameless spectacles and a lean, tight build that suggests he might be a runner like me.

'Who the hell are you?'

'Mum!'

The man stands up, and holds out his hand. 'My name is Tim Anderson. *Pastor* Tim Anderson.'

As his words sink in, I slowly begin to take in my surroundings. The hall is plastered with posters: *'Messy church every Monday and Wednesday'*, and on the far wall is a poster with the words, *'Christ Has Risen'* written in rainbow colours. I look at the man's outstretched hand.

'What are you doing meeting my fifteen-year-old daughter at ten o'clock on a Monday night?'

The Pastor's face freezes. 'If you'll let me explain, Grace–'

'And how the hell do you know my name?'

'Mum, don't be such an idiot!'

'Jodie,' says the pastor, in a calm tone I never seem able to manage anymore. 'The kettle's still warm. Why don't you go and make your mother a cup of tea?'

'But–'

'There's nothing to worry about; I just want to have a quick word.'

Jodie gives me a scathing look and stomps off.

Tim indicates a chair opposite. 'I promise you, there really is nothing to worry about.' I reluctantly take a seat and let the dog lead fall to floor. Bismarck sniffs around the table, lapping up a few stray biscuit crumbs, before wandering over and settling himself directly next to Pastor Tim.

'Bismarck, come here.'

'It's fine,' he says, reaching down and patting the dog's head. 'I know him well.'

My eyes widen. There is a lot I want to say to this person, this pastor, but conscious of Jodie, I try to rein in my temper. I'm also aware of the fact that I am wearing one of Alex's old T-shirts, and no bra. I'm certainly not giving the impression of a responsible parent. Tim rests his hands on the table in front of him. 'It's nice to meet you, Grace.'

26

I won't be drawn by pleasantries. 'Will you please answer my question?'

'Here's your tea,' says Jodie, thumping the cup down on the table in of front me. I watch as the beige liquid sloshes over the sides and onto the Formica tabletop. 'Just to make things clear, Mum,' she says. 'And before you make any more ridiculous assumptions. I've been helping Tim out with the youth club, okay?'

'Youth club?'

Jodie points to one of the posters on the wall opposite. *The Loft Teen café: Every Monday, Wednesday, and Friday Night. This week's film,* The Fault in Our Stars.

Tim clears his throat. 'But surely you knew that?'

'I'm not sure–'

'I told you!' Jodie's lips are drawn back, exposing expensively straightened teeth. 'You signed a consent form!'

Somewhere amidst a chaotic kitchen refurb, my developing relationship with Marcus, and the relentless horror of an internal investigation questioning my professional conduct, I seem to recall my daughter having said something about going to a club.

'I thought it was at school,' I look around the empty church hall, 'not here.'

Tim raises an eyebrow. 'Here?'

'Well, you know, a church.'

'I gather you're not a person of faith?'

'Faith yes, religion no.'

'I can see where Jodie gets her candour.'

'I'm not like *her!*' Jodie's face is tight, her eyes burning with resentment. I feel my heart falter.

'I don't think speaking to your mother that way is very helpful,' says Tim, a hint of censure in his voice.

I look at this man with a mixture of suspicion and displeasure. *Who is he to tell my daughter off?*

Jodie looks away. 'Sorry, Mum.'

I try to hide my surprise at this rare apology, but I suspect the sharp-eyed pastor has already noticed.

'It's after ten o'clock,' I say, furious that this stranger seems to be achieving better parenting results with Jodie than I have been. 'You have yet to explain what my daughter's doing here.'

'Believe me,' he replies, 'I wasn't expecting to see Jodie tonight... Well I was, but at six o'clock, not ten.'

'Pardon me?'

'As Jodie mentioned, she's been helping out with the youth club, along with a number of other projects at the church.'

'And tonight,' says Jodie, her voice thick with self-reprisal, 'I was covering for Hannah, who has flu. I was supposed to get here at half past six, set up the AV equipment and run the film,' she stares at her hands, 'but I forgot.'

'You were busy revising,' I reply. I feel I need to defend her. 'You have mocks in a few weeks.'

'I'm supposed to ring if I can't make it.'

'It really wasn't a problem,' says Tim, 'I was just trying to tell her that.'

'I should have rung.'

'Jodie,' says Tim firmly, 'I have been running film nights almost as long as I have been a pastor. I can certainly manage on my own for one night.'

'But I let you down.'

That familiar forlorn expression on my daughter's face fills me with an aching sadness. I long to reach out and touch her and say something reassuring. Instead, I sit mute and inept.

'Well now,' says Tim, 'there's no harm done, and now that we all know what's what, I don't expect it will happen again.'

He stands up and reaches over to rub Jodie's shoulder. If I was Bismarck, my hackles would be up. 'Feeling better?'

For the first time that evening, I see my daughter smile.

'Yeah,' she says, 'I am.'

'And that's all that really matters,' says Tim. 'Though perhaps in future you'll let your mother know where you're going so she doesn't worry.'

'Yes, Tim,' she replies. 'It's like they say, *do unto others as you would have them do unto you.* That's right, isn't it? Matthew. Chapter seven, verse ten?'

'Twelve,' says Tim, 'but you've got the gist of it.'

I stare at my daughter in amazement.

'When did *you* start learning the Bible?'

Jodie glances away. 'I sometimes come to Bible study after hip hop class on Saturday.'

'I thought you went out for McDonalds with your mates?'

'Used to,' Jodie replies. 'I have new friends now.'

I try to shake away my anger and confusion, to replace it with something more productive. 'How is it that I don't know any of this?'

'I–'

'Don't say that you told me you were going to Bible studies, Jodie, because you didn't.' Something strikes me, and I shake my head in sudden understanding. 'And all those Sunday brunches with your friends?'

Jodie looks away, her cheeks pink. 'Either you're at the office,' she mutters, 'or working late at home. It never seems to matter what I'm doing.'

'That's not fair.'

Tim clears his throat. 'I wonder if Jodie is trying to communicate something very important to you here, Grace?'

I can't help but sense a hint of self-righteousness in his voice.

'And what is that, *Tim?*'

'Mum, *please.*' Jodie's voice has dropped so low that I almost can't hear her. 'It helps – you know, being here – with everything.'

I think of her recent diagnosis, of the divorce, and all the uncertainty. Is this why she sought solace in a church of all places?

I force myself to step back, pause, and take a breath.

'Why didn't you tell me?'

'I was afraid.'

'Afraid of what?'

'That you wouldn't let me come.'

Those words silence me, because I can't deny that she might have been right, but this isn't about me. This is about my daughter; my beautiful, intelligent, overwhelmed daughter.

'I'm really glad you found somewhere that you feel safe and happy, honey, I really am, but not telling me?'

'Jodie,' say Tim, gently. 'Your mother is right. You should have told her.'

'I wanted to,' she replies. Fat tears are streaking her cheeks, leaving dark blots on her Pixies T-shirt.

'It's okay.' I can't bear to see her this way. 'The most important thing is you're doing something that makes you happy.' God knows, my daughter hasn't been happy in a long time. 'It's fine with me if you want to come to youth club.' She seems to relax slightly, 'But I'd really like me or your dad to drop you off and pick you up.' I'm not going to make things worse by telling her why. Most of the city must know about the attack on Nicky White by now.

'Okay.'

I take her in my arms for a moment, and feel ridiculously grateful when she doesn't resist.

'The power of Christ,' says Tim softly, 'enables divine healing.'

I resist the urge to tell the pastor to sod off with his divine healing, because suddenly my daughter is smiling – really smiling – a wide grin that dimples her lightly freckled cheeks. I haven't seen those dimples in months.

'Now I really must finish putting the chairs away, and lock up,' says Tim. 'Ingrid will kill me if I'm late home again.'

6

I wake up at five, the echo of a nightmare in which I'm chasing Jodie down a dark corridor still lingering. With little hope of getting back to sleep, I make coffee, check my emails, and take Bizzy for a run through the park. At half past six I sneak into Jodie's room, gently push back her fringe, and kiss her on the forehead. I make her a packed lunch and leave a note on the fridge, reminding her that her father is picking her up after school.

It's still early by the time I make it to Tamar House and into main reception. Even after all these years, it still amazes me how much it resembles a GP's waiting room. Rows of seats covered in faded tartan material curve their way towards a small table dotted with discarded leaflets offering support for depression, substance misuse, and debt. Just ahead of me is the reception desk. The built-in counter reaches to chest height and is plastered with a large, laminated sign that reads:

Please do not use abusive, profane, or racist language when dealing with National Probation Services staff.

Above the desk, a blockade of reinforced glass rises to ceiling height. Any communication between visitors and those interned behind the barricade is via a small opening that's wide enough to slip through an A4 envelope, but not to fit a fist.

I give a quick wave to my colleagues at the desk, punch my security code into the adjoining door, and enter what is jokingly referred to as the grey mile. A drab corridor stretches out before me like a monochrome road. To my right is the high-risk interview room, in which I spent most of yesterday, and will probably spend most of today. Inside, there are two panic alarms: one by the door, and another secreted under the desk. This is where some of the most dangerous offenders in the country are interviewed. A card has been slipped into a plastic frame on the door. It reads: *Midwinter 09:00*. I do my usual prep of reviewing the risk assessment and the psych report, then fill my water bottle – hot drinks are not allowed – grab my notepad and appointment diary, then go to collect William Vale from reception.

When I arrive, he's chatting merrily to our eighteen-year-old admin apprentice through the security glass. Hearing the door open, he glances my way. He isn't tall, maybe five seven, but with a tight, wiry frame that suggests suppressed energy and violence. He has dark hair, a strong chin, and very blue eyes.

'Mr Vale?'

His eyes narrow as he takes me in. *Friend or foe? Easy mark, or by-the-book bitch?*

'It was really nice talking to you, Alice.' He gives her a wide, cocky grin that I imagine has taken in a lot of Alices in its time. *Maybe she would be better suited to working in the office.* I make a mental note to mention it to Simon.

'This way, please.' I hold the door open for him. 'First door to your right.'

I wait until he is seated, him by the window and me by the

door, for if a quick escape is necessary. 'Mr Vale... Billy... May I call you Billy?' He's leaning back, posture loose, legs wide.

'Billy's fine with me, luv.'

I push the table forward a little, jarring his chair, and forcing him to sit upright. 'I'm Grace Midwinter, your interim probation officer.'

'Where's Sophie?'

'She's unavailable I'm afraid.' I'm not going to tell him about her staffroom meltdown, the rumoured suicide attempt, and how she's been signed off for at least three months. 'As we've only got half an hour together this morning, Billy, I would suggest that the most appropriate way forward would be for us to focus on what happened a few days ago, and how best we can deal with it.' His face is a fortress. 'Maybe find some common ground?'

'Yes, Grace,' he says, visibly relaxing slightly. 'Common ground would be good.'

I can't decide if he's being sincere, or just saying what he thinks I want to hear. I'll find out soon enough.

'Well now, there seems to be plenty of information about what happened – reports from the police, social services, solicitors. There's even witness statements from half a dozen neighbours in the flats across the street.' His look hardens, and for a moment I can see the danger in him: the short fuse, raised fist, and an unending need to make the pain last.

'I know I messed up big time,' now he's the frightened schoolboy, 'but I really want to make things right.'

He's got the look: contrite, hopeful, compliant, down to a tee. I wonder what's really going on behind those sharp blue eyes. After last night's chaos with Jodie, I need to refresh my memory, so speed-read my notes. *Twenty-four, originally from Bristol.* I go through the list of his previous offences: common assault, possession, but nothing that had earned him a spell

34

inside, and certainly nothing to suggest that he would one day tie his girlfriend to a bed frame and torture her while their six-month-old daughter slept peacefully in the room next door.

'So, you've been out of custody for eighteen months without a single incident. I see you've completed all the required programmes, Building Better Relationships, Horizon, Intimate Partner Violence.' He winces slightly at the last one. 'How did you find those?'

Billy nods vigorously. 'Good. Really, really helpful.'

"Full attendance and excellent participation," according to these notes. You even became a peer mentor on one of them. That's pretty impressive.' I lean forward. 'So, what happened?'

'I don't know what all the fuss was about,' says Billy, shaking his head. 'Stuck a couple of Post-it notes on her front door, and all hell breaks loose.'

'You frightened her, Billy.'

'I didn't mean to.'

'What *did* you mean to do?'

He pauses, and studies the wall above my head. 'I just wanted to say sorry.'

'Sorry?'

'For what I'd done... for hurting her.'

'What made you decide to do that?'

His eyes find mine. 'I found my way back.'

'Back?'

'Back to myself, back to truth.'

'Truth?'

'To choosing my attitude, you know?'

'Your... attitude?' I'm unable to censor the scepticism from my voice.

'Yes, my attitude!' He lurches forward, and I realise that his choice of attitude at this moment might not be a wise one. I slip my hand under the desk and feel for the smooth reassuring nub of the panic alarm. 'In the disarray of my life,' he says, suddenly calm again, 'I lost sight of my pathway to certainty, to the real me.'

'The real you?' I realise I'm repeating his words verbatim, but I can't help myself. I'm baffled by the psychobabble. It's just not what I had expected.

He leans forward, his elbows almost touching mine.

'When you read that,' he says, pointing towards my notepad. 'What you see is a cruel bastard who's spent most of his life taking his shit out on the rest of the world and taking it out hard. I had no insight, no authenticity. I hurt my girlfriend, ruined my relationship, lost my daughter, and spent three years in prison.' He takes a deep breath, holds it, then exhales. 'Now, I realise that being true to myself involves embracing all aspects of my existence, including the harm I've done to others.' He spreads his arms wide. 'It's the only way for my offences to be swept away.'

'If only it were that easy,' I mutter. God knows what the judge will do if Billy presents in court like this. I scan my notes to see if there was anything on his psyche report to suggest a history of psychosis or delusion, but aside from anger issues, there's nothing. *Could he be sincere?*

'I see you've been doing voluntary work?'

'For the last year,' he says proudly. 'That's been a big part of my healing.'

What about your ex-girlfriend's healing? I wonder. *What about your daughter's?* But that's not why I'm here. Simon instructed me before going in this morning that the holding cells at Charles Cross Police Station were full, and that a lockdown at Channings Wood Prison means that any new intakes will have to go to HMP Exeter. To top it all off, most of the prisoner transport is booked, or out of commission. My remit is clear. If safe and appropriate, keep Billy Vale out of prison while making sure his risk stats are below 5%. Shame I haven't brought my calculator with me.

'What exactly do you do? Your voluntary work, I mean.'

'Help out in the local community, handyman work mostly.' He sits up a little straighter. 'I built the raised beds for the community gardening project at Victoria Park.' I feel that familiar inward lurch. Victoria Park is where I run with Bismarck every morning. Jodie walks through there every day to get to school. 'Everyone at the project has been really good to me,' continues Billy, 'offered me lots of support, guidance, you know.'

'That's great, Billy. I'm really pleased for you, but why–'

'Screw it all up by leaving a note on my ex's door asking her to forgive me?'

'Exactly.'

'I don't know.'

I give the clock a few ticks. I have a good sense of what might have inspired this act. Fifteen years' experience has given me an instinct that rarely lets me down. 'She was seeing someone else, wasn't she?'

There's a long pause. 'Yeah,' he says finally, 'me mate Ozzy saw her with a bloke in Prezzo.'

'And did you really think that leaving that note on her front door would change things?'

Billy shakes his head. 'It was sincere,' he says, and lifting his hands in subjugation he whispers the next bit. 'I was seeking forgiveness.'

In the distance, a slow wail of a police siren gains volume as it nears Tamar House. I glance out of the window and watch as a squad car speeds past the building, towards the harbourfront. I pull my mind away from the image of Nicky White's body beaten, bloody, his lungs filled with seawater.

'Forgiveness or not, Billy, it was very lucky that you didn't have any actual contact with Nicole, because if you had, you'd be in holding cells right now, waiting to go back to prison.' I return to my notebook, which I unthinkingly marked up with thin strips of Post-it notes half an hour before our meeting. Feeling my cheeks begin to glow, I quickly peel away the strips of brightly coloured paper, and crumple them into a ball. I hear Billy clear his throat. When I look up, I see that he has a wide grin on his face.

'Well,' I say, returning to professional mode. 'It looks like you have quite a few prominent character witnesses. Your GP. The local Conservative counsellor.'

'I really haven't put a foot wrong since I've been outside.'

'Aside from last week, of course.' Billy gives a defeated sigh, and lets his head fall back against the back of the chair, before covering his face with his hands. 'The thing is, Billy, you messed up. You messed up big time, but thankfully you didn't have any direct contact with Nicole, and as soon as you realised what you had done you handed yourself in to the police. It's probably those things, along with your recent clean record and character references, that have kept you out of prison.'

He sits up and fixes me with his cobalt gaze. 'Does that mean I won't have to go back inside?'

'Well, it's still early days, and I gather you've already had a provisional court date.'

'But?'

'Considering the nature of the breach (no direct contact with your ex or your daughter), and your recent exemplary behaviour, I would be hoping for a medium level community order. If it goes our way, you'd be looking at supervision, maybe an extension to your probationary period, and most likely a return to some of your previous courses.'

For the first time I see hope in his eyes.

'I don't want to go back inside, Grace.'

I am always amazed at this point in an interview, when all the bullshit and bravado is stripped away, and the real person emerges. Rarely are they charismatic or exciting – the Tony Sopranos or Hannibal Lecters from fiction. Normally they are sad, desperate, damaged people.

'I don't want that to happen either,' I say sincerely. After all, that would be detrimental to my monthly outcomes. Time to drive it home. 'First, to ensure there are no repeat breaches and to give you the best possible chance at your court appearance in a few weeks, I would like us to continue to meet regularly – at least weekly for the next few months.'

Billy nods enthusiastically. 'I can do that.'

'Good.' I glance through my diary.

'Final warning, Billy. If anything like this happens again, if you even sneeze within five miles of Nicole's flat, you will be back inside, no questions asked.'

'Anything else?'

'I'd like you to revisit the victim empathy module of the Building Better Relationships programme. Do you still have the booklets?'

'Yeah, I guess so.'

He sounds like a bored teenager, *just like Jodie.* 'I would also like you to consider some counselling, particularly if you are sincere about addressing the harm you've done to others. Your notes indicate you've had a few sessions already, but it may be worth exploring this a bit more.'

'Whatever you say, Grace.'

I look up, wondering if he's taking the mick, but his expression is genuine. *It's not often they cooperate this readily. It must be my week.*

'I want to make clear what you're going to do next. You're to maintain your voluntary work if it complies with your licence conditions, and you are absolutely *not* to go anywhere near your ex-wife or daughter. Is that clear?' He nods. 'I'll put this all in an action plan document, which you will read, sign and adhere to. Is that also clear?'

'Clear,' he replies.

'Your word is your bond, Billy.'

7

I make my way back to my desk to discover a note from Simon saying he wants to see me in his office *ASAP*. I discreetly tear it into tiny shreds, deposit it into the bin, and head for his office. A heavy sigh is forming in my chest, one that I expect will need to stay buried for the duration of our meeting. In the early days, Simon and I were friends. Not close – he was a bit too driven for that, continually striving for that next promotion – but close enough to look out for each other. We lost touch when his marriage disintegrated, and he retreated to Bristol. I was hoping his return to the Plymouth office eighteen months ago would re-establish some of that camaraderie, but then the Senior Probation Officer vacancy came up. We shook hands and declared magnanimously, 'May the best person win,' but the rumour was that I was a shoo-in for the role, and Simon knew it. I have to give him credit; he did everything he could to stand out, working overtime and taking on additional duties.

I was just preparing for my interview when nine-year-old Katie Cross was murdered, and the spotlight fell on probation services, and any poor sod the press could think of who might have sent her safehouse address to her deranged father. The scrutiny was relentless, and my life both personal and professional fell apart. I withdrew my application and retreated into a world of misery and self-pity. Had it not been for Jodie, I would probably still be there today. Simon got the job, became my line manager, and micro-managed the hell out of it.

His office door is conspicuously open, a clear indication that he's annoyed. I slip in and take a seat opposite his desk.

'Glad you could make it.'

'I've just gotten out of a possible recall meeting,' I reply. 'One of my guys needs help accessing counselling services.'

'Counselling services?' Simon's voice has a hint of censure. 'What have we said about boundaries, Grace?'

'Boundaries?' I try to disguise the defensiveness in my voice. 'Surely I don't have to tell you how important it is for our clients to have the right support?'

'For goodness' sake!' he snaps. Suddenly, I can see the strain he's under. 'I've got a service to run, a service that's under a hell of a lot of pressure at the moment, including a visit by Her Majesty's Inspectorate of Probation in six months.' His voice softens. 'Look, Grace, we're not social workers, and we are not a charity. Okay? We're here to manage risk. Risk to the public, risk to law enforcement services, and risk to themselves. There are plenty of other resettlement agencies designated to sort out their personal problems.'

I can feel the heat creeping up past my chin. 'Not if you're on the sex offenders register there aren't.'

Simon sighs, but doesn't argue. He knows I'm right. Instead, he picks up a leather-bound notebook on the desk in front of him.

'Let's just get on, shall we? I assume you're aware of Tel's arrest?'

'What?'

Tel Denzies is one of my oldest clients, a user and dealer

with a propensity for hiding heroin in some pretty creative places. This has included inside nappies, empty soft drink cans, and following a nasty bust-up at his local pub, which resulted in a fractured shin bone, the hollow tubes of his aluminium crutches.

'Found shoplifting again,' says Simon. 'He's in custody cells at Charles Cross, pending a court appearance first thing tomorrow morning. A remand is looking likely.'

'Not like he'll mind.' I sigh. As a prolific offender Tel has spent nearly half of his thirty-nine years in prison. 'Was he carrying?'

Simon responds with a nod. 'Just under an intent to supply.'

'That's a relief. At least he won't be charged with dealing.' I stand up to leave. 'I'd better speak to the custody officer.'

'No need to worry about that.' Simon's tone is caring, but I can detect just the subtlest hint of a rebuke. 'I've asked one of the juniors to follow it up for you.'

'What?' I can feel my fingernails digging into my palms. 'He's *my* client.' I'm acutely aware of the open door, of the fact that most of my colleagues in the office might be able to hear, but I don't care. 'You should have asked me first.'

'You were busy, Grace, and I have a job to do.' Then he says something completely unexpected. He rests his elbows on the desk and leans forward. 'Everything all right with you?'

'I beg your pardon?'

'In the workplace, I mean. Are you happy?'

'Christ, Simon, is this some sort of joke?'

For a moment he looks embarrassed. Touchy-feely is definitely not Simon's thing.

'The new civil service protocols for staff well-being require that we ask,' he mutters.

'I see.' I know that Simon is under considerable pressure to turn around the nearly non-existent morale of the team. I also know there is little point in reminding him about my crushing workload, or the fact that after fifteen years in the National Probation Service I'm finding it increasingly difficult to reconcile a criminal justice system based on risk and outcomes with my desire to make a difference. As one of the few functioning probation officers in the overstretched, under-resourced office, happy in the workplace doesn't even come into it. While I realise Simon has a job to do, and wants to do it well, it's a bit too late in the day for this kind of conversation.

'And with the internal investigation?' he continues. 'It's just a case of formal notification now, isn't it, but it looks like you're in the clear?'

I stare at him in disbelief.

'You've read the interim report, Simon. The Deputy Director has indicated that however Anton Cross got access to the report with Katie's safehouse address on it, it was unlikely it was through this office.' I try to stop the uncertainty from creeping into my voice, and block the crime scene images from my head. I was so busy that week. Simon had asked me to help out with Katie's child protection report, to comment on whether I felt Anton's visitation rights should be suspended. I had to make copies and, depending on whether the relevant parties had secure Wi-Fi, email or get them posted by the end of the day. Then there was a letter to Anton for his missed probation appointment, which needed to be printed out and sent to his approved premises. It was time consuming and stressful, everything having to be put in the postal out tray by four thirty at the latest. We were running late, and even though I had asked Simon to peer check my work, I still wonder if I could have mixed up the documents, put the child protection report with the safehouse address in the envelope addressed to Anton by mistake. *Could I be responsible for the death of an innocent child?* I'll never stop asking myself that question. 'And as they never found the envelope–'

'Which would have had our franking mark showing that you had sent it.'

'I did not send it.'

'No, of course not. What I mean is, *had* you sent it.'

Not much better.

I force my frustration deep into that dark place where I keep all the other crap in my life.

'I guess the only question is, who actually did send it?'

'Indeed,' says Simon. He picks up a pencil and begins twiddling it through his fingers. 'How's Jodie?'

'I'm sorry?'

'How are things with Jodie, the recent diagnosis mental health wise?'

'I appreciate your concern, but–'

'I realise it's all been a bit of a strain for you. The divorce, Katie's murder, the internal investigation, and now Jodie.'

God, could this conversation be any more awkward?

Then he says something that surprises me most of all.

'You know you can always talk to me.'

I pause, struggling with how best to take this in. Simon was always a 'keep your private life private' sort of person, referring us to HR whenever there were personal issues. I get that bungling government policy, staff dissatisfaction and the bottoming out of public confidence in the probation service means he's probably been under enormous pressure to engage more effectively with staff, but I liked the outcome driven Simon. I always knew where I stood, and always had a clear, if sometimes rigid structure to follow. If only that structure hadn't collapsed around me. I'm about to reply in a way that will certainly raise his eyebrows when we're interrupted by the sound of someone clearing their throat. I turn. My case assistant Viola is standing in the open doorway.

'Yes,' barks Simon.

'Grace,' she says softly. 'Your next appointment is in five minutes.'

'Oh yes. Cheers, Vi.' I jump up, grateful for an escape. I catch the delicate scent of Viola's perfume as I follow her into the open-plan office. 'What appointment?'

She turns and gives me a stern look. 'Let's just say he's called John Doe, and his bus has broken down, so he'll have to reschedule.'

'I don't–'

She shakes her head at my witlessness. 'For goodness' sake, Grace. Somebody's got to keep you out of trouble.'

8

I claim I have an appointment in Stonehouse, but instead walk the one and a half miles northeast to Charles Cross Police Station in the city centre. I check in at the desk and am buzzed through to the small waiting area. A few minutes later, a burly custody officer ushers me in. He waits until the door closes behind me, before turning and enveloping me in an enormous hug.

'Grace,' he says. 'How the hell are you?'

'Better for seeing you, Mick.'

Mick Williams and I first met fifteen years ago, when I was a junior PO and he a newly qualified PC. We were forced together on a particularly nasty domestic violence case and found ourselves meeting for drinks after work to decompress. We dated, slept together once, and broke up after I met Alex. A few years later, he transferred to custody and is now a sergeant, happily married father of four, and my first point of contact when I need anything to do with clients in holding cells.

Mick holds me at arm's length, and studies me closely. 'You okay?'

I nod, but don't meet his gaze. 'Just a lot on at the moment.'

'Tell me about it.' He runs his thumb and forefinger thoughtfully along the edge of his ginger beard. 'Nicky White's been dead two days, and we're already seeing the fallout.'

'Already?'

'Just low-level gang stuff at the moment, but if one of those idiots gets hold of a real weapon...'

'I'm here about Tel.'

'Yeah,' he says. 'I was here when they brought him in.' He shakes his head sadly. 'I kind of thought that maybe this time he might have made it.'

I know he's just being kind. No experienced copper dares hope for too much from a prolific offender and long-term addict.

'Can I see him?'

'He's had his visit,' Mick says, clearly confused. 'Some newbie who quite frankly looked scared shitless.'

'I was tied up.' I try to keep the vitriol from my voice. 'Simon sent someone else.'

He gives me a knowing look. 'So, is this official?'

'Let's just say I'm here as a friend.'

'Righto.'

Mick checks me in, then leads me to the detention cells, stopping at a blue metal door identical to the twelve others we have just passed. He squints into the peephole, then slides open the hatch. 'Tel,' he calls softly. 'Someone here to see you, mate.'

Mick opens the cell door, and I feel myself falter. Tel is sitting on the small platform with the thin blue plastic mattress that serves as a bed. He is shirtless, his scrawny chest and arms covered in faded homemade tattoos. He's lost weight since I last saw him, and I wonder if his darkened skin tone is due more to his hepatitis C than our recent bout of nice weather.

'Can I speak to him in here?'

Mick gives me a warning look. 'Five minutes, Grace, and you stay the required distance, right?'

'Thanks, Mick.'

He wanders down the corridor, checking the neighbouring cells. I know he should have been home a half hour ago. I take a small step forward.

'Hey, Tel.'

He looks up at me.

'Hey, Grace.'

Ignoring Mick's warning, I move forward. 'How are you doing, matey?' Tel's battered face represents a history of misdiagnosis, neglect, and abuse. 'Sorry to see you back inside.'

'Me too,' he says, sadly.

'Got into a bit of bother, I hear.'

'Yeah.'

'Want to tell me about it?'

'Not much to tell.' He picks at a scab on his elbow, and I resist the urge to reach forward and stop him. 'Just needed some stuff, you know.'

'You were found with twelve packets of razor blades on you.'

'Easy to sell on, you know?'

'You dealing as well?'

He looks at me with wide, innocent eyes. 'Just a bit of weed here and there. No class A, I promise.'

The next sentence proves difficult. 'Using?'

'Just my script,' he says, referring to his methadone prescription. 'I haven't touched any gear for six months.' He gives a proud, gap-toothed grin. 'Just like I promised.'

Ignoring Mick's instructions, I sit down on the bunk beside him. Reaching into my handbag, I remove a Mars bar and hand it to him.

'You remembered,' he says, his eyes creasing with pleasure. Tel meticulously tears open the wrapper and takes a tiny nibble before re-wrapping it and slipping it into the pocket of his jeans. 'Don't want to eat it all in one go.'

Days like these make me wish I had become a nurse or an accountant, but there's work to be done.

'Why, Tel?' I say, softly. 'You were doing so well.'

It's a good twenty seconds before he replies.

'It's daft really.'

'But?'

'It's just that ever since me dog Sparky was run down, well, you know. There just didn't seem no reason to carry on.'

Now I'm confused. 'But why the shoplifting?'

'I seen a sign at the pub for these Jack Russell puppies. Three hundred quid each.'

'Ah,' I reply, my voice catching in my throat.

Tel gives a deep, sorry sigh. 'It's easier inside anyway,' he says. 'You get your own cells up Dartmoor, as long as you don't mind mixing with them nonces, and three squares a day. Being spring and all, I might even see if I can get on gardening duty.'

I squeeze Tel's bony hand. 'I'm going to speak to the judge, your drugs worker, mental health nurse—'

'I don't want you going to no trouble, Grace.'

I hear someone clear their throat, and I look up to see Mick standing in the doorway.

'Why do I bother?' he mutters, then pointing to his watch he adds, 'Any longer and I'll have to log this as an official visit.'

'I'd better go, Tel.' I'm conscious that he's only allowed limited visits, and I don't want to take up time that may be better used by his brief.

'Will you be in court tomorrow, Grace?'

'Course I will, mate.'

Something about seeing the sad, emaciated Tel makes me long for the comforts of home, so I stop at my local Tesco Express and pick up all the fixings for a roast dinner. I'm just basting the chicken when I hear Jodie arrive, and then, 'Mmm, what's that lovely smell?' Gone is the truculent adolescent of last night, now replaced by a smiling cherub. *Are all teenagers like this?*

We eat our dinner in the garden, and then drive to The Hoe where we eat ice cream and watch three young tombstoners jumping off the stone parapets and into the water below.

'Don't even think of it,' whispers Jodie, as I consider warning the boys about the dangers of shallow water. At the sight of an approaching police car, they vanish. We leave with the setting sun. This cheerful tourist location takes on a very different aspect with darkness and the night-time economy.

'So about this church thing,' I say to her later, as she's getting ready for bed. We're relaxed, comfortable with each other again... Maybe it's the right time to ask her about what's been going on.

'What do you mean, church *thing*?'

'The youth club I get,' I say, feeling like I'm tiptoeing, 'but Bible study?'

Her eyes narrow. 'Why do you have to say it like that?'

'Like what?'

'Like it's something freaky?'

'I don't think–'

'Just because I'm not an *avowed atheist* like you.'

'I'm not an avowed atheist, I'm just–'

'Why do you always have to go and ruin things?' says Jodie, with unexpected vitriol. 'We were having such a nice time.'

'I don't want to upset you,' I reply with the calm clarity I often use with my clients. 'I just want to make sure you're okay, that this sudden interest in religion isn't because of—'

'A father who screwed around?' Jodie's voice is high, shrill. 'A workaholic mother, and both of you using me as some sort of emotional ping-pong ball to score points off each other?'

This is the first time Jodie has expressed anything even close to these feelings. I know I should be understanding, supportive, but old habits die hard, and I find myself defaulting to the defensive.

'That's not fair.'

'Fair!' she screams. 'When has anything in this house been fair?'

'Jodie!'

'If either of you really care about me,' she speaks with a calm that is concerning, 'you and Dad should get your shit together, and stop acting like idiots. You should also stop disrespecting the things I like. Paradise Church really matters to me.'

'I'm sorry, honey, I didn't mean to—'

'I'm tired.' Jodie gets under the bedcovers and turns away. 'I don't want to talk about it anymore.' Reaching forward, she turns off the bedside light, leaving me standing in darkness.

I wait until I can hear her heavy breath of sleep before going downstairs and calling Marcus.

'Everything all right?' He sounds as concerned as anyone receiving a call at eleven o'clock at night might be.

'You okay to talk?'

'What's up?'

'I just wanted to hear your voice.'

'Is it work, Jodie, or Alex?'

Am I that transparent?

'Never mind. It's late.'

'I was kidding.' His voice is deep, warm, and comforting. I only wish he was here and not a hundred and thirty miles away in Bristol. 'How much have I gone on to you about my access issues?'

'Any improvement?'

'I've got Kian for two weeks over the summer.'

'That's great news.'

'I was thinking we could come down to Devon for a few days. You could meet him.'

'Would he be okay with that?' I try to manage the uncertainty in my voice. Marcus meeting my fifteen-year-old daughter was awkward enough.

'He likes ice cream,' Marcus replies, and I can tell he's smiling. 'Just buy him an ice cream, and he'll be yours.'

'I miss those days.'

'So it's Jodie, then.'

'I can see why you're in intelligence.'

'What's up?'

'Nothing really. I mean, I don't want to make a big deal about it.'

'But?'

'She's volunteering at some weird community church on Paradise Street.'

'Weird?'

'You know,' I continue, 'all that evangelical "Praise Jesus!" stuff.'

'Any problem with that?'

I feel myself sitting up a little straighter. 'What do you mean by that?'

Marcus clears his throat. 'It's just that tone you get in your voice when you're not happy about something.'

'What tone?'

'That tone.'

'I really don't mean to, it's just that–'

'Just that what?'

'I'm not sure about Jodie getting involved with that kind of place.'

'What kind of place?'

'Some way out there church.'

There's a pause before Marcus replies. 'It's called NCM,

Grace. New Church Movement. All above board, and legitimate.'

'Oh man, you're NCM, aren't you?'

'Not me,' he replies, 'but my mum and gran are. Hope Evangelical in Fishponds.'

'I'm so sorry, Marcus.' If I could throw my mobile out of the window, and hide under my duvet right now, I would. 'I seem to have gotten everything wrong tonight.'

'Not wrong, Grace, maybe just slightly off-kilter.'

I try not to sound as tearful as I feel. 'I just wish you were here.'

'Me too, babes.'

'Can I ask you something?'

'Is it what I'm wearing right now?'

It's amazing how that man can change the mood with a few well-chosen words.

'I wish it were.'

I hear him sigh. 'Now I can tell it's about work.'

'Well, yes, but I promise I'll make it up to you.'

'Will you now? Okay, go ahead.'

I give Marcus a quick overview of the comms meeting yesterday. It's not unusual for me to ask his advice. What's shared between us, stays between us.

'Do you think it's drugs related? Organised crime, I mean.'

'Not sure,' he replies. 'I mean from what you've told me, the Whites are small-time, Plymouth-based, not got that much to do with the big boys.'

'But if they were trying to move in on someone else's operation? Would killing Nicky send a signal?'

'A signal, yes,' said Marcus, 'but it would also mean a shedload of police, DCI, and possibly even NCA officers sniffing around.'

'Are your guys involved in this?'

'I imagine we'll be getting some intel.'

'But you don't think—'

'Look, Grace, from what you told me the guy was a lowlife with offences for possession, and sexual assault. It sounds like there were probably a lot of people gunning for him.'

Something about the tone in Marcus' voice reminds me of Ryan's words from the day before. 'So, you think he deserved it?'

'Of course not. It's just that the guy probably had a lot of enemies. Any of them could have done it. It also sounds like somebody really wanted him dead.'

'They achieved that for certain.'

'Why are you so interested in all of this?' he crunches, through a mouthful of what might be his favourite balsamic vinegar crisps.

'I'm not really sure. I mean, I know he wasn't a very pleasant person, but to be beaten up and thrown in the harbour like that? Who would do something so brutal?'

'Plenty out there,' he sighs, 'plenty.' Marcus' work on county lines, human trafficking and organised crime means he's probably seen more violence than I ever will. Not for the first time, I wonder if it was foolish of me to get involved with another law enforcement officer. Probation, police, National Crime Agency, we all think the same. Work comes first, family a worthy sacrifice. We're saving lives, aren't we? *Is it only Jodie's recent, diagnosis that has made me start to think otherwise?*

'Anything else on your mind?' he asks.

I tell him about my interview with Billy Vale. 'It was just so weird. All this talk about being authentic, and true to himself. I can't figure out if he was being genuine, or trying to mess with me.'

'What was his name again?' He's trying to sound casual, but I've known Marcus long enough to realise he's intrigued.

'Billy Vale. Originally from Bristol. Do you know him?'

Marcus doesn't answer, only makes a small *hmm* sound.

'And his history?'

I tell Marcus a little about Billy's background, no real breach of confidentiality because as a NCA officer he can access the Police National Computer anytime he wants to. Tired of talking shop, I try to change the subject, but he seems eager to hear more. Finally I decide to put a stop to it.

'You free this weekend?'

'Not sure,' he replies, 'something's brewing, but I won't know for a few days.'

'But if it doesn't?'

'I just might be able to make my way down the M5.'

'Jodie's doing her Duke of Edinburgh training this weekend. Camping on the moors in preparation for the real thing in a few weeks.'

There's another reason why I don't want to be alone this weekend, which I keep to myself.

'You don't say.'

'So, if you're free…'

'Friday, 8pm,' he growls. 'Be ready.'

I love that man.

9

I wake up early, change my Outlook diary to say I'll be working from home, and email the junior Simon assigned to Tel yesterday, informing him that I will be attending the court hearing. Simon can have a go at me later. The most important thing is that I keep Tel out of prison, or at least negotiate the shortest sentence possible.

The court appearance is brief and to the point. I tell the magistrate that Tel has been a model client, that he's been attending Narcotics Anonymous meetings, keeping off the hard stuff, and that I will continue to support him in his ongoing endeavours to engage positively in the local community. She looks down at me through her half-moon spectacles, unconvinced. A sentence of six weeks is handed down. Tel gives me a sad backward glance as he is led out of the courtroom. I feel hopeless and furious. I'm about to leave when Justice Matthews points a perfectly manicured finger in my direction, and beckons me to the bench.

'Diane,' I say, my voice sounding gritty. 'Having a good day?'

'Don't be a smartass, Grace,' she replies sharply, then her

voice softens. 'I'm recommending he's put back into the DRM Wing for his period of incarceration. He did all right there before.'

I give a half-hearted smile. The Dialogue Road Map Project is probably the safest place in Dartmoor for Tel. Not only are DRM prisoners supported by trained peer mentors and offered regular drug and counselling sessions, they're also housed in a specialist wing that most inmates would give their right hand to get into.

'He's clean, Di. Going inside with ready access to drugs might change all that.'

'He's also homeless, vulnerable and a risk to himself and others, and I still have a job to do.'

I make my way back to Tamar House in time for the afternoon brief. In the grey mile I come across the junior PO, who asks how the hearing went.

'Six weeks in Dartmoor,' I reply, 'but his brief is trying for an earlier release.'

He shifts uncomfortably. 'The thing is, I haven't mentioned to Simon about you going instead of me.'

The poor kid looks terrified. 'Don't worry about it,' I say. I still remember what it was like the first few months in the job. With so much to learn, and so much potential for things to go wrong, you're pretty much on tenterhooks for most of the working day. Also, Simon isn't always the most understanding of bosses. 'I'll tell him,' I say. Which of course I won't.

He smiles gratefully, and we head down the corridor to the meeting room. We enter with two other POs also just back from outreach work. Simon, already in full force, is standing at the front of the room holding up the front page of the local newspaper.

'So, as you can see,' Simon distributes copies of the *Plymouth Herald* around the conference room table, 'the press is going to town with conspiracy theories about Nicky White's death.'

He holds up the front page of the local newspaper with its screaming headline.

WELL KNOWN CITY CRIMINAL FOUND DEAD IN SUTTON HARBOUR!

'Unfortunately,' he continues, 'they've dragged up every rumour and bit of gossip you can imagine – ranging from a full-on gang war, to a late-night stalker targeting pub leavers.' His voice pounds through my head like the start of a migraine. 'There is also some indication that this news story contains confidential information about Nicky's previous, which could have only come from an internal source.'

The junior PO nudges me, and whispers, 'What does he mean by that?' I silence him with a shake of my head.

'I'm sure I don't need to remind you,' continues Simon, 'that any staff member found disclosing confidential information to the press will face immediate disciplinary action including dismissal. I've already made a brief statement to the press, clarifying that Probation Services operates under a strict code of conduct, and that we will not be answering any questions.'

I let his voice fade from my consciousness as I stare out of the window at the street below. I wonder about Simon's interest in the case. Clearly this information could have been handled by Alex, or someone else from the serious crimes team, but over the last couple of months Simon has become even more obsessive about protocol and procedure. I can't say I blame him. *Is this what the job does to you, strips you down until you become something less than yourself?* Maybe I'll ask Simon if he wants to go out for a drink after work sometime, try a bit harder to re-establish some common ground. I'm grateful for the end of the information session, and I'm hurrying from the conference room when I hear my name being called.

'Just a quick one please, Grace.'

What the hell does he want now?

'Don't look so worried,' Simon says, in a cheerful tone that immediately puts me on edge. 'That chap you saw yesterday, Sophie's client. Michael, ah...' I watch as he struggles for the name.

'Fellows,' I reply. 'Is there a problem?'

'Not that I'm aware of. However, in light of the situation with Nicky White, I thought it would be prudent for me to do a technical review on some case files.'

'For the entire department?'

He holds my gaze. 'No, just a few.'

I don't like where this is going.

'I've inputted my notes from yesterday's interview.' I try not to sound defensive. It's one of our internal protocols for interview records to be logged on the same day, although whether that actually happens is another thing altogether, particularly with ongoing problems with the database. 'I haven't quite finished reviewing Sophie's, though.' I decide not to mention the gaps in her recordkeeping. She doesn't need any more shit in her life.

Simon gives me a look that suggests he's not surprised Sophie's notes aren't up scratch.

'In light of what's happened, it might be an idea for us to ensure that all Sophie's notes are complete.'

'How complete?'

'Concluded.' He clears his throat. 'Any irregularities, inconsistencies, unfinished sections, addressed and notated. Then I want the cases closed.'

'But it will be date stamped.'

Date stamped means anyone reviewing the records will know that someone else had to go in to amend the files in order to complete them to the proper standard – essentially a really big signpost that Sophie wasn't doing her job properly.

'I'm fully aware of that,' says Simon. 'I could bring in one of the regional supervisors if that would be easier for you.' I stare at him, wondering how to interpret this. Is it a threat, or a not-so-subtle hint for me to tidy up Sophie's mess before it reaches senior management level? He clears his throat. 'I'm just trying to protect you, Grace.'

Protect me from what?

'Whatever you say, Simon.' I know the disastrous part-privatisation of probation services, and its return to the public sector, means we've been racing to catch up ever since. I also know that the review at the end of the year by Her Majesty's Inspectorate of Probation has been on every team meeting agenda for the last six months. *Is that what's causing him so much worry?* It's just one more reminder that I'm not the only one under scrutiny. Maybe Simon needs my support as much as Sophie does, though he'd never admit it. 'Don't worry, Simon. I'll sort out her database entries, and do her exit reports.' I want to say more: how Sophie is a highly skilled and diligent PO, how she goes above and beyond to support her clients, how her job is her life, or once was.

'And one more thing,' he adds, as if what he's already said isn't enough. 'I'd like you to email me with an update on all your client meetings.'

'What? That will take–'

'The regional director has asked me to monitor some staff members for reporting purposes.'

I really didn't think things today could get any worse.

'And you chose me?'

Simon doesn't even blink.

'Seemed like a sensible choice.'

I spend the rest of the afternoon catching up on appointments; a fraudster, and a civil servant possessing indecent images are midweek standards. Alongside that, I'm doing my best to try and tidy up Sophie's case files before Simon has a chance to scrutinise them. It appears both Billy Vale and Michael Fellows haven't received full inductions, and there's some suggestion that Michael had been given the okay to move into a shared house with another ex-offender, which is a situation that might compromise his bail conditions. I drain the dregs of my coffee cup, wondering how a talented probation officer like Sophie could have so spectacularly dropped the ball. I glance at my mobile. Only this morning, she texted asking to meet up. I want to be supportive – she's a good friend after all – but I'm also genuinely uncertain I want to be her saviour. I've got enough on my plate as it is. Then I consider my own predicament, that of Katie Cross and the disastrously misdirected child protection report and decide not to be so critical. I also refuse to be just one more victim of compassion fatigue. I send her a text, to see when she's free. She replies minutes later, suggesting Friday. Her slightly desperate tone makes me feel uneasy. The situation with Sophie has been awkward for all of us. How *do you* support a close friend who's seriously lost the plot? Send a card? Meet for sushi? Maybe that's one of the modules they should offer on our Continual Professional Development Portfolio.

It's nearly six by the time I finally finish tidying up Sophie's case files. Simon also asked me to clear out her desk drawer, as a new regional directive has required us to move to hot-desking.

After today's conversation there are a few bits of hers that I'd like him to see – thank you cards, a testimonial, an award from the local mental health charity – just to remind him that she's still a good PO, but he's gone for the day. I ask the cleaner to unlock the door so that I can leave them on his desk, with a note saying:

I thought you might like to see these before I return them to Sophie.

That's when I notice his open notebook. Something catches my eye.

Risk review Nicky White:

I glance up and scan the office. A few remaining colleagues are still diligently working, heads down. We're in and out of Simon's office all the time, so my presence won't be regarded as unusual. As casually as possible, I flip the page. It's clear that Simon has been looking through the database too. There are comments about Nicky's history in the cobbled shorthand he uses, which from years of working alongside him, I can decipher. He's listed meetings, referrals, and action plans. There is also a note regarding an assault Nicky White made on a PO at the beginning of the year. Next to it, and underlined heavily, is the word **confidential.**

The date links to around the time I was on a six-week training course in Exeter. I had no idea it had even taken place. Assaults on probation officers happen all the time. Depending on the severity, which ranges from verbal abuse and stalking to common assault, we just tend to get on with it or park it in the *I hope it won't happen to me* category. As I continue reading, I spot something that makes my jaw drop. The person who was assaulted by Nicky White earlier this year wasn't his current PO – a highly experienced professional – it was his original probation officer Sophie... my good friend Sophie. Is that what tipped her over the edge?

10

Two days later I find myself manoeuvring around tourists on the narrow, cobbled streets of the Barbican. I pass the cafes and souvenir shops selling ice cream and West Country fudge, and make my way towards the far edge of the harbourfront. It's not long before I spot the yellow and black crime scene tape blocking access to where Nicky White's body was found. The scene ahead is average, unremarkable. Just an inlet with oil slicked water, and plastic bottles being bashed against a stone jetty by the rising tide. I wave as I approach, hoping to disguise my growing sense of unease with a pasted-on smile. Normally Sophie is a confident, effervescent personality. In the early days she struggled to be taken seriously, but her intelligence, work ethic and tendency to swear like a navvy meant any sceptics were quickly silenced. Now, she looks ghostly pale, her eyes desperate and wide, someone clearly in the throes of crushing anxiety. I know that look. *I have felt that look.*

'Hello, my lovely,' I say, kissing her cheek. She's chosen an outside table, with a view of the marina. I find my eyes straying the few hundred metres past the yachts and fishing boats, to where Nicky's body floated face down in the water for nearly five hours. I wonder about his last moments: the murky water filling his mouth, nose and lungs, the sense of absolute helplessness as darkness came.

'Wine?' Sophie pours me a glass from a half empty bottle, then raises her hand to a nearby waitress. 'Another please.'

I take a reluctant sip. I'd hoped the meeting would be a social one, but considering Sophie's circumstances, how can we not talk shop?

'So how are things?' she says lightly.

'Fine,' I reply. And then, knowing I must ask, 'And with you?'

Sophie downs her wine in one gulp. 'How do you think? I've been signed off with stress for the foreseeable future, given a shitload of anti-depressants, and this morning I received a voicemail from Simon asking about my case notes.'

'He shouldn't be doing that,' I say, 'not while you're signed off.'

'Like he gives a shit,' Sophie snarls. 'Said it was just some general information he needed so he could temporarily reassign my caseload.' She closes her eyes as if the thought is too much to bear, 'But, you know.'

'It could be that.'

'Yeah, right. The caring sharing Simon.' Sophie snorts.

'I'm sure there's nothing to worry about.' I try to console her, but I know different. Among the comments in Simon's notebook was a telling list of actions in preparation of the Inspectorate's visit in November.

> *Check all files for missed signatures.*
> *Check for inappropriate guidance/bias.*
> *Have they followed all protocols to the letter?*
> *Have appropriate referrals been made/followed up?*

The final note is what really got me worried.

Are there any fitness to practice issues for Sophie?

'I've spoken to my union rep,' says Sophie, sounding less than hopeful. 'She says not to worry.'

'I'm sure she's right,' I reply, with forced optimism. I genuinely want to support her, but I'm also feeling horribly guilty for the fact that I'm relieved it's Sophie under the microscope, and not me.

'You know they're trying to cull staff, don't you?' Sophie's look has hardened, and there's a discernible bitterness in her voice.

'I haven't heard about another call for voluntary redundancies.'

'Not voluntary,' Sophie spits the words, 'mandatory.' The waitress arrives with another bottle, and Sophie hurriedly refills our glasses. I don't touch mine. 'Who do you think is going to get the chop first? The newly qualified POs, easily mouldable and on the lowest pay grade, or the more seasoned staff with a few issues, and maybe one or two skeletons in the closet?' I stare at her, uncertain of what to say. 'I guess you've heard about Nicky White?' Sophie points towards the far end of the marina. 'They found his body right there. What's the intel?'

I hesitate, but decide I owe her something.

'Beaten up, dumped in the water. The consensus seems to be that it was a drug deal gone bad.'

'I thought he was with a girl before it happened?'

I stop mid-sip. 'Who told you that?'

Sophie gives a noncommittal shrug. 'I still like to keep in the know, and one hears things.'

'I suppose one does.'

'I was hoping for a custodial sentence when he was last up

in front of a judge.' She gives a bitter snort. 'I knew one more spell in Dartmoor wouldn't change him, but at least it would keep other women safe.'

'Because of his assault on you?'

Sophie's eyes flash. 'How did you find out about that?'

I can't tell her it was from sneaking a peek at Simon's notes.

I throw it back at her. 'Why didn't you tell me?'

Sophie stares into the distance, and sighs.

'You had enough crap going on in your life with the divorce and then, you know, Katie.' She pauses, sensitive enough to know not to go there. 'And anyway, I was advised to keep it hush-hush.'

'Hush-hush?' I stare at her in disbelief. Who would advise her to do that? 'Did Simon know about this?'

Sophie's eyes widen, and then she begins to laugh, a deep throaty cackle that puts my already jangled nerves even further on edge. 'It was his idea.'

That's when I realise just how out of the loop I've been.

'I'm so sorry I wasn't there for you, Sophie.'

'Why should you be?' she says softly. 'And anyway, like I said, I kept most of it to myself.'

'And that trip to the hospital?'

'The suicide attempt you mean?'

'Maybe I could have helped.'

'*No* one could have.'

I feel suddenly overwhelmingly sad. Once, Sophie and I were close friends. Now we feel like strangers. The words come before I can stop them.

'I'm scared.'

Clearly taken aback, she reaches not for her wine glass, but for my hand.

'Oh shit, Grace.'

'Yeah,' I reply.

She rifles through the bucket bag at her feet, and emerges with a packet of cigarettes, points one my way.

'Want one?'

'God yes!'

She leans forward with her lighter, then we sit back, inhaling the carcinogens with a guilty sense of enjoyment.

'So you know it's not just me he's after.'

I watch as she exhales, the smoke clouding her face.

'I know.'

'And you know he got the Anton Cross case passed to you.'

'He was busy. I was just helping out.'

Sophie speaks slowly, emphasising each word. 'It was supposed to be *his* case. He was Cross's Offender Manager and was supposed to be dealing with all that bastard's issues with missing appointments, and contravening restrictions. Instead, he got it shifted to you.' I try to look away, but she holds my gaze. 'He knew it was going to be time consuming and complex, writing up the report and dealing with all the crap that came along with it, which knowing Anton, there was bound to be.' She pauses to take a long drag on her cigarette. 'Maybe he thought all that work would stop you being able to give your all to the Senior Probation Officer application.'

Is she saying what I think she's saying? That Simon deliberately got the Cross case transferred to me, in order to give himself leverage for a promotion opportunity? Has Sophie gotten so paranoid that she really believes this?

'I don't think–'

'Has he asked to see my records yet?' she asks. Clocking my expression, she adds darkly, 'I thought so. I'd watch my back if I were you.'

'Sophie, please.'

'Why do you think they had the internal investigation in the first place?'

'You mean about Katie Cross?' I'm not sure what she's getting at. 'It's standard procedure for a serious further offence.'

'SFO or not,' she says, beginning to sound testy, 'why the particular emphasis on you? I mean, it *was* your signature on the report with the safehouse address, but there were copies of it all over the place.'

She flicks her cigarette end into the harbour, where it floats briefly before being submerged by the wake of a passing fishing boat. 'It's all changed.' She reaches for another cigarette, then decides against it. 'We all used to look out for each other.'

I find myself feeling tearful, again. 'There doesn't seem to be the time to do that anymore.'

'Or the interest.' Sophie lifts the wine glass to her mouth and, finding it empty, puts it down again. 'Do you know after Nicky assaulted me, I had nasty phone calls, people watching the house, dog shit through my letter box? I had to have it sealed up after someone tried to put a burning rag through it. They even tried to hack into my bank account.'

'What? How–'

'Bit of a tech whiz kid was our Nicky.' In any other context the words could be interpreted as complimentary, except for the look of absolute hatred on Sophie's face. She points to the inlet where Nicky White's body was found. 'I'm glad that little bastard is dead. I only wish I was the one who put him there.'

I insist on taking Sophie home, because the wine has hit her. Once inside her flat, I help her get undressed and into bed. I check the windows and balcony doors are locked, and make a mental note to speak to the Police Protection Unit about security advice.

I place a large glass of water and two paracetamol tablets on the bedside table. I'm just leaning over to kiss her forehead when her eyes open. They're bloodshot and groggy, probably a mixture of the wine and prescription medication I've seen on her bedside table.

'There's one more thing you should know, Grace,' she whispers, 'because I've been looking into things.'

'Things?' I ask. I'm not certain what sort of information she'll be able to offer in her current state, but I still sit down on the bed next to her. 'What things?'

She gives me a look that suggests she's aware I'm humouring her, but carries on.

'You know Anton Cross had minors before he killed Katie? In and out of Dartmoor for DV, common assault, you name it.' I don't reply. He was never one of my clients, and I haven't had the courage to look at his case file. 'One of those times was in 2021,' she continues. 'July 2021.'

'Okay?' I really have no idea what she's getting at.

'At exactly the same time Nicky White had a spell inside.'

It takes a few seconds for me to process the information. 'Nicky and Anton were in Dartmoor Prison at the same time?'

'Only for about two weeks,' she replies, 'but it's possible they might have hung around in the same circles.'

'It's a big prison–'

'They're connected, Grace.' Sophie's eyes begin to flicker shut as the booze, pills and fatigue take over. 'Somehow they're connected.'

I arrive home with a heavy heart and a ready meal, my mind racing. *Was what Sophie said all just some kind of paranoid fantasy, or could she have a point?* It *was* eminently possible that Nicky and Anton could have been in Dartmoor together, as

Sophie suggested. They were both repeat offenders, and most Category B or C offences tried in Plymouth are either sent to Dartmoor or to HMP Exeter. Those two 'hanging around in the same circles,' however, was not a good thing, particularly as Nicky's family had been known to handle stolen weapons. Could the Whites have provided Anton with the weapon that he used to kill Katie? This thought is almost unbearable. There's also the problem that the gun itself was never found, so there was no way of actually linking it to anyone one person or criminal organisation. It all may seem like a bit of a fluke, but after so many years working in the criminal justice system I tend not to believe in coincidence anymore.

I check my texts. There's one from Marcus confirming he will be *incommunicado* for a while, which is code for saying he's going covert and won't be down this weekend as promised, and one from Jodie reminding me she's staying at her friend Jasmine's house tonight.

I pop the ready meal into the microwave. It comes out looking like something I would feed the dog, which I do, and instead seek solace in a packet of crisps and my laptop. I find myself searching the Paradise Church website for more information about Pastor Tim Anderson. If my daughter is spending time with him, I want the full intel.

Paradise Church, the friendly community church in the heart of
Plymouth.
We're a group of friendly, supportive people from all kinds of
Backgrounds, who have all been touched by the love and grace
of God.

I glance through the events section, which includes group meetings: *AA, NA, Women Moving Forward, Victim Support, Community Outreach and Counselling,* as well as lists of weekday and Sunday services. I scroll down to the youth club section of the website, where I am surprised to discover a *zine* with practical suggestions on how to deal with exam stress, designed by Jodie. There's also a list of youth committee members, with Jodie's name front and centre. Time to find out more. I make my way upstairs, where I slip into a pair of Lycra leggings, a running top and trainers.

'Fancy a run, Bizzy?'

The dog jumps up from where he has been napping on the bed and begins barking. It's been weeks since I've mustered the energy to go for a proper run. The workload and worries have prompted an inertia that has not only left me unfit, but with a few unwelcome extra pounds as well.

We run through the park, past the bail hostel and along the tree-lined path behind Paradise Church. Even though I'm puffing heavily, I run on. 'Come on, boy,' I call, quickening my pace. 'Let's go for it!' The dog yelps in excitement and in a moment of confusion, crosses directly in front of me, causing the lead to tangle between my feet, and sending me hurtling to the ground. I land heavily, banging my knees and elbows, and grazing my cheek on the pavement. It's a few seconds before I'm able to push myself into a sitting position. I give silent thanks that there are no broken bottles on the path. As I get to my feet, I feel the world around me begin to spin, and find myself staggering towards a nearby retaining wall for support.

'Oh, my goodness,' comes a voice from nearby, 'are you all right?' I look over to the church car park, from which a slim, blonde woman is hurrying towards me. 'What happened?'

'I was running,' I say. The words feel scrambled, barely coherent. 'I tripped.' Bismarck nuzzles up against me, in apparent apology. 'It's all right, Bizzy,' I whisper. 'Just an accident, you silly thing.' I bend down and scratch him under the chin, but as I lift my head, I feel my legs begin to give.

'Easy now,' says the woman, slipping an arm around my waist to keep me from collapsing. 'You had better come with me.'

'Really, I'm fine. I just—'

'You're bleeding.' It's only then that I realise the liquid on my cheek isn't perspiration; it's blood. 'There's a first aid box in the church hall.' The sight of blood dripping onto my arm halts any desire to argue further. Instead, I allow myself to be led across the car park, into the same back entrance I had passed through only a few nights before. I find myself being seated on a chair in the small back office, and a clean, damp tea towel is gently pressed against my elbow.

'Looks like just a few grazes,' the woman says, opening the first aid box and taking out some cotton wool and disinfectant. 'Can you tell me your name, and what day it is?'

'I'm fine,' I reply, feeling much more clear-headed now that I'm sitting down. 'I didn't really fall that hard. It was just the shock of it.'

'Good.' The woman hands me a wad of cotton wool moistened with disinfectant. 'Why don't you do your face while I make us a cup of tea?'

As I wait for the British cure for all, I dab at my blazing cheek, and gaze around the office. There is an outdated PC, with an even more outdated printer. On the shelf above it is a Bible, and next to that a small, framed photograph. In it, the blonde woman is sitting on a bench, and next to her sits Tim Anderson. He has his arm around her shoulders, and they both look terribly serious.

'Here you go,' says the woman, placing a cup of tea in front of me. 'Are you certain you don't feel dizzy?' She deftly places two fingers on the inside of my wrist and begins taking my pulse. 'Any headache, nausea?'

'I'm fine, Ingrid, really.'

She looks up in surprise. 'Have we met?'

I indicate towards the photograph. 'No, but I met your husband on Monday night. I'm Grace Midwinter; my daughter is Jodie Treglann.'

'Oh yes, of course,' says Ingrid, 'I thought I recognised the dog. Jodie is a much-valued member of our youth congregation. Such a lovely girl. Her contribution to the teen mental health support group has been invaluable.'

I try to keep the curiosity from my voice. 'Mental health support group?'

'She's been so articulate about her struggles,' continues Ingrid, brightly.

I feel an acute sense of jealousy. Jodie has categorically refused to discuss her mental health issues with me, beyond the basic confirmation that she is attending her counselling appointments and taking her medication.

'Yes,' I lie, 'so articulate.'

Ingrid doesn't look up from where she has been gently cleaning my knee with an antiseptic wipe.

'Tim told me there was a little, ah, uncertainty on Monday night?'

I put the crimson cotton wool pad on the desk in front of me and reach for my tea. 'Jodie missed youth club. She wanted to say sorry to Tim, so came by late.'

'Ah,' replies Ingrid, apparently not the least bit surprised that a fifteen-year-old girl would be visiting her husband at ten o'clock at night. 'Tim also mentioned you weren't aware she was with us – in the congregation, I mean?' I shake my head no, too embarrassed to speak. *What kind of mother doesn't know her own daughter has been attending a church group for months?* I recall all those times when I'd thought she was going to the gym or hanging out with her friends. *What about the weekends she stayed with her father? Did he know?*

'It looks like the bleeding has stopped now,' says Ingrid. Gently taking my chin in her hand, she turns my head slightly to the left. 'Let's have a look at that cheek, shall we?' I sit quietly, studying the pastor's wife more closely. She must be in her early forties, with the strong bone structure and the icy blue eyes of someone with clear Scandinavian origins. I note the hint of a north-eastern accent, perhaps Newcastle? Durham?

'Looks fine to me,' she says, 'but I would expect some rather colourful bruising in the morning.'

'Are you a nurse?'

'Just a first aider.' Ingrid reaches for another wipe, to clean her hands.

'Thank you for looking after me.'

'It's what we do.' She pauses, and gives me a searching look. 'I hope you don't mind me asking, but Jodie has mentioned some, ah... difficulties at home.'

Humiliation hits me hard. I find myself on the defensive. 'I don't think–'

'Please,' Ingrid interrupts. 'This is in no way a judgement or criticism. Tim and I weren't blessed with children of our own, but we have fostered many over the years. Believe me, I know how difficult it can be,' she touches my arm, 'and how lonely.'

I close my eyes, willing myself not to cry. *What must she be thinking of me, this pastor's wife? That I'm some crazy woman, falling over outside her church, smelling of wine and desperation?* I open my eyes again, to see Ingrid smiling at me.

'Be crumbled,' she says softly, 'so wildflowers will come up where you are.'

It's one of my favourite poems, from a collection Jodie gave me for Christmas. It's a few seconds before I'm able to speak. 'You know Rumi?'

Ingrid chuckles. 'I'm not just full of Bible quotes, you know.'

There is a moment of relaxed stillness between us, of ease...

then I remember that I've got case files to review, and there's been a funny smell coming from the dishwasher.

'I'd better go.'

Ingrid opens a drawer and removes a leaflet. 'Take one of these. It lists all our services, the support we offer.' She writes a mobile number on the back. 'My personal number if you ever fancy a chat. Along with coordinating all the community and outreach groups, I'm also a trained counsellor. I've done a lot of work with people going through difficult transitions.'

'Thank you.' I attempt to push myself out of the chair, but my body aches and I inadvertently make a small squeal of pain.

'I'd better drive you and Bismarck home.' Ingrid takes my hands and gently helps me to my feet. 'You know, you'd be most welcome to attend our church service on Sunday. You could find out a bit more about us.' There's a questioning, almost challenging look in her eyes. 'It could also be an excellent opportunity for you to engage with Jodie, perhaps find some common ground?'

'I'm not really the religious type.'

Ingrid shakes her head. 'It's not *all* about religion, Grace. Yes, worship and prayer are essential to our beliefs, but that's only a part of what we do. We're also about community and looking out for one another.' Her voice drops to a soft whisper. 'And I sense you could do with some support.'

I'm not sure how to respond to her invitation. I'm still not comfortable with this whole set-up, but there is one thing she's right about; getting involved with Paradise Church could be a way of bringing me and Jodie closer together.

'I'll think about it.'

'Good,' she says calmly, 'that's a start.'

We're just making our way out of the office when the back door springs open.

'Tim?' Ingrid's voice has gone up an octave. 'I thought you weren't back until later?'

'The meeting finished early.' He sounds different from the easy-going pastor I met on Monday night. I step into the hallway to stand beside her. It takes a second for him to register my presence.

'Grace. What a surprise.' He attempts to sound cheerful. 'Have a thing for late night visits?'

'I found her outside,' says Ingrid. Gone is the calm professional, replaced now by someone walking a tightrope. 'She fell over.'

I know this scenario. Have seen it hundreds of times before. 'I was running,' I add quickly. 'Bismarck cut in front of me.' I hold up my battered elbow. 'Ingrid's been looking after me.'

He looks to his wife. 'Of course she has.'

Ingrid vibrates with tension. 'I was just going to drive her home.'

'I'm sure I can manage.' I'm not a part of this conversation, not yet.

Ingrid rests her hand on my arm. It's cold. 'Are you certain you don't want a lift?'

'I'll be fine, honestly.'

'Well at least let me see you out.'

I wish Tim goodnight, and follow Ingrid out of the back door and into the cool night air.

'Are you going to be okay?' I whisper.

'Okay?'

'Safe.'

'I don't know what you mean.'

I tread very carefully. 'It's just that Tim seems rather edgy.'

'Oh that.' Ingrid dismisses the awkward tension with a flick of her wrist. 'He's just worried about his mother. His father passed away a few months ago, and along with all his other responsibilities, Tim now has to travel up the country regularly to support her.' Bitterness seeps into her voice. 'His brother lives ten miles away from her, but he can't be bothered...' She stops herself, realising that perhaps she has said too much.

I reach into the zip pocket of my leggings, remove my mobile, and text the number she has written on the back of the leaflet.

'Now you've got my personal number. If there's ever anything that you need, call me – day or night.'

Ingrid's expression has become indecipherable. After a moment, she reaches forward, and gently squeezes my hand.

'Thank you, Grace.'

Maybe it's not me who needs *her* help, but the other way around.

11

I wake before dawn and stare out of the bedroom window as darkness slowly eases into light. Every inch of my body aches, and there are smudges of blood all over my sheets where my cuts and grazes have oozed in the night. My bedside clock reads 5.04 am. A year ago today, Anton Cross shot and killed his nine-year-old daughter Katie on her front doorstep. During the inquest there was evidence that Anton had discovered the safehouse address where his wife and daughter were staying, but no evidence of how. The coroner had introduced several possibilities, such as a lack of due diligence from a number of agencies including probation services, but nothing had been proved. His final words, *'We may never know,'* were as painful and ineffectual then as they are now. None of that matters though. The fact is that the first two pages of the safeguarding report that I had commented on, and which had included Katie and her mother's safehouse address, had been found at Anton Cross' bedsit. What if I *had* sent it? *Could I be responsible for the death of an innocent child?*

I walk the dog, shower, dress smartly and make my way to the local florists, where I collect my order of nine white tulips.

I'm relieved that Jodie is on a school trip trekking across the moors, not having to deal with her mother's distress.

It's nearly eleven by the time I arrive at the crematorium. I wander past tidy identical rows of pale war graves, past the sombre memorial for the hundreds killed in the Plymouth blitz, and towards the cemetery. Even from a distance, I can see Katie's grave is already overflowing with tributes. I place the tulips next to a large arrangement that reads *Our Angel*, then sit on a bench near a gnarled yew tree and ring Alex.

'Grace.' He sounds surprised. 'Are you okay? Is Jodie okay?'

'Can we meet?'

'What, today?'

'Never mind.' My voice sounds as dull and hopeless as I feel. 'I imagine you're busy.'

'I've got a few things to do, but could meet you a little later. Lunch maybe?'

'Only if it's no trouble.'

'Of course it's not.'

We meet at a pub on the Barbican when I'm already halfway through my second glass of wine.

'Starting a bit early, aren't we?' says Alex. 'And what the hell happened to your face?'

'I fell over.' I note his sceptical look. 'I was running.'

'I'm getting a beer.' He glances at my glass, and says, 'I expect you'll want another.'

He returns a few minutes later, sits down opposite me, and sips his lager.

'So, what's up?'

'I wanted to know if you're still looking into the Anton Cross case?'

There's a sudden look of recognition on his face.

'Shit! Today's the anniversary, isn't it?' He gets up and

comes over to sit beside me. 'I should have remembered. I'm sorry.'

'It's okay,' I reply, but it isn't. 'You've been busy with the murder case.'

'Not so busy that I shouldn't have remembered.'

'So, the Cross investigation.'

'Honey,' Alex lets out a deep sigh, 'the coroner returned a verdict of unlawful killing. The case is closed.'

'Closed but not resolved,' I reply, 'because we still don't know how my report got to his bedsit.'

'*Grace.*' Alex is sitting so close that our shoulders are touching. In the cool of the air-conditioned pub, I welcome the warmth of his skin against mine. 'You've got to stop torturing yourself like this. There are tens of ways that report could have got to Cross, none of them to do with you.'

'Can you guarantee that?' Alex looks away. 'It's a year today since she was murdered, and we're not really any closer to discovering how my report got there.'

He points to the empty wine glasses on the table in front of me. 'Is that the reason for all the liquid pain relief?'

'What do you think?'

'And Marcus?'

'What about him?'

'Why aren't you talking to *him* about this? I thought Jodie said he was coming down this weekend?'

'He had to go undercover on a drugs thing.'

'Sounds exciting,' Alex mutters, 'but if it were me...'

'Yes?'

'Well, if you were my partner, or *still* my partner, knowing what day it is today, I would be here.'

'And so you are.' I lift my glass in a mock toast.

'Look, Grace.' He sighs. 'I've told you everything I can about the investigation, about who had access to your report.' Alex rubs his jaw. 'There was the CPS, police, social services, probation, Sally's solicitor—'

'I know, I know. They all had copies.'

'We visited every office, checked all their governance procedures, file storage, data protection.'

'Nothing?'

'Nothing.'

'If you could get me a copy of your investigation...'

Alex puts his beer glass down with a thump. 'Come on, Grace. You may be NPS, but you know there's no way I can do that.'

I consider telling him what Sophie disclosed to me last night, but he probably won't have any more information about Anton and Nicky's previous detentions than I do.

'Maybe there's something we've missed.'

'You mean *I've* missed,' he says, his voice tight. 'I've done everything I can to protect you, Grace. You've just got to believe that there is no evidence linking you to that court report.'

'It's not about the evidence, Alex; it's about the truth.'

Alex speaks slowly, as if to a child. 'The Coroner's Court has declared it impossible to determine who sent that letter. You're in the clear.'

'Is that all you think I care about?'

'Jesus.' Alex's lips have thinned into a straight line. 'Have you ever considered just how much this obsession of yours is affecting our daughter?'

I open my mouth to snap a reply when I catch sight of my reflection in the mirror across from me. My cheeks are flushed from the wine, I've got dark circles under my eyes, and there's an angry scrape on my left cheekbone. *I look like something out of a zombie movie.* 'I'm sorry,' I mutter. 'I shouldn't have called you.'

Alex sighs. 'Of course you should have. It's a difficult day for you. Have you eaten?'

'Not since breakfast.'

Alex stands up, holds out his hand, and helps me to my feet. 'I think we'd better get some food into you, don't you?'

We wander to the Italian cafe we used to frequent when we were married, and order old favourites: bruschetta, anti-pasti, and olives. We're just finishing our espressos, when Alex clears his throat in a way I know means he's about to say something serious.

'I know that the timing isn't great, Grace, but Jodie has asked if she can come and stay with me for the summer.'

I feel a sickness deep in the pit of my stomach. 'Are you kidding me?'

'I know.' It's not the first time we've had this back and forth from Jodie since the divorce. 'After she finishes her exams. She said she needs a bit of space.'

'A bit of a space from *what*?' I shake my head. 'No, Alex. I won't have it. I know Jodie and I have our challenges, but I'm really not prepared to be messed around like this.'

'It isn't always about *you*, Grace.' I can see the muscle in his jaw pulsate as he tries to calm himself. 'I know you and I need to present a united front, but I also think Jodie has the right to make some decisions for herself. I'm going to pay the bill and walk you home. We'll have another cup of coffee, and talk about it like adults, okay?'

I say nothing. The last thing I feel like doing is behaving like an adult. We walk the half mile to Penzance Street in silence. It takes me a few tries to unlock the door.

'Hey, Bizzy!' cries Alex, as the dog jumps on him in excitement. 'How've you been?' The dog whines in pleasure at seeing his former master. 'Why don't you make the coffee?' he says to me. 'And I'll take the old fella for a walk.'

He returns a half hour later, the smell of fresh air on his skin.

'Still one sugar?' I say, putting the pod in the coffee maker and turning it on. He's standing in the kitchen, looking at the noticeboard. 'Since when did you do mindfulness?'

'Just something I thought I'd try.'

'Hmm.' He turns to me. 'The handle on the downstairs loo is wonky.'

'I'm not much of a handyman.'

'And Marcus?'

I give him a look, and hand him his coffee.

'I know things are tough for Jodie,' I say, returning to our previous subject. 'She's got her exams coming up, and there are a few issues with school, but I've been doing everything I can to support her.' I debate whether to mention her late night visit to Tim, and the whole Paradise Church thing, but decide against it. The last thing I need right now is for Alex to further question my parenting skills. 'I've been trying, you know. I drive her to counselling appointments, make sure she takes her meds, does her coursework.' *Why am I suddenly so tearful?* 'I just worry.'

'I know,' he whispers. 'I do too.'

Something undoes me, and suddenly I'm crying.

'It'll be all right,' Alex whispers, 'we'll work it out.' When he takes me into his arms I don't resist. His lips touch my forehead, the bruise on my cheek, and then settle on my mouth. I feel his hands move to encircle my waist. Against my better judgement, I find myself responding. Our lips part, his tongue touches mine. He pulls me in closer. The familiarity of his body, the feel of him, is overpowering. When his lips travel to the curve of my neck, I moan softly. His hands slip under my blouse.

'*Grace,*' he murmurs.

'Yes,' I reply. *God knows I'll regret this in the morning,* 'Yes.'

I wake to an empty space on the bed beside me. I give a small sigh of relief, then I hear the pop and hiss of the coffee maker and shortly afterwards, footsteps on the stairs.

'White, no sugar,' says Alex, entering the bedroom with two steaming cups of coffee. He's wearing boxer shorts, and a hopeful smile.

'You're still here.'

He pauses. 'I thought we could have coffee in bed like the old days.'

I throw on a T-shirt, and a pair of knickers.

'This isn't the old days, Alex.'

He places the mugs on the bedside table. I feel the give of the mattress as he sits on the bed next to me.

'Can't we just enjoy this moment, just for once?'

I stare at the swirling wisps of steam rising from the mugs. A few years ago, this would have been nice, *normal.* Early morning sex, then coffee in bed. An image of Alex and Denise at the staff Christmas do bursts into my brain. How close they stood. The way his hands rested on hers shoulders that little bit too long as he helped her on with her coat.

'This was a mistake.'

'Not a mistake.' Alex reaches for my hand. 'How it should be.'

'No.' I pull my hand from his. I think of Jodie and Marcus, of my colossal betrayal. 'Jodie will be home any minute.'

'You wanted this,' his tone shifts to something more severe, 'were a part of this.'

I only wish I could deny it. 'We've divorced, Alex. I'm with someone else now.'

'Oh yeah, the wonderful Marcus. Only he's not the one you called yesterday, and he's not the one you're with right now.'

'It's not that simple.'

'Or that difficult!' Alex grabs his T-shirt and jeans from the chair next to the bed and begins getting dressed. 'Only like everything else in your life you have to make it into a huge drama!'

'What?!'

'You need to get your shit together, Grace.' He's standing in front of me now. 'I know it's been a tough year for you, for all of us actually, and I realise this may not have been the wisest thing for us to do, but it's happened, and we need to deal with it.'

'I can't do this right now.'

'You've got to.' I can hear the frustration in his voice. '*We've* got to, for Jodie's sake.'

'Can't we just forget this ever happened?'

'But it *has* happened!' During our marriage Alex was always the rational one, the argument winner. 'Whatever happens from here on in, we need to agree that Jodie is our priority.'

'Of course she is!'

'Then if she wants to come and stay with me for the summer, we should let her.'

Whammo! Fell right into that one.

I hate the idea of Jodie leaving me, of the possibility that she might just want to be with her father more than me, but digging my heels in will only make Jodie more adamant. In that way, she's much more like Alex than me.

'Can I think about it, please?'

He offers that sad, gentle smile that won me over all those years before.

'Of course.' He reaches over and touches my cheek. 'I'll ring you later, okay? We can talk some more.'

The last thing I want to do is talk, but he's right; this is about Jodie, not me.

I watch him disappear downstairs, and then hear the soft

click as he pulls the front door shut. I follow, making my way to the kitchen, where I scramble for a tissue from a box on the table. As desperate and unscrupulous as it might seem, I need to do something to get Jodie on *my* side. Lying prominently next to some unopened post is the brochure from Paradise Church that Ingrid gave me last night, a few dots of blood from my accident spattered across the front cover, the memory of her words an invocation: *'Coming to Paradise Church could also be an excellent opportunity for you to re-engage with Jodie, perhaps find some common ground?'*

12

I am on Sunday morning is the first time I've seen the front entrance of Paradise Church, my only experiences so far having been stealing in through the back door after Jodie, or being led in there bloody and bruised by Ingrid. The building is unremarkable, just a block of prefabricated pebble-dashed concrete, clearly post-war, and clearly not expected to last beyond the eighties.

Not quite Notre Dame.

I chastise myself for being so ungenerous. Church really isn't my thing, but if it gets me closer to Jodie, closer to keeping her with me, then I'm all in. I've parked across the street, unable to ingratiate myself into the communal parking lot. I'm now on foot, just waiting for a gap in the traffic, when I have a crisis of confidence.

'Who am I kidding?' I mutter, and turning, make my way back towards my car.

'Grace!' I sneak a backwards glance, and spot a familiar face bobbing towards me, a hand raised high in greeting. I pretend not to hear, groping instead for the car door handle. 'Grace?' Ingrid is standing next to me. 'I'm so glad you came.'

'I don't think this is such a good idea.' I'm gripping the car door handle so fiercely my fingertips have gone blue.

'You'll be fine,' whispers Ingrid. 'I'll look after you.'

'I'm not sure I'm ready for this.'

Ingrid chuckles. 'I imagine not!'

'Pardon?'

'Do you think any of us is really ready for salvation?' I feel her arm around my shoulders. 'Relax. Taking part in our service this morning is not about anything other than spending sixty minutes with God and some very kind people. There is no objective, no outcome, no risk to assess, and no strings attached.'

I find myself relaxing slightly, and then unexpectedly, I'm being led across the street to where a handful of friendly looking parishioners are smiling at me.

I'm welcomed into the hall and led to a seat near the front. The inside of the building is as nondescript as its exterior. Magnolia coloured walls, rows of conference centre style chairs, and at the front a small, raised stage area where four musicians are warming up.'

'Are you visiting?' I turn to see a woman sitting down next to me.

'I'm a friend of Ingrid's.'

'Wonderful,' she replies. 'You may find our service a little bit different, but don't let that put you off.'

I swallow hard. My mouth is dry. The room seems hazy, and I'm feeling more than a little uncomfortable. The band begins to play, and a pretty, dark-haired young woman starts singing something about God being a lion, or is it a lamb? The room seems hot. I feel a bead of sweat roll down my spine. The music fades. A voice begins to speak.

'We lift our hands to the Lord.' It's Tim, his deep baritone soft, yet compelling. 'We lift our hands in praise to our saviour Jesus Christ, to our church, our community and to our kind sisters and brothers who sing to his glory.' There are a few faint calls of *hallelujah,* and some scattered applause. I find myself mustering the courage to open my eyes.

'But did you know,' continues Tim, 'that in lifting our hands as we do now, as we do every Sunday, does not always imply joy or praise? In the Bible this gesture is actually recorded as a sign of surrender.'

I glance around the room. Young people, couples, families, single women, and men of all ages, they're all here. Normal, happy, committed. This is definitely not what I expected. I take a deep breath and relax a little.

'So, I am asking you now,' continues Tim, 'asking each and every one of you here today to surrender yourself to God; to give yourself to his kindness and his grace; to throw away your fears, your self-obsessions, your wantonness. I want you to surrender your heart and soul to our Lord so that he can cleanse you of your sins and help you find a new path to salvation. Surrendering is what makes us powerful.' Tim's tone is resolute, but kind, his conviction clear. 'I am asking each one of you today to surrender your guilt, your fears, your anger.' I look up to see Tim standing in front of me. He takes my hands and gently lifts me to my feet. 'Surrender your feelings of unworthiness, Grace.' He moves on to the woman next to me. 'Surrender your fears about loss.' Again and again, Tim repeats this act until he has made his way around the room, and back to the stage. He places his hands on the lectern and bows his head. 'Pray with me.' He drops his voice to a whisper, but it still seems to reach every corner of the room. 'Say it with me. I surrender myself to you, oh Lord. I surrender myself to you, oh Lord.' With each repetition his voice grows stronger. The entire congregation is testifying, repeating the phrase softly, no different to reciting the Hail Mary during mass at my Catholic secondary school.

As the service ends, I make my way out of the hall and into the small foyer area. People are milling around, smiling, chatting to each other. There's a genuine sense of community and support. I can see why Jodie likes it here. There's a hand on my shoulder. Ingrid is beside me, pressing her cool cheek against mine.

'How did you find it?'

'It was, well, interesting.'

'I knew you would like it.'

'Thank you for inviting me.'

'I was hoping you could stay for a bit.' Ingrid sounds determined. 'I could really do with some help serving the coffees and teas.' I hesitate, but after all the help and support she has given Jodie recently, the last thing I want to do is appear ungrateful.

'Grace is a probation officer,' Ingrid announces to one of the other volunteers as I hand out mugs of instant coffee. Betty, a sprightly OAP with a shock of white hair, reaches forward and pats me on the back of my hand.

'A noble occupation.'

'I'm not so sure about that.'

The actual truth is, Betty, that for most of yesterday, I was completely pissed, and then I had sex with my ex-husband even though I have a steady partner. Not quite Mother Teresa, am I?

'Why don't you help me with the washing up?' says Ingrid, interrupting the exchange. 'We can talk some more.'

I find myself being led into the small kitchen area. Ingrid ties an apron around my waist, and hands me a tea towel. I'm just starting to dry off the coffee mugs, when half a dozen people enter the hall, led by Tim. They're all wearing purple fleeces with the words *Paradise Church Street Pastors* written across the back in gold lettering. Tim unlocks a storage cupboard at the rear of the hall and removes two large boxes with the words *Stoke Cash & Carry* stamped on them. He claps his hands to call attention. 'Come on, everyone. Let's not forget it's another bank holiday. We've got a lot to do before tonight's Go Out.'

I turn to Ingrid. 'Go Out?'

'Have you not heard of the street pastors programme?' she says, handing me a tray of hot drinks. 'We go out most weekends, helping the homeless and vulnerable. We provide food, toiletries, make referrals to support services, but perhaps most importantly we offer service to young people emerging from pubs and clubs a little worse for wear.' I'm surprised I haven't heard of this already, in my line of work. 'We give them water and lollies to help with dehydration, and any other general support, such as ensuring they get home safely.' She shakes her head sadly. 'With the number of incidents of spiking and sexual assaults lately, we're finding this takes up a good proportion of our time.'

'What an incredible thing to do.'

Ingrid gives a good-natured shrug. 'It's nothing really, just us as church members following the example of our Lord and Saviour.' She scrutinises me. 'You know, we're always looking for more helpers.'

I'm taken aback. While the service was pleasant enough, I am no convert and probably never will be... but if there is some way I could be involved with Paradise Church it might just help to keep Jodie on my side.

'It's been wonderful being here, and the work you're doing is amazing.'

'But it's not right for you.'

I think about Jodie, about last night with Alex.

'I'm not quite sure what's right for me at the moment.'

Ingrid places her hand on mine. Her expression is warm. 'Is there anything I can do to help?'

Ingrid takes me by the arm, and leads me to the back office, where only a few days before she treated my cuts and bruises. She pulls a chair forward. 'Sit.' Her face is filled with kindness. 'There's still some tea in the pot. I imagine we could both do with another drink.' She returns minutes later, with two cups of tea and a plate of Bourbon biscuits. She pushes the plate towards me. 'Take your time and tell me what's on your mind.'

'My relationship with Jodie has always been strong, until recently.'

Ingrid reaches across and takes my hand. 'Believe me, Grace, we all have periods in our life where we feel that way. The important thing is to have faith and carry on.'

'But I'm a fraud.'

'How is it that you are a fraud?' Ingrid's tone is challenging. 'You work with some of the most awful people in the country, keeping us safe.'

'My work used to mean everything to me,' I say. *Sometimes taking precedence over my own family*, is the bit I don't tell her. 'Did you know that until very recently I was under investigation for professional misconduct?' Ingrid does her best to hide her surprise. 'And that Jodie wants to go and live with her father?' The confessional is now wide open. 'The youth club, Bible studies, newsletter. Did she really think I wouldn't understand?' Ingrid smiles sympathetically but says nothing. 'Do you know how it feels, to find out that your own child is keeping secrets from you?'

'I'm well aware of the damage caused by secrets.' Ingrid leans closer. 'Perhaps now is the time to start doing something to change your situation?' Shame washes over me.

'Does Jodie really think I wouldn't understand about her wanting to be here? Does she really think I'm that bad a mother?' I know I sound pathetic, but I can't stop myself. I put my face in my hands.

There's a long pause, and then the sound of a chair being pushed backwards. Suddenly Ingrid is beside me, her arm around my shoulders.

'Rock bottom became the solid foundation on which I rebuilt my life,' she whispers.

I wipe my eyes with the tea towel I had tucked into my waistband, then toss it on the desk. 'Another Bible quote?'

Ingrid gives me a sheepish grin. 'J.K. Rowling.'

13

I arrive at Tamar House early on Monday morning, to find Michael Fellows already waiting for me.

'Me mum always said if you're early you're on time,' he says brightly, 'and if you're on time, you're late.'

I was hoping to access the database records to check if what Sophie told me about Anton and Nicky being inside at the same time was true, but that will have to wait until later. I buy Michael a coffee from the kiosk opposite, and we walk in easy silence for ten minutes to a nondescript building incongruously situated between a tyre garage and a carpet shop.

'The St Benedict Centre,' reads Michael, from the sign above the door. He turns to me. 'I'm kinda not into religion, Grace.'

'Neither am I, but this isn't all about religion.' I'm struck by the fact my words almost echo those of Ingrid's from the day before. 'St Benedict's is a charity that helps with homelessness, mental health, well-being and in your case, training to get you back into work.'

In fact, St B's, as it's known, is one of the few charities that accepts high risk offenders on their programmes. It's known to most POs as the last chance saloon.

'What work?' says Michael.

He knows as well as I do that finding a job when you're on the sex offenders register is no easy task.

'The kind of training you'll get here,' I say, with forced optimism, 'plastering, bricklaying, construction, means you'll be working on locations that won't contravene your licence conditions.' He looks sceptical. 'No one will care about you or your past, Michael,' I continue, 'only that you can show up at 7am and do a full day's hard graft on the tools.'

'Really?'

'Really,' I reply, but in truth I'm not sure. His time inside, nearly three years, means he'll probably be on the register for life. Not all employers are willing to risk hiring someone with that sort of history, and I can't say I blame them. That bit of judgement I keep to myself, out of my professional realm. If I allowed my personal opinions into the mix, I'd never get the job done, and my job is to keep the public safe. Getting ex-offenders into sustained employment is one of the best ways to do that.

Michael shifts uneasily, and I realise I'm nervous too. I give his arm a gentle punch, unexpected and nerdy. 'You ready?'

'Ready,' he replies, with just a hint of hopefulness in his voice.

We go into the small drop-in area, with a large table, chairs, and people of every age, description, and background sipping hot drinks and eating biscuits. Michael seems to relax a little.

'Grace, it's been ages!' I feel unexpectedly relieved to see Carrie, a long-time volunteer at St B's. Carrie is in her sixties, looks forty, and has had a previous career working in social housing. Now retired, 'busier than ever,' she's been a mainstay at the drop-in centre for years. She welcomes Michael with her typical warmth and enthusiasm. Next to her sits a woman wearing earphones and typing away on a laptop – late-twenties, blonde, gorgeous, but with a gentle disposition that hints at vulnerability and history. She turns, and her face explodes into a smile.

'Grace!'

She jumps up from her seat and embraces me in a warm hug.

'Layla, how are you?'

Layla was someone I mentored a few years back as part of some pro bono work I did with St Benedict's. Sex worker, addict, I did my absolute best to help get her off the streets and get clean. Not all my mentees were successful, but this one was. We connected, and after the mentorship was completed, stayed friends.

'I'm doing great.' Layla is glowing. Her skin is clear, eyes bright. 'Starting an access course in September, and then I'll be going to uni.'

My heart swells just a little.

'That's fantastic news, Layla.' I give her a little wink. 'Time for a fry-up?'

When Layla was still on the streets, I used to take her out for breakfast. Full English with extra toast. I knew it would probably be her only meal of the day, and I'd often ask for the extra sausages to be put in a takeaway bag for her for later.

'That would be lovely.'

Carrie gives me a gentle look. She knows more than most that getting too involved with clients, or ex-clients in my case, can open up a world of pain, but sometimes it just feels right.

'I'll ring you,' I squeeze her arm, 'I want to hear all about your plans.'

The phone rings, and Layla rushes to answer it, blowing me a kiss goodbye as she does.

'Nice looking girl,' says Michael when I return to his side.

I give him a warning look, and hand him a brochure. 'There's bricklaying, garden services, plastering, and there is an expectation of doing some of their personal development courses.' I point to one called *The Better Me*.

We spend nearly an hour at St B's, where Michael finally decides on plastering, '*kind of artistic,*' but shies away from the personal development course.

'It's not going to be easy,' I warn gently, as we make our way back to the city centre, 'and there's no backing out. This is about sticking to it, otherwise...' He gives me a look which suggests he knows where I'm going.

'If I do that *Better Me* rubbish, will you give me the okay to move in with me missus?'

Is that the reason for all this compliant behaviour?

'Let's see how it goes, Michael, but that would be a good start.'

For now, it's a good day, a positive day. I leave Michael with another cup of takeaway coffee, and an appointment card for next week. *I have a good feeling about this one.*

When I get back to the office, I check both Nicky and Anton's prison records, and make a phone call to Dartmoor Prison records office.

'It's Grace Midwinter from Tamar House.'

'Hey, Grace, it's Jenna.'

Jenna was a trainee PO I mentored for a while a few years ago. Smart, compassionate, and maybe just that little bit too soft hearted, she eventually opted for an admin job instead of one-to-one contact.

'How are things?'

I hear Jenna chuckle on the other end of the phone. 'There I was moaning about all the paperwork in the probation service, now my life is all about paperwork.'

'Well maybe that's where you can help me.'

'Fire away.'

'I wanted to check on the custody dates in 2019 for Anton Cross and Nicky White.'

'Mind if I ask why?'

'Just for our records.'

'Records, eh, nothing to do with Nicky's recent murder?'

'I'm no detective, Jenna. I just want to make sure Sophie's files are up to date.'

'Got ya. I'd hate to see any more crap go flying her way.' I hear the tap of fingers on a keyboard and then, 'Anton Cross, detained 29 June 2021, for a period of eight weeks. Charged with criminal damage to the property of a spouse.' She makes a tutting sound. 'He was out in four.' There's more tapping. 'Nicky White, incarcerated 3 July 2021 for a period of four months, charged with...' There's a long pause. She clears her throat. 'Possession of an imitation firearm.'

'What?'

'Part 3D printed.'

I think back to what Sophie said about Nicky being 'a bit of a tech whiz.'

I force myself to speak. 'What kind of weapon?'

'Rifle of some sort.'

'Christ.' I sit back in my chair. Nicky was in Dartmoor for possession of an illegally made firearm at the same time as Anton, and then three years later Anton shoots his own daughter with an illegally obtained firearm. What did I say about coincidences?

'Did no one ever clock this?' I ask.

'You'd have to check the court transcripts,' she replies, her voice sounding hollow.

I find myself thinking out loud. 'Why was Nicky's sentence so light?'

'It was deemed by ballistics experts to have the potential for firing capability,' she replies, 'but not proven conclusively in court. He went down for other charges,' there's a short pause, 'possession I think.'

I'm still reeling from this discovery, but have one more question.

'What wing were they in?'

Another long pause. 'They were both in G wing.'

When I get home that evening, Jodie has managed to leave a pile of dirty laundry from her weekend away directly in front of the washing machine. I hear the sound of muted thumping, and when I make my way upstairs, I see the loft ladder has been lowered and two feet are descending from the roof storage space.

'What on earth?'

'Grab one of these, will you, Mum?' Jodie hands me a suitcase. She follows soon after with another.

'It's a bit early to be packing, isn't it?' I try to keep the worry from my voice. 'And two suitcases? You won't be staying with your father that long, will you?'

'Of course not,' she replies, but with a hint of evasiveness.

'I'm ordering pizza,' I say, unwilling to take this conversation any further. 'Want your usual?'

After dinner, I drop her off at the youth club, but don't go in. I don't think I can bear Ingrid's feel-good philosophy tonight. Instead, I drive the twenty-five minutes to Wembury, to the identical row of bungalows that lines the gently sloping road that leads to the sea. I knock on the door and wait.

I see a figure approach, amorphous through the smoky glass.

'Grace?'

My father always seems to say my name with a question mark, as if I'm some kind of mystery to him, which I suppose I am.

'Hey, Dad.'

'Everything okay?'

He's clearly as surprised by my unexpected arrival as I am by my decision to visit. It's not as if we don't like spending time together; we do. It's just finding time that seems to be the problem.

I suddenly feel the need to retreat back to the security of my house on Penzance Street with the creaking stairs and stuccoed ceilings. 'It's kind of late, you're probably busy.'

'Not at all.' He glances around. 'Did you bring the dog?'

We walk to the beach, Bismarck running ahead in excitement. It's nearing dusk, and the sun is quickening its way past the Mewstone, a rocky outcrop that thrusts its way through the water like a knife tip. We sip from our tins of Bud Light and watch as the last of the surfers disappear. In the distance, dark clouds are forming on the horizon.

'So,' he says, finally.

I've always admired his patience.

'Jodie says she wants to go and stay with her father for the summer.' No point in beating around the bush.

'Ah.'

I take a long sip of beer, hold the bitter bubbles on my tongue. 'I told Alex I would think about it, but...'

'You don't want her to.' My father was never the overly empathetic type. He was always more of a 'get on with it' person. 'And what's wrong with that?' he adds. 'You not wanting her to go and stay with him? Don't you have a say in the matter?'

'Alex thinks Jodie is old enough to make these kinds of decisions.'

'Old enough, maybe,' he stares out at sea, his expression unreadable, 'but mature enough?' I nod, silently. I know what he's saying. Jodie is my daughter and I love her, but she can be impulsive, manipulative, changeable, all traits not uncommon in teenagers trying to find their way.

'Have you considered what might be behind all this?' I stare at him in surprise. Where our relationship has always been cautious, tentative, his bond with Jodie has been one of fervent love and support. 'Could there be some other reason for her wanting to stay with her father?' He gives a muffled burp. 'His job is pretty demanding, with more out of hours work than you, which means he probably won't be able to keep an eye on her as much as you do.'

I find myself feeling unexpectedly defensive. 'Are you saying I don't give her enough freedom?'

He turns to me and smiles. 'You give her just the right amount.'

My father and I have always spoken in code, his praise hidden within directives, my replies economical and uncertain. This unqualified accolade hits me like a brick in the chest.

'Thanks, Dad.'

'You're a great mum, Grace, always have been.'

I turn to him, suddenly aware of the hidden cipher.

Nothing like my mum, you mean.

My mother left my father and me the day after my sixteenth birthday.

So as not to ruin my special day.

There were no sit downs, explanations or discussions, no tearful, regretful goodbyes, just a short note (which I found years later hidden in his desk drawer) saying she was in love with someone else. She lives up north somewhere with her new family. Children, grandchildren, and a second marriage that has long outlived her first. We don't talk about her much. I don't talk to her at all.

My father checks his watch. 'What time are you picking Jodie up?'

'Nine thirty.'

'Still time for a cup of decaf, and bit of homemade Victoria sponge, then?'

I follow him back to the house, trying to get my head around the fact that my father has taken up home baking.

'I read about that boy in the *Herald*,' he says a half hour later, as he walks me back to my car. 'His brothers were in and out of the cells, as I recall.'

Before retiring, my father was a custody officer like Mick. Just one more twisty tendril holding me to the world of criminal justice.

'It was pretty nasty stuff.'

'It was always nasty with that lot.' Normally a robust presence, my father suddenly looks all of his sixty-seven years. 'I remember their mother kicking off whenever she tried to come in and see them. Quite a handful.' He gives me a knowing look. 'You stay out of it, Grace, promise?'

I collect Jodie from youth club, an unexpected rainstorm soaking us both as we hurry our way back to the car. When we get home, I run her a bath, make hot chocolate, and we sit on the settee watching TV until she falls asleep, her head on my shoulder. The feel of her soft curls against my cheek, the gentle puff of her breathing, fills me with such a profound sense of love and devotion that I ignore the crick in my neck, and let my arm go numb. I try to rationalise my fear of losing her – it's only for a few months, after all – but it feels deeper than just her going to live with her father. *Is it something to do with my own mother abandoning me, or is it Nicky White's murder that has made me feel this uneasy? I know what's really out there, who's really out there.*

14

You stand in a halo of murky orange light, and watch the third-floor window of the white building opposite. You've positioned yourself next to an all-night burger van, pretending to eat a greasy disc of gristle that the sign next to you proclaims is 'PLYMOUTH'S BEST BURGER!' It isn't. Opposite, one of the building's inhabitants stands bare chested by the window, blow drying his hair. If only he knew how much could be seen from outside. A few minutes later, the room grows dark. You deposit your uneaten burger in the bin, then wait. The security light in the building's front entrance sparks into life, and suddenly he's across the street, cocky and full of energy. He turns right towards the city centre, and for a second you're confused. Then you remember, he likes to keep his fun for later. He makes his way along Union Street towards the strip, a half mile of seedy nightclubs, derelict buildings, and fast-food outlets. *Gomorrah.* It's still early, and the clubs aren't open. Their front entrances are still littered with empty beer bottles, and cigarette ends from the night before. He stops at the pedestrian crossing where a painfully thin girl dressed in a onesie is asking passers-by for a cigarette. He strides past her without a glance. He eases his way around a group of forty-something women vaping outside Wetherspoons. One of them makes a joke, and he gives her his best Hollywood smile. You follow him into the anonymity of pub darkness and allow yourself to be absorbed near a group of women drinking pitchers of watered-down cocktails. You've been doing this long enough to know how not to be noticed. You watch as he checks his reflection in the mirror, smooths back his hair, and finds an empty stool by the bar. He turns and looks to the front entrance. The vape girls are making their way towards him.

'Has anyone ever told you that you look like Brad Pitt?' one of them says. He grins and pulls up a bar stool. The other women crowd around him. *It's going to be a long night.*

It's late now, and he is pissed. He's spent most of the evening being bought drinks and having his ass squeezed by the girls. There will be no action with them. You know he has only one girl in mind. There's a loud ping of an incoming text, and he angles his phone so that he can read the message in the flashing lights of the fruit machine.

'Gotta go,' he says, above the rehashed eighties soundtrack. There are faint protestations from the women as they dig into their plates of fish and chips.

He heads north towards Mount Wise, stopping first at the all-night chemist on King Street. You watch through a side window as he purchases a box of condoms. *This time there will be no DNA.* You take your phone out, send a text.

He walks at a steady pace, taking long, energetic strides. You follow, enjoying the feeling of your legs working, the muscles flexing. It won't be much longer. You know where he's going. He passes Neptune Yachts, and then turns left towards

Richmond Walk. The road is an odd mix of properties – building merchants, a boat upholsterer, car parts distributor. A little further down the road there is a drug and alcohol recovery day centre he knows well. Beyond that, just past the marina, is a row of three terraced houses that are tidy, nice, and painted periwinkle blue. That's where she lives. He stops, taps his hand on the back pocket of his jeans, then carries on. You glance at the streetlight opposite. The CCTV camera mounted on the top has been out of operation for nearly a year. The other one, mounted on the side of the used car dealers a few feet away, has been dealt with.

Just ahead, a large figure steps out from behind a gate which encloses an old boatyard, the hulking frames of decaying fishing trawlers swallowing the night.

'Got a fag, mate?'

He shakes his head then tries to walk on. The big man steps in front of him, blocks his way.

'Where you off to in such a hurry?'

'None of your business,' he says, feigning confidence.

A second figure, small and wiry, steps forward from behind the gate. He's holding a cricket bat in his right hand. He slaps it against his thigh. It makes a sharp whacking sound.

'It is now,' he says.

You wait until it is over, until they are done with him. He's lying on his back next to an overturned rowboat. He's semi-conscious but breathing steadily. Blood trickles from a wound on his temple, and down along a sculpted cheekbone. His eyes flicker, and he whispers something. 'Yes,' you reply, 'I know you too.' Then you lean over, lift his right hip, and reach for what is in his back pocket.

15

The next morning, I wake early, still troubled. I lace up my trainers and take the dog for a run, making it up to Devil's Point and back without stopping. Once I'm back, and while the coffee is brewing, I make Jodie's lunch and sneak a peek at her planner:

> *Maths revision session. Dealing with exam nerves. Make the most of your summer break to prepare for A-levels.*

Don't they ever give these girls a break? I'm just about to text Marcus when I remember he's deep undercover and won't have his phone with him. That's probably a good thing, as I desperately need more time to get my head straight. Sleeping with Alex was a mistake, pure and simple. I was drunk, vulnerable, and needing reassurance. History isn't always possible to erase, but when it comes to Alex, I'm really not sure I want to repeat it. As far as I'm concerned, it's already ancient history. I hope Alex feels the same.

I decide to walk to work, picking up some doughnuts for the

team on the way. Arriving at work, I slide a couple of iced chocolate ones under the glass partition, and then make my way along the grey mile and into the main office. I glance at my desk, and the checkerboard of Post-it notes Viola has left for me. I'm just heading towards the kitchen to make myself a cup of tea, when I catch a glimpse of a familiar figure in Simon's office. *Christ! Can't my sense of peace last for a few hours at least?*

'Grace?' Simon has spotted me. 'Could you come into my office please?'

Since the Katie Cross incident, my default response in situations like this has always been a deep-seated gut ache that hurries my pulse rate and slows my thinking. *What bit of bad news will be coming next? What error or protocol breach have I missed?*

'Grace?'

'Sorry, Simon.' I fumble for a notepad and pen, and hurry into his office. Sitting in one of the two chairs opposite his desk is Alex. I give him a nod, but do my best to avoid eye contact.

'Why don't you sit down?' Simon says, indicating the chair next to Alex.

'What's happened?' A thread of panic is starting to unwind within me. 'Is it Jodie? Is she all right?'

'It's nothing to do with Jodie.' There's apprehension in Simon's voice. 'Why don't I make us all a cup of tea?' He slips out of the office, leaving me alone with Alex.

'*Grace,*' he begins, his voice warm, appeasing.

'I don't want to talk about it, okay?'

'Well, we can't bloody ignore it, can we?'

'Why not? It was a mistake. We both know that.' His expression suggests a different sentiment, but I'm not prepared to have this conversation. Not here, not now.

'I want your promise that what happened on Saturday night

stays between you and I.' He raises an eyebrow. 'Jodie is never to know about it.'

'And Marcus?'

The hint of self-righteousness stokes my temper. 'I think that's my business, don't you?'

'If you say so.'

Simon returns with our cups of tea. Clearly sensing the tension in the room, he hands us our mugs before quickly returning to safety on the other side of his desk. I stare at the murky brown liquid in front of me, feeling resentful and uncertain.

'Will you please tell me why I'm here?'

Alex turns to face me. Gone is the affable countenance of a few moments before. This is business.

'There's no real easy way to say this, Grace, but I have to inform you that one of your guys was found murdered last night.'

'What?!'

'One of Sophie's that you were covering,' says Simon. 'Michael Fellows.'

'Michael?' I can feel the blood draining from my face. 'I only saw him yesterday. We went to St Benedict's. He signed up for some courses.' I know I'm babbling, but I can't help myself. 'We're scheduled to meet again next week.'

Alex leans forward, seeking my gaze. 'He was discovered at four this morning in a boatyard near Mayflower Marina, beaten to death.'

'Oh God.' I feel the sting of tears, and professional demeanour or not, I don't hold them back. No matter who they are, or how serious their offences, I never stop caring. I feel something soft being slipped into my hand and look down to see it's Alex's handkerchief.

'The thing is,' there's a shift in Alex's tone as he moves from sympathetic back to professional. 'He was discovered near the residence of his last victim, Chantal Atkins.'

Who he was convicted of raping. I know the case notes.

'How near?'

'It also appears,' continues Alex, 'that Michael stopped at an all-night chemist on King Street and purchased some condoms. There was a receipt in his wallet from 11:50pm.'

'So?'

'So, he was in the vicinity of his victim with a packet of condoms.'

'And?'

'Seems pretty clear to me,' says Simon. 'He was planning to go to Chantal Atkins' flat, and sexually assault her again.'

'Pretty clear?' I regard Simon with a mixture of disbelief, and contempt. 'Since when did you become a police detective?'

He does that thing – head wobble, jostling of shoulders – that clearly indicates I've hit a nerve. He ignores me and turns to Alex. 'Well, it's obvious, isn't it?'

I snap. 'What happened to innocent until proven guilty?'

'Give it a rest, Grace.' Alex points to the case file. 'We know Fellows had a history of coercive behaviour. Even though none of his other partners would testify, there was considerable evidence to suggest that Chantal wasn't the first girlfriend he sexually assaulted.'

'Speculative and unproven!'

'And yet he was still in the area of Mayflower Arena,' Alex counters.

'Breaking his curfew, and contravening his licence conditions by being within a three-mile radius of Chantal's residence,' adds Simon.

'Did he actually have any contact with her?' I'm trying hard to keep my voice at a suitable level. 'With Chantal?'

'Not sure,' says Alex. 'I expect Major Crimes will be asking that question.'

I am not having this.

'Yes, he broke curfew and was near to where a previous crime took place,' I say, 'but what does that have to do with him being beaten to death?' The two men exchange glances.

Something strikes me, and I turn my attention to Simon. 'He was in approved premises, the bail hostel on Paradise Road. Did they contact the police for immediate recall when he failed to show up for curfew?' Simon shrugs. 'So, you two are sitting here giving *me* the third degree, when it appears that you really should be speaking to MOSOVO and Balliol House.'

'This isn't about blame, Grace,' says Alex, his voice tight. 'This is about damage control.'

'Damage control?'

Simon leans forward on his desk. 'Alex came here to give us the heads-up that the investigation will be coming our way. Just what I need,' he mutters, 'six months before a major inspection.'

'And rightly so. What are you two so worried about? I completed all of Sophie's paperwork, got all the necessary signatures, did my bit to the tee. I was also explicit in my warning to Michael not to go anywhere near Chantal Atkins.'

'Yes, yes,' says Simon, 'it's clear you covered everything.'

'So, what's the problem?'

Simon shifts in his seat. 'We just don't want any of this reflecting badly on probation services.'

'Why should it?' Then I realise the actual subtext to this conversation and why he's so anxious.

I try to hold my temper, but my voice wavers. 'You don't want this office associated with any further scandal, and you definitely don't want it associated with me.'

'Will you two just stop,' says Alex. 'I'm just trying to ensure that we're all singing from the same hymn sheet when the Major Crimes Investigation Team comes knocking at our door.'

I still can't believe I'm having this conversation. 'Why wouldn't we?'

'Indeed,' says Simon. 'But,' he continues, sounding more officious than ever, 'as of Saturday night, Michael Fellows was still a resident at Balliol House, and still expected to adhere to his licence conditions and curfew. The fact that he may have decided to go to the residence of one of his previous victims has nothing to do with us, particularly as he was clearly informed by his PO, and duly recorded that this was against his licence conditions and grounds for recall.' It's as if he's practicing for an interrogation. 'It was clearly up to the team at Balliol House to contact one of the relevant police units the minute he failed to check in.'

'At least we've got that on our side,' Alex mutters.

'What the hell is wrong with you two?' I'm astounded by both men's callousness. 'A person has been murdered and all you can think about is damage control?'

'Believe me,' says Alex. 'In the end that's what it will all come down to.'

'Have you read his report? I mean *really* read it?' Both men give me a questioning look. 'Michael's new partner lives in Mount Wise, a few miles from Chantal Atkins' residence. There is a possibility he was in the general vicinity because he was on his way to *her* flat, not Chantal's. That could explain the condoms, as well. Michael told me he had been given the okay by Sophie to engage in a sexual relationship.' Simon raises an eyebrow at this potentially dubious decision-making by my colleague. Recently released individuals on the sex offenders list are often required to complete all their resettlement programmes before being allowed to engage in intimate relationships. I feel like I'm dropping Sophie in it, and I hate myself for it. 'It might be worth checking with Balliol House to see if he'd been approved a home visit.'

Alex shakes his head. 'That's all irrelevant as far as I'm concerned. The boatyard where we found Michael was less than half a mile from Chantal's flat.'

'But–'

'And the direct route from Balliol House to Mount Wise doesn't go anywhere near Chantal's house. He shouldn't have been there.'

'It doesn't necessarily mean that he was–'

'For Christ's sake, Grace!' Alex smacks his hand on the arm of the chair, making me jump. 'This guy was no boy scout. He systematically abused and manipulated Chantal, and when she finally gained the courage to chuck him out, he raped her.'

'Once a rapist,' mutters Simon.

I stand up and push my chair back so hard that it hits the wall with a loud thump.

'I appreciate you both giving me the heads-up, but as far as I'm aware, I haven't done anything to be worried about. I don't think damage control is required, and by the way, thank you for the vote of confidence. I will be perfectly happy to speak to your senior colleagues at Major Crimes, and anyone from the Deputy Director's office, in a completely open and transparent way.' I glance from one man to the other. 'I've got absolutely nothing to hide.'

There's a pause, perhaps even a sense of begrudging respect from both men as they consider my words. Alex clears his throat.

'There is one more thing you need to know,' he indicates towards my chair. 'Sit down. When the paramedics first arrived, they thought the cause of death was due to the obvious head injury.'

'Yes?'

'But when they were trying to determine an airway, they discovered that his mouth had been stuffed full of condoms. He choked to death.'

I can't speak, just stare open mouthed. Over the years, I've been exposed to some of the most violent crimes imaginable: murders, sexual assaults, child exploitation. You would think I would have become desensitised by now, but each new brutality still hits me like a fist in the chest. Alex hands me my tea. It's lukewarm and too sweet, but at least it lubricates my bone-dry throat. The words finally come.

'Who would do something like that?'

'That's what I wanted to ask you.' Alex clears his throat. 'Are you okay to go on?' I nod and take another sip. 'Simon's talked me through your case notes. Initial assessment, clarification of licence conditions, signatures on the appropriate paperwork.' I nod, grateful I followed protocol to the letter. 'You were meeting with him weekly, is that correct?'

'Yes, that's correct.' This is starting to feel more like a formal investigation than damage control. 'We got him registered for some courses at St Benedict's, and I was going to action the Thames Valley Sex Offenders Programme, maybe a referral for further alcohol misuse support.' I can't bear to mention how thrilled he was at starting the plastering course. 'He was genuinely trying to move forward.'

Both Alex and Simon give me looks that suggest they are unconvinced.

'Was there any indication from Michael that he was being threatened, maybe by Chantal's family, or someone else? Was he nervous, frightened?' Alex asks.

'No more than any other recently released sex offender,' I reply, and then inwardly chastise myself for being flippant. 'No, he seemed okay, but then you don't come out of prison after three and a half years without feeling apprehensive.' Something strikes me. 'Could this have anything to do with Nicky White?'

Alex gives me a hard stare. 'It's too early to make those kinds of assumptions.'

'But it can't just be a random attack, can it? Especially after they were badly beaten?'

Alex sighs heavily. 'People like Michael and Nicky carry their crimes around with them like a noose. Perhaps it was someone with a score to settle – and let's be honest, there were plenty with those two – but more often than not, they're on a timer.'

'A timer?'

'Prison or death.' He rubs his eyes, and the veil falls. *God, he looks tired.* 'For all we know, Michael may have simply been in the wrong place at the wrong time.'

Simon glances at his watch. 'I've got a meeting in a few minutes. Can I leave you two to finish up on your own?'

'Of course,' Alex replies. 'There are just a few more things I need to run through with Grace.'

'No problem,' says Simon. 'Just shut the door behind you when you leave.'

Alex waits until Simon has left, before continuing. 'You're absolutely certain that Michael Fellows didn't say anything to you about visiting Chantal?'

'If that was the case, don't you think I would have actioned it?'

'It's just that you can sometimes get a little, ah...' I'm curious to hear what he has to say next, 'overly invested.'

This hits a sore spot. 'Are you suggesting I don't have professional boundaries?'

I realise that he's referring to my behaviour on Saturday, the drunkenness and desperation.

'Last year is over, Alex. I've been cleared of any wrongdoing. I'm just waiting for formal confirmation.'

'I'm worried about you, Gracie, that's all.' His use of an old pet name rankles. 'This obsession with the Cross case just isn't good for you.' *Obsession? How can he say that?* A nine-year-old girl was murdered on her own doorstep – and maybe, just maybe, I could have done something to stop it. 'It wasn't your fault.'

'So everyone keeps telling me.' Conscious of the thin office partitions, and my colleagues' curiosity, I lower my voice. 'But *I* wrote that report. It had my name, and the name and address of Sue and Katie Cross on it.' I stop to catch my breath as I always do when thinking about it. 'And somehow it found its way to Anton Cross' bedsit. Don't you think my obsession is somewhat justified?'

'I wish you could let it go.'

'This is pointless.' I know I'm being an ass, but I can't help it. 'He killed her, Alex. That's the only truth there is.' The often-imagined scene floods my brain. Sue and Katie walking home after school. Katie munching on a packet of crisps she had convinced her mother to buy her from the corner shop, mother and daughter chatting about the upcoming school disco, and what to have for tea, then two of them arriving at the flat to discover Anton waiting for them on the doorstep with a rifle under his coat. It's always with me, no matter how many times I am reassured or vindicated. *An innocent child is dead, and I should have done something to stop it.*

Alex's phone buzzes. He glances at the message. 'I've got to go,' he mutters, and stands to leave. 'We do need to communicate a bit better though, for Jodie's sake if nothing else, especially if she's going to be staying with me for a while.'

It takes a few minutes before I can return to my desk.

Viola approaches and puts her cool hand on my arm.

'Um, Grace.'

She's holding a sealed white envelope. On the front, in bold lettering, is written:

```
From the Office of the Deputy Director,
National Probation Service.
```

Shit.

'I'm sure it's good news,' she says, trying her best.

'Sure,' I reply, with what I know sounds like forced brightness. 'I'm just going to nip to the loo. Can you let my next client know I'm going to be a few minutes late?'

16

I lock the door in the far cubicle, sit down, and carefully tear open the envelope. The letter is short and to the point.

Dear Grace,

Further to our investigation regarding the possible disclosure of confidential data to unauthorised parties, after extensive investigation and consideration, the investigations conducted by The Office of the Deputy Director have agreed that there is no evidence to suggest that you acted in any way to contravene General Data Protection Regulations, or acted in a manner that constituted professional misconduct. No further action or investigation will take place unless further evidence is submitted to the department. A full report will be

> forwarded to yourself and the Senior
> Manager in due course.

That's it – formal notification, of a sort. I lean forward and force myself to exhale, long and deep. For me, the letter isn't so much a resolution as a placation. Maybe what's really bothering me is that it doesn't focus on the fact that I am innocent, but rather that I couldn't be proven guilty. *And if it wasn't me, then who was it?*

I work through the rest of my morning appointments on automatic pilot, asking the standard questions, grading ex-offenders on risk levels, arranging referrals. After lunch, I attend a public protection meeting, in which I nod at all the appropriate places but offer little input.

It's nearly 3pm before I have time to open my laptop and review Michael's case file, a copy of which has already been sent to the Major Investigations Team. As our first meeting had only been for an initial assessment, there were no in-depth conversations about his psychological state and possible wider support, just the standard initial risk assessment tick-box exercise, clarification of his licence conditions, and an appointment for our next meeting to visit St Benedict's. Notes about our second meeting were all about our morning at St B's, how enthusiastic Michael was about a new start, how I felt it was a positive intervention with potential long-term results. Reading through my notes I'm struck by how clinical they are, how soulless. Maybe I should have asked him if he felt he was vulnerable or at risk, or if anyone had threatened him. He certainly didn't present that way. The thing that keeps sticking in my mind though, is how anyone could possibly have known where he was going that night. I doubt very much that he would have confided in his bail hostel housemates, and if he was planning to wander into restraining order territory, he certainly wouldn't have told the lead PO at the hostel. *Maybe Alex was right. Maybe Michael was just in the wrong place at the wrong time.* It's common enough in Plymouth for groups of lads to go out after a few drinks and look for trouble. I watch the clock until I can go home and have a bath, a glass of Merlot, and a good cry.

———

I arrive home to find a note on the kitchen table from Jodie, saying she's gone to the cinema with a friend, and will be dropped home by 10pm. Michael's murder still on my mind, I text and tell her to be careful, to call if she needs anything. Then I fill the bath and slide beneath the bubbles, but duty calls: the dog scratches at the door begging for his bedtime Bonio, and I need to put a wash on.

I slip into my bathrobe, run a comb through my damp hair, and am just about to pour myself a glass of wine when I hear a knock at the door. Bismarck does his usual watchdog thing, a high-pitched bark that if not so effective at keeping cold callers away, would be annoying. He's already waiting by the front door when I get there. I tighten the belt on my bathrobe, check that the security chain is fastened, and cautiously open the door. With the porch light long out of commission I strain to make out the figure in the darkness.

'Ingrid?'

'Grace,' she says my name in one great exhalation, 'I wasn't certain this was the right house.' We stare at each other. Bismarck's growls have turned into yelps of pleasure at seeing her. 'May I come in?'

'Oh, yes of course, sorry.' I step back, nearly tripping over the dog, and invite her into my home. 'Have a seat.' My brain feels muddled by this unexpected visitor, but I default to good manners. 'Would you like a cup of tea?'

'That would be lovely. Herbal if possible. I don't take caffeine.'

I make my way to the kitchen, and search through the cupboard for the box of fruit tea I bought for my last detox diet.

'Blueberry and elderflower,' I announce, placing the concoction on the coffee table in front of her.

'Thank you, Grace, that's most kind.'

I sit down opposite with my mug of Yorkshire Gold.

'So, to what do I owe the pleasure of this visit?'

'I was in the area visiting an elderly parishioner,' she replies, 'and I thought I might pop in and say hello.'

'How nice.' I take a sip of tea. 'But how did you know where I live?'

Ingrid blinks. 'Didn't you mention it to me when we first met?'

'I don't think so.'

'It must have been Jodie, then.' She places her mug down on the table in front of her, and comes to sit beside me on the settee. 'You've been on my mind all day, Grace.'

'Have I?'

'Not just because of our conversation the other night, but because I wanted to ask you a favour.'

'A favour?'

'First of all,' she places her hand on mine, 'how have you been feeling?'

I wish I could say 'better, happier, calmer', but all those descriptors would be a lie. The news of Michael's murder, and the thought of Jodie going to live with her father, makes me wants to toss my tea into a nearby plant pot and down the entire bottle of Merlot.

'Well, you know.'

Ingrid nods sympathetically. 'One can't fix things overnight.' She takes another sip and pauses. 'Have you considered my offer of counselling? It doesn't have to be anything formal. I often find that I'm just a facilitator helping others to find their own pathway to certainty.'

That sounds so nice, and so damn unachievable.

'I'll think about it.'

'Good!' She looks pleased. 'But that's not the only reason I've sought you out.'

Her enthusiasm is infectious, and I find myself curious.

'Go on.'

Ingrid clasps her hands together and takes a big breath. 'Do you remember on Sunday after church, when we spoke about the street pastors programme?'

I recall the people in purple fleeces packing rucksacks full of bottles of water, lollies, and silver space blankets.

'The volunteers that help people who are off their faces after partying all night?'

Ingrid gives me an indulgent look. 'Not just partygoers, Grace, but the homeless, the needy, the lost.'

'Sorry.'

'I'm not here to make you feel guilty. I'm here to offer you an opportunity.'

I'm torn between being intrigued and wishing she would leave.

'And what opportunity is that?'

'Come out with us this Friday!' Ingrid is beaming. 'Come with the street pastors on a Go Out, where you'll be able to see our work firsthand. There is no obligation to do anything; you can just come as an observer.' Her tone turns serious. 'And with the amount of violence we're seeing on the streets at the moment, your knowledge and experience would be extremely helpful.'

I'm about to politely decline, then I consider my own life. There is work of course, plus Jodie, trips to the gym, dog walking, shopping, and my guilty pleasure of weekend binge watching cheesy romances on telly. It all seems so shallow, compared to the work that Paradise Church is doing. I also recall Ingrid's comment about how getting involved with the church could be a good way for me to improve my relationship with Jodie, speaking of which, she'll be camping on the moors on Friday, so I don't have to worry about her being on her own overnight. The timing seems perfect, particularly as the way things are going at the moment, I need all the help I can get.

'Just as an observer?'

'Yes of course,' says Ingrid.

'Okay, I'm in.'

Though I'm slightly uncertain, there's a chance this may be the best decision I've made in a long time.

17

I wake to the sound of Jodie singing in the shower. I make coffee, her lunch, and leave her something for breakfast. In a month or so, she'll be off to stay with her father, and very happy about it too by the sounds of things.

My first appointment isn't until nine, so I decide to do a large loop and walk to work through Central Park, its wide expanse of green contrasting with the large yellow brick of a leisure centre. There are early morning joggers, teenage girls heading to the nearby grammar school, and pedestrian commuters like me taking a green route into town. When Jodie was little, Alex and I used to bring her here for picnics. She first learned to ride a bicycle along these leafy paths.

I make my way uphill past the train station and university, through the shopping mall that smells of coffee and Krispy Kreme donuts, then down towards the grubby end of the town with its greying postwar architecture, vape shops and the homeless. As I climb the slope to Tamar House, I catch a whiff of salty air. In the distance, past the parked cars and B&Bs, I spot a glimpse of the sea. I briefly consider ignoring everything, and walking onwards to The Hoe, where I could spend the morning drinking windswept cappuccinos and gazing at the breakwater.

I take the back stairs into Tamar House, neck my takeaway espresso, pop a breath mint into my mouth, and go to collect Billy Vale for interview number two.

With no Alice at the reception window, Billy has taken a seat in the far corner. When he hears the click of the door opening, he looks up, his penetrating blue eyes holding mine.

'This way,' I say, holding open the door. Billy takes his time getting up, smooths back his hair, tucks his T-shirt into his jeans, and picks up a plastic shopping bag from the floor next to him.

What is he up to?

'How are things, Billy?'

'Good.' That cocky grin is still on show, but today it's looking a little forced.

I lead him to a regular interview suite – high risk is occupied – and pick up from where we left off last week.

'So,' I begin. 'We decided last time to look at revisiting some of your training modules.'

'Yeah, about that,' he says. He taps a finger to his forehead. 'It's all in here, from the first time I did them, Grace. Do I really need to go through all that bullshit again?'

Gone is last week's talk of 'authenticity' and 'choosing his attitude', replaced by a sharp edge of hostility.

'No negotiation, Billy. If you've lost the booklets, I can get you new ones.'

He reaches into his bag, and emerges with a handful of training manuals. 'Victim empathy,' he throws a booklet down on the table in front of me. 'Life skills,' he continues, a second leaflet full of information slapped on the table. 'Better lives.' Another tome is added to the pile.

'Having a bad day?'

'Letter from Nicole's solicitors,' he replies, after twenty seconds of pugnacious silence. He retrieves a carefully folded letter from his stash. 'No visitation rights for the foreseeable future.' He appears to be reading from the document, but I can tell he knows it off by heart.

'It'll happen, Billy. You've just got to be patient.'

'You think?' He leans forward, splaying his hands across the table, sending the documents flying.

'Do you feel we should end this interview?'

He knows full well an aborted interview won't look good on his record and won't help his court appearance next week.

'No, Grace, no.'

I stand up and step back. 'Why don't you pick that all up, and we'll start again?'

I wait while he gets on his hands and knees to retrieve the booklets, never once looking up. Anger radiates from him like a sunburn. Once all the booklets are returned to his shopping bag he resumes his seat. I take a sip of water from my flask.

'It feels like there's still a bit of work to do on your anger issues.' He gives me a furious look. 'Did you manage to get in touch with St Benedict's about the anger management course I mentioned?' He shrugs. 'We'll add that as one of your conditions, shall we?'

'For fuck's sake.'

I try to sound casual. 'It's up to you, Billy.'

'We done?'

'For today.' Sometimes it's good to know when to call it a day. I scribble on an appointment card and hand it to him. 'Same time next week?'

'Whatever,' he replies. Gone is last week's enthusiastic new age charmer, now replaced by a sullen adolescent.

'And, Billy?' He's busy sorting out the contents of his plastic bag, so I'm not sure if he hears me. 'Be careful out there, okay?'

Something has clearly struck a chord, because for the first time during our meeting Billy looks at me, really looks at me.

'Nice that you care, Grace,' he says it without a hint of sarcasm, 'but you don't need to worry about me. I can look after myself, though can't say the same for some of your other guys.'

'Pardon?'

'I know all about Nicky White,' he replies, 'Michael Fellows, too. One of yours, wasn't he?' He gives me a look that suggests superiority, one-upmanship. 'How they were both beaten up and left for dead. How they both had a thing for messing with girls.' The temperature in the room seems to have dropped. 'Both better off dead if you ask me.' *Is he testing me?* 'Maybe the Devonport Crew has decided to start imposing its own form of justice sorting out those nonces.' He gives me a smug grin. 'Even crims have principles, you know.'

I lead him out to the reception, realising how relieved I am that the interview is over. Billy Vale gets my senses tingling. His record of violence, unscrupulous behaviour and hostility makes me think that his current situation won't be resolved by a simple action plan or anger management course. His comments about Nicky and Michael, while manipulative, are not in any way insightful. *Just one more criminal lowlife trying to provoke me.*

I let reception know I'll be out for a few hours, then make my way back to my part of town, and then onwards to Paradise Place. I pass the turn for my street, the further education college, and stop in front of a familiar white Georgian townhouse, Balliol House. I ring the bell, announce myself, and wait to be buzzed in.

'Grace.' My good friend Rose Evans hugs me and then leads

me into the back office, where an array of CCTV monitors display flickering images of hallways, bedrooms, a lounge area, and a courtyard. 'Cup of tea?' I nod and watch her progress on the monitors as she makes her way to the kitchen, makes our drinks, and returns. 'I can guess what this is about.'

'I just wanted to see if you were okay.'

'And ask about Michael?' I nod. 'Well,' she says, 'he appeared to be a pretty model resident. Engaged with his key worker, met with the community forensic team, complied with drug and alcohol testing.'

'Was he using?'

'Some traces of cannabis,' Rose replies, 'but any issues were mostly to do with alcohol.'

'And *were* there any issues?'

'Not hugely,' she sighs, 'yes, he came back over the limit once or twice, but he was never dangerous or abusive.'

'And curfews?'

'He always got back before eleven.'

'Except for on Tuesday.'

Rose gives me a look. 'Unfortunately, I wasn't working, but the duty PO did make the call to say he hadn't checked in.'

'And?'

'The police said they would send a call out.'

'That's it?'

'There was some big bust-up on Union Street,' says Rose. 'They were pretty pushed.'

'But if he *was* going after Chantal?'

'Do you really believe that?'

It's clear that Rose is thinking along the same lines as me. *If Michael was being allowed conjugal visits with his girlfriend, would he still be interested in Chantal?* The trouble is there was no documentation in Sophie's notes to confirm this, just a supposed okay for him to engage in a sexual relationship.

Michael also had history, and a dubious one at that. It's this kind of ambiguity that leads to disciplinaries, dismissals... and possibly even murder.

'And things were okay here? Did he have any issues with the other residents?'

'Not the residents,' replies Rose, 'but Chantal Atkins' family had a thing about him.'

'A thing?'

'They'd show up outside, a bunch of angry white guys saying people like Michael should be hanged, castrated, you know the kind of stuff.' *Unfortunately, I did.* 'They're part of some Facebook group her brother Callum got involved in after Michael's release. *'Justice South.'*

'I thought those kinds of groups were mostly paedophile hunters.'

'Sex offender hunters too,' says Rose. 'Especially if your sister's a victim.'

'Could they have been enacting some form of vigilante justice against Michael?'

Rose shrugs. 'From what I understand they mostly deal in online stings. Some middle-aged white guy posing as a vulnerable fourteen-year-old girl, setting up a meeting with the interested party, and letting the police do the rest. I've never heard of any actual violence on their part.'

'But there's always a first time.'

Rose doesn't answer. I finish my tea, thank her, and leave. My visit to Balliol House has raised more questions than answers. *Could Michael have been the victim of a vigilante group like Justice South? Was his murder really as random as Alex suggested, or was he keeping the full truth from me so that I wouldn't get overly invested?* Once again that familiar narrative floods my brain.

Could I have done anything to stop it?

Something keeps nagging at me, a connection I'm just not making. My conversations with Sophie, Rose, Alex and Billy seem to be leading me to one person who might be able to help.

I hurry home for some lunch, give Bismarck a quick walk, and block out my calendar for the afternoon. I make a phone call, grab my car keys, and head out.

I follow the long line of traffic that leads out of the city towards the moors. Persistent frost has meant a late start to spring, and the russet-coloured landscape is just now bursting into life. Wild daffodils have appeared in roadside clusters, along with scattered dots of yellow and pink primroses. I know that inland, where the land eases its way towards the Tamar River, the last carpeting of bluebells will be dying away to make way for wild garlic and honey-coloured gorse. As I carry along the B3212 towards Princetown, the scenery becomes increasingly beautiful and bleak, the faded gold and green interrupted by ragged shards of granite forcing its way up through the shallow soil.

I arrive at my destination just before one, turn left at the roundabout, and pass a few small shops and cafes. To my right, the silhouette of Dartmoor Prison rises above the village like a dark grey spectre. I find a space in the visitor's car park, walk the few metres towards the unassuming front entrance, ring the bell and wait. There's the click of a lock, and I enter a small reception area. The desk in front of me, like most reception desks in my world, is barricaded by a large armoured window. A young prison officer peers at me through a zigzag of wire reinforced glass.

'Hi, Dave.'

'Nice to see you, Grace.'

I place my ID in the metal drawer below the window. Dave examines it, checks the visitor list, and nods. He points to a sign to the left of the window.

'Same old, Grace. Can you please confirm that you are not carrying any of the listed items?'

As a courtesy, I scan the list, which by now I know almost off by heart. It includes chewing gum and Blu-tack, which can be used by prisoners to make impressions of keys, plus black or white clothing, so that they can't be accidentally mistaken for uniformed staff, and cling film, which can be used to wrap and hide drugs in body orifices – an unpleasant though inventive practice, known as plugging.

'None of those,' I confirm.

'No mobile phone, smart watch or any other recording devices?'

'All left in the car.'

'You don't need an escort, do you?'

'After ten years of visiting this place, I reckon I could find my way around here with my eyes shut.'

Dave smiles and returns my ID along with my temporary pass through the metal drawer. I wait for the electric door to slide open.

Once inside, I follow a small corridor that leads to a quiet outside courtyard. I turn left, past a group of inmates tending a flower garden, and towards a two-storey building with a sign that says *Legal Visits*. I check in with the Duty Officer and am directed towards a meeting room. A few minutes later, Terry Duggan is led in by a prison officer.

'Tel.' I wait to see if he is open to physical contact, and when he holds out his hand, I shake it warmly. 'Sit,' I say, indicating towards a chair on the opposite side of the desk. I look to the guard. 'Would you mind waiting outside?'

'Got to leave the door open though, ma'am. He's been a bit edgy today.'

'That's fine. Much appreciated.'

Tel looks at me in hopeful anticipation. I hand him a Snickers bar and he gives me a look.

'Sorry, mate. They were out of Mars.'

He gives a disappointed sigh. 'No worries, Grace. Maybe next time, eh?'

'*Definitely* next time.' We sit for what seems like ages. 'So, how are things?'

Tel looks at me as if I've asked him if the moon is made of cheese.

'Fine, Grace, just fine.'

'I've spoken to your solicitor. An early release is looking likely.'

'That's good news.' He picks at a thread in his prison issue jeans. 'I've stayed clear of the gear too,' he adds proudly.

'I'm pleased for you, Tel. I really am.'

'Me too.' He looks around the room, stopping to gaze through the barred window at the blue sky beyond.

I clear my throat. 'Could I ask you something, Tel?'

'Yeah, Grace, anything.' He says it with such trust that I wonder if it was fair of me to come here. After Sophie's bombshell the other night I was hoping he might have been inside at the same time as Nicky and Anton, and that I could get some intel. Checking his records, however, I discovered that this was sadly not the case. He'd been inside plenty of times that year, but not July. Still, I'm glad to be able to check on him, make sure he's okay.

I lean forward slightly so that the guard can't hear. 'There were a couple of guys on your patch, Nicky White and Michael Fellows.' Tel looks at me through heavily lidded eyes, and I wonder if he was telling the truth about staying off the gear. 'I was wondering if you were–'

'Their dealer,' says Tel, good-naturedly. 'Sure. I done some deals with Nicky before he started dealing himself, yeah.' He scratches his chin. 'Coke and a partiality to ketamine, as I recall.'

'And Michael? He was mostly weed, might have bought off you in Stonehouse.'

'Nope,' he shakes his head. 'Never dealt to him.' He gives me a cheeky smile. 'What you after, Grace?'

Maybe it's the upheaval of the last few days, or because I'm so tired, but I find myself thinking aloud. 'I was just sort of wondering if there might have been a connection between the two.'

Tel gives me a knowing, gap-toothed smile. He has endured a life of hardship, addiction, and abuse, but is still relatively switched on.

'Because of what happened to 'em?'

'Yes.' There's no point in denying it. Their murders must be common knowledge inside and out by now. 'I was just wondering if you'd heard anything about them,' I whisper, 'about what might have happened?'

Tel chuckles. 'You a detective now, Grace?'

I find myself smiling. 'Maybe.'

'Were they yours?'

'Yes,' I reply, 'well Michael was, anyway. I didn't really have that much to do with Nicky.' I run my fingertips along a thin groove in the table. 'It's just strange that they were from the same part of Plymouth, that they were both dealers, offenders with–'

'Sex offenders,' says Tel, his distaste clear. 'From what I heard they both had a nasty way with women, too.'

I decide to ignore his comment. 'I was thinking it might be something do with the drug connection, or that they might have been involved with the Devonport Crew?'

Tel looks at me for a long while. 'I reckon you may be barking up the wrong tree, Grace.'

'What?'

'Word on the street is that if you're a sex offender living in Stonehouse you'd better watch your back.'

'Where'd you hear that?'

'It's been going around,' says Tel, 'ever since those two boys were beaten up a few months back.' He yawns, exposing his missing teeth. 'Rumours it was them Justice South people what beat them up.'

Justice South was the group Rose had referred to. The ones who organised those protests against Michael outside Balliol House. I know too, that they regularly 'outed' paedophiles and sex offenders, including posting their photos and addresses on their Facebook page.

'But surely you don't think–'

'Get what you deserve in this life, Grace.'

'But to murder two people?'

'Plenty in here that would do it, believe you me.' He leans forward and whispers, 'Word is they have a contact inside.'

'Inside?'

'In the police. That's how they finds 'em. Someone gives 'em the names, addresses, when they're out, what they done. And then they sort 'em out.'

'Come on now.'

'I'm only saying what I heard,' says Tel, glancing around the room suspiciously, 'and that's probably too much already.' He wiggles an index finger, beckoning me closer. 'They bug the light switches, you know.'

'The light switches?'

'And underneath the chairs.' He stands up, picks up his chair, and flips it over. Within seconds, the prison guard stationed outside is charging into the room.

'It's okay, Tel,' I say, gently. 'There's nothing there. You can see that. Put the chair down.'

Tel looks up at me, his face a mixture of confusion and despair. 'They bug our cells too, you know,' he says, his voice gaining volume. By now the guard has removed the extendable baton from his belt, and is carefully approaching Tel.

'Put down the chair!' As if the sound of the guard's voice frees Tel from some sort of trance, he puts the chair down and returns to his seat.

The guard, gruff, grey-haired, and built like a Mexican wrestler, puts a hand on Tel's shoulder. 'Come on, buddy, time to get back.'

'But I still have a few things to discuss with him.'

The guard gives me a stern look. 'I really don't want to have to report this, ma'am.' It's clear from his face that this isn't Tel's first transgression of the day.

'I'm going to have to go now, Tel,' I say softly, 'but I'll try to come and see you again soon. Next time I'll even try to bring not one Mars bar, but two.' Tel grins in delight. 'But only on one condition.' I raise my finger in a warning. 'You stay calm, and behave yourself. No more swinging chairs about, okay?'

'Okay,' says Tel, apologetically.

'Good.'

'Let's leave it there then, shall we?' says the guard, and taking Tel by the arm, leads him out of the room. 'I gather you can see yourself out?'

'Yes, thank you. I'll be fine.'

In truth, I don't feel fine at all. I leave the prison, feeling anxious and uncertain. *Could what Tel have suggested actually be true? Could someone out there be targeting sex offenders, seeking revenge? Is that what links the attacks on Robert Lawson, Darren Murphy, Nicky White, and now Michael Fellows? More alarmingly, is someone within Devon and Cornwall Police leaking confidential information to them?*

Once back in my car, I take my mobile from the glove

compartment and dial Alex's number. It goes straight to voicemail.

'Hi, Alex, it's Grace. I need to speak to you urgently. It's a professional matter. Can you ring me back as soon as possible?'

I drive back to Plymouth, my eyes fixed firmly on the road ahead, the beauty of the moors no longer offering its normal consolation.

18

It's nearly 2pm when I park in the multi-storey car park behind the police station and make my way along the long line of bars and cafes that stretch out behind the nearby art university campus. I take a seat outside, on the veranda of the Cappuccino Club, and order a coffee. It isn't long before Alex arrives. He gives me a nod and walks straight past me to the bar.

'Tough morning?' I say, as he sits down and takes a large gulp from his pint. He's wearing a dark suit and has recently had his hair cut. I wish I could turn off that part of me, no matter how small it is, that still fancies him.

His pained expression relaxes into a smile. 'You are *so* not someone to lecture me about day drinking. So what's up?'

'I just got back from Dartmoor after seeing Tel Duggan.' Alex rolls his eyes. 'It was a personal visit.'

'So, how is old Tel?'

'Mental health problems, and possibly back on gear.'

'Surprise, surprise.'

'I need to get him out of there.'

'Is that why you asked me here? Because if you think I have any influence with the CPS, you're sadly mistaken.'

'That's not the reason.'

Alex raises an eyebrow, clearly intrigued. 'Fire away then.'

'It was just something Tel said.'

'Which was?'

'He said there was a rumour going around Dartmoor that sex offenders in the city had better watch their backs.'

'Sex offenders anywhere had better watch their backs as far as I'm concerned,' Alex replies, 'but what has that got to do with me?'

'Tel also said that the rumour was that someone from Devon and Cornwall police, someone inside, was leaking information about them.'

'What?' Alex wipes a thin layer of froth from his upper lip. 'What kind of information?'

'Tel suggested someone was leaking information about sex offenders – their histories, convictions, home addresses, name changes, that kind of thing – to an online vigilante group.'

Alex's face turns crimson. 'You're kidding me, right? Do you know how many times I've heard some banged-up lowlife blame the system for what's gone wrong in their life? "The cops set me up, the cops are corrupt, if only the cops hadn't told social services that I was a convicted paedophile I might still be living with my new girlfriend and her three-year-old daughter."'

'Alex–'

'Tel Duggan is a convicted drug dealer with a long history of mental health issues. He'll say just about anything to get some attention. I cannot believe you were stupid enough to visit him in prison, and even so stupid that you took him seriously.'

'You took him seriously once upon a time.'

'That was a long time ago.'

I lean across the table so that my lips nearly touch his cheek.

'One of your best informers, as I recall.'

'I should never have told you that.'

'So why don't you believe him now?'

'He's messed up, Grace,' says Alex, 'no use to anyone.'

'I've heard Ryan in PPU.' I'm determined to say my peace. 'Talking about what he'd do to sex offenders if he had a chance. The other day he was blabbing confidential information about Michael Fellows all over the shop. Maybe it wasn't intentional, but if he's that indiscreet in the office–'

'Come on, Grace. He's just a kid. Just because he said something slightly inappropriate in the office, doesn't mean he's part of some major conspiracy to rid the city of sex offenders. Do you know how ridiculous that sounds?'

'I know it may be a bit way out there, but–'

'It's not just way out there,' says Alex, 'it's downright crazy and, even more than that, insulting. The fact that you could really think that any of our guys are a part of this just beggars belief.'

'It's not like there haven't been–'

'Stop it, Grace, just stop it!' I'm surprised by how vehemently Alex is protesting. As a detective, I would have expected him to be open to every possibility, even corruption. He stands up to leave.

'I'm sorry,' I say, desperately trying to calm him down. I need his help. I need *him*. 'I press my fingers against my aching temples. 'I'm just all over the place at the moment.'

'You need to take a break, Grace. Step back.'

Stepping back is the last thing I need to do.

'Did you know that Nicky White and Anton Cross were in Dartmoor at the same time?'

'What are you on about?'

'July 2019. Nicky was in for a firearms offence.'

Alex tries but fails to hide the look of surprise on his face. Not surprise like he didn't know that, but rather surprise that I found out about it.

LOUISE SHARLAND

'How did you—'

'Sophie told me.'

'I should have known.' He nods. 'It's not enough that she's buggered up her own career, now she wants to do the same to yours.'

'I checked. It's true.'

Alex takes a long sip of his pint.

'As far as we could tell there was no interaction between the two men when they were inside, and certainly no indication of any when they were out, either.'

'They're all connected, Alex.' I feel breathless but carry on. 'Anton, Nicky, Michael, Darren and–'

'Woah, woah, woah. Anton and Nicky were prolifics. The fact they ended up in the same place at the same time is more than likely pure coincidence.'

'But two murders in as many weeks,' I say, unable to let it go, 'and two serious assaults in the last six months? Don't you think there's a–'

'Connection?' says Alex. 'That's a strong possibility, and one we're looking into, but it isn't to do with some ridiculous theory about violent sex offenders being knocked off by vigilantes. And it's *not* connected to Cross.' He's sounds so resolute. 'If there is a connection, I would suggest it has more to do with organised crime than anything else. Just like I mentioned in the comms meeting.'

'Drug crime?'

'You've been doing this long enough to see that. Both Nicky and Michael have previous, for possession with intent to supply. Nicky's family has been trying to extend their patch into Devonport.'

'What about those two assaults – Lawson and Murphy?'

'They've all been connected to dealing and violence in the city in some way or other for years. Tension among dealers has been escalating for months now. Maybe there is a turf war going on, but more than likely it's just the usual double-dealing and backstabbing that goes with the territory.'

'But you agree that there may be a connection between the assaults and the murders?'

'Possibly,' he replies, 'but that's as much as I'm saying.'

'But Michael was one of mine!'

Alex puts his pint down. 'Bloody hell, Grace. You don't have to be everyone's fucking saviour!' A few heads turn, and he lowers his voice. 'Look, I know you've been through a tough time, but your behaviour lately has been erratic and self-destructive.'

'You think I'm losing it?'

'Not losing it, just under a lot of pressure. I've seen too many police and POs go down with stress, ruin their careers, their marriages.' He looks away before finally re-establishing eye contact. 'I did it to you, didn't I?'

'That's history.'

'Grace, I regret it every day.' *This is not the conversation I was planning to have. It feels like a deflection.* 'Last Saturday was–'

'Please don't.'

'It's still there, Grace, between us. I know I screwed up, but I'll do everything I can to make it up to you. Just give me a chance.'

The last thing I want to do is hurt my ex-husband's feelings, but that's what he is – my ex.

'I don't think we should consider getting back together.'

'Just say it like it is eh, Grace?' He stands up quickly, his chair making a loud scraping sound on the wooden floor that makes me jump. 'Forget I said anything. That I was there for you when Katie Cross died, and throughout the investigation. That I supported you last Saturday, and that I came here as soon as you called.' His voice is thick with anger, sadness, and regret. 'That we had something good once, and could have that again. Just forget it.' He walks off without looking back.

I keep my eyes lowered, unable to face the curious looks of strangers. I wait a few minutes for my breathing to slow, then get up to leave. 'I will get answers, Alex,' I whisper under my breath, 'just you watch me.'

I head back to the office feeling more uncertain than ever. I'm just finishing some case notes when I get a text from Jodie:

> Can you pick me up after school?

I leave work a bit early, ignoring Simon's questioning looks, and manage to find a spot on a lay-by opposite the girls' grammar school. My eyes scan the pedestrian footbridge, looking for a pair of black Converse, a source of endless conflict with her head teacher, coming across the bridge. Finally, I see that familiar gait, and feel an almost overpowering surge of gratitude and love. By the time Jodie reaches the car I am feigning an interest in my mobile phone. All I really want to do is hug her tightly.

She glances over shyly. 'You okay?'

'All good,' I reply, trying my best to sound casual. 'Fancy some sushi?'

'Yes please!'

I feel an irrational sense of victory then force myself to acknowledge that this is not a competition. Our daughter is not a prize to be haggled over, someone whose affections can be bought through fast food outings. Alex, Jodie, and I will continually have to navigate our lives together: boundaries, respect, kindness, and who she lives with... but that can all come later. For now, all I want is to revel in her presence.

We go for sushi, talk about school, her friends, and her first proper Duke of Edinburgh Award camping expedition this weekend. Then, I gently lead the conversation towards Paradise Church.

'So, I was sort of thinking of getting involved myself.'

'With the church?' says Jodie, through a mouthful of tekka maki.

'I happened to meet Ingrid, and we got talking about the street pastor work she does. She asked me to shadow at one of the Go Outs tomorrow night.'

'*You* with the Street Pastors?' Jodie's eyes are wide with disbelief, though interestingly she doesn't seem angry, only hugely curious.

'Ingrid said they could do with someone who has experience of working within the criminal justice system.' I lean forward so the couple in the booth next to us doesn't hear. 'And let me be completely clear. This is in no way a religious conversion.' Jodie risks a smile. 'It's really just an opportunity to help out.'

'Do you mean that?' Jodie is serious now, with a hint confrontation. 'It's not just an excuse to keep an eye on me?'

'Unless you plan on being off your face on Union Street this Friday night, I doubt very much our paths will cross.'

Her smile is wider now, and genuine. 'Cool.'

'Cool?'

'If you want to help out at the church, I think it's cool.' She gives me a goofy grin. 'Can I have some of your Korean fried chicken?' she asks, her chopsticks coming my way.

19

I go through the rest of the week with a surprising lightness, convincing myself that volunteering will be a good thing for my relationship with Jodie. I can't deny we've been getting on much better since it was agreed. This morning when packing up her camping gear for the weekend, she said casually, 'Why don't you invite Marcus over? That way you won't be on your own.'

When did she get so grown up?

I spend most of the day in a personal safety training workshop, and by five thirty I am counting the minutes. Finally, the day is done and I pack up my desk, grab my keys and head out. I'm making my way through the car park when I hear footsteps behind me. *Shit. Has a disgruntled client waited for me outside Tamar House?* The footsteps are getting closer. I try and recall that day's training, and turn around, preparing to yell 'Back off!', or run to the nearest place of safety. My brain struggles to remember the major pressure points should I need to defend myself. *Groin, knee, eye sockets.* I take a breath, brace myself, and turn.

A young woman who looks to be in her mid-twenties, brunette and pretty, is standing behind me.

'Ms Midwinter?' Her voice is shaky, her face pale.

'Yes,' I reply uneasily. 'Who are you?'

She takes a breath. 'I'm Jade Weller. I was Michael's girlfriend.'

I buy Jade a coffee, and we find a secluded bench behind the Civic Centre.

'I'm so sorry about Michael.' The words sound shallow, and ineffectual.

'I know he did a terrible thing,' whispers Jade, 'but he did his time.' She dabs at her red-rimmed eyes. 'He *was* trying to do better.'

I reach into my bag for a tissue and pass it to her. 'He seemed genuinely committed to his rehabilitation.'

You can do better than that, Grace.

I squeeze her arm. 'I was proud of him.'

'Me too.' Jade tells me she and Michael had been friends since secondary school and had dated for a while until Chantal came on the scene.

I'm expecting some attempt at justification, but she only says, 'He knows what he did.'

I watch a pair of seagulls picking at a crisp packet. 'I just can't understand how this could have happened.'

'He was afraid,' Jade's voice is barely audible, 'terrified.'

'Terrified?'

She glances around, clearly still frightened herself. 'He started getting really paranoid, you know? Telling me not to post anything online or tell anyone stuff that might let people know where we were going to be living.' I'm reminded of our very first meeting where Michael told me he was planning to move in with his missus. Jade leans a little closer. 'I think someone was threatening to put our new address on social media.'

'Which would get Chantal's family at your front door.' She nods sadly. 'Why didn't you go to the police?'

'The police!' She laughs an angry, bitter, heartbreaking sound. 'He thought it was one of them what was doing it.'

I get home still mulling over my meeting with Jade. *Could someone have been blackmailing Michael, threatening to expose his personal details online?* It was hard for ex-offenders, particularly sex offenders, being googled or having their details posted on crime and punishment Facebook groups. More often than not they were forced out of their accommodation, or like Michael, threatened with having their convictions, photographs and address posted online. I take the dog for a walk, make myself something to eat, then text Jodie to see how she's getting on with her trek. No signal.

Just after 10pm I change into a pair of jeans, a lightweight waterproof, and slip on the high vis jacket Ingrid has given me. I put on a slick of lip balm, and rifle through the top drawer of my bedside table until I find a hair bobble, which I snap around my wrist. My eyes fall to the far corner of the drawer where, next to an expired passport and a yellowing plastic keychain with a picture of me, Jodie, and Alex at Legoland, is a slim leather case. Inside that is an unexpected gift I received from my father when I was ten.

'*Any girl can have a Barbie,*' he had said, once the birthday wrapping paper was cleared away, '*this just might save your life one day,*' and he had watched me open the narrow wooden box. I thought it might have been a watch, but when I slipped off the lid I was astonished to discover a pocketknife, with my initials engraved into the dark sycamore handle. My mother had protested at the inappropriateness of the gift, but I had loved it. After Alex and I got engaged I even ridiculously carved our initials in a sticky pine somewhere along the Southwest Coastal Path. When our divorce was being finalised, I had tried to find that tree, but gave up after a few fruitless hours.

I take the knife from the drawer now, slip it out of its leather pouch and, easing open the polished blade, carefully balance it in the palm of my hand. 'Feels just right,' I whisper, just as I did thirty plus years ago when my father first gave it to me. I carefully close the knife and slip it into my pocket.

When I arrive at Paradise Church, I discover the rest of the street pastors already congregated in the church hall. I glance around hoping to spot Ingrid, but she's nowhere to be seen. I find myself loitering awkwardly by the back door, hoping someone will eventually speak to me.

'Grace!' Ingrid's cheerful lilt cuts through my anxiety. She leads me into the throng, where there are friendly greetings. I find myself working alongside Betty, the elderly lady I met last Sunday, helping to fill large flasks with tea and coffee for the night ahead. The room is filled with the steady sound of work, and I am unaware of Tim's arrival until a sudden, reverent silence fills the hall.

'Good evening, everyone. Glad to see you could all make it.' He spots Ingrid and heads our way, his brow creasing as soon as he recognises me.

'Grace has so much to offer,' says Ingrid, deflecting any potential criticism with ease. 'Her experience of working within the criminal justice system, and her contacts with other support networks in the city will be invaluable.'

'I'm really happy to help out wherever I can,' I add, picking up the baton. Tim regards me with a mixture of curiosity and caution. I get the clear sense that he still doesn't trust me.

'Considering how much you've helped Jodie, I'd really like to give a little something back if I can.' That little homily seems to do the trick.

'Well,' says Tim, with a sigh. 'We could do with someone with your level of expertise.' I hear Ingrid's tiny exhalation of relief. 'You've read the volunteer guidelines, and signed the agreement?' I nod. 'You're to follow them to a T, understood?'

'Understood.'

'If all goes well tonight, we can see about getting you on the volunteer induction programme next month.'

'Thank you, Tim.' Of course I want to help out, what community minded person wouldn't? But I also want to get to know Tim a little bit better. *See if the man who has been so involved in my daughter's life has any secrets to hide.*

Tim claps his hands, and almost immediately, the assembled crew forms a small circle around him. I feel a gentle hand on my elbow, and am led into the circle, where I find myself standing between Ingrid and Tim.

'Dear God,' says Tim, his voice resonant. 'We ask for your blessing on this night, and we pray that all that happens will be guided by your Holy Spirit and that God's presence is with us in this city tonight, so that it is a safe place for everyone. We also welcome our sister Grace into this circle of care, compassion, and trust. May you guide her to serve you with integrity, faith, and good will, and to always be on the side of righteousness. In Jesus' name, Amen.

'Amen,' echoes the group, and I find myself saying it as well.

We take the minibus into the city centre, and park up behind the British Red Cross charity shop, which had once been a Toys R Us.

'This will be our base for the next few hours,' says Tim, as we begin unloading the tea and coffee flasks onto a collapsible picnic table. 'The full moon tonight should be useful.'

'It's always mad on a full moon,' says Ingrid, her tone playful.

'We'll have none of that,' snaps Tim. In the eerie glow of the LED streetlights his face is fluorescent.

'We could do with some more bottles of water,' says Ingrid, ignoring her husband's reprimand. She takes my arm, and I find myself being pulled back towards the minibus. 'I do love the Go Outs,' she confides as soon as we're out of earshot, 'but I sometimes think Tim would rather I didn't come along.'

This is a surprising revelation. 'Why not? You organise most of it.'

'He thinks I become too, ah...'

She struggles for the right word. I recall my conversation with Alex in the office a few days before.

'Invested?'

'Exactly.' She sighs. We grab the supplies and begin slowly making our way back to the base. 'Some nights, it's just handing out a few bottles of water, helping those in need get home safely. Others, it's about discovering a level of depravity in your own city that you never knew existed.' She shakes her head as if trying to dislodge a memory. 'He thinks I don't know when to stop. Every down and out, addict or working girl.' The moon appears from behind a cloud, and I can see the look of fierce determination on her face. 'More than ever, I need to protect those who can't protect themselves.'

We make it back to the meeting point to find Tim handing Ingrid's rucksack to one of the other volunteers.

'What's going on?'

'Change of rota,' replies Tim, brusquely. 'I'd like you and

David to stay with the van to manage the supplies and any drop-bys.'

'But—'

'It's decided.'

An awkward hush falls over the group. I get the impression that this sort of about-face from Tim isn't uncommon.

My earlier assessment of that man stands!

Ingrid takes her demotion with practised grace. The rest of us pack up and walk on. It's not long before we come across a pair of drunken young men staggering their way towards us.

'You all right, lads?' says Tim.

'Ace,' replies one, who seems to be having trouble getting his lighter to meet the end of his cigarette.

'Have a drop of water.' He hands them each a bottle. 'You need to keep hydrated.'

'Good thinking,' says the second lad, who opening the bottle, proceeds to spill half of it down the front of his shirt. 'Help us to keep drinking for longer.'

'Wasn't quite my objective,' says Tim, as we watch the duo stagger down the road. Something about the calm compassion with which he has just dealt with the two young men, no stern judgement or lectures, makes me reflect on my first impressions of the Paradise Church leader.

It's not long before it's kicking out time at the pubs, and the pavement is flooded with drunken bodies. We spend the next hour handing out water and lollies to a torrent of partygoers ranging in age from sixteen to sixty, some barely able to stand. The pervading smells of body odour and lager seem to permeate the night air. *I'm definitely going to have a long, hot shower when I get home.* By 1am the team is flagging, and Betty and I stop to sit at some benches at a small park just off the main strip.

'Is it what you expected?' asks Betty, handing me a cup of hot chocolate.

'Yes and no,' I reply, grateful for the warm liquid. 'Ingrid's a real inspiration.'

'She loves the night work,' Betty gives me a rueful look, 'that's what we call it. Is very good at it, too.'

I sense she wants to say more, but just needs a little push.

'But?'

Betty makes a soft tutting sound. 'Tim has always been very protective,' and then, glancing around to make sure that he isn't within hearing distance she adds, 'one could almost say controlling.'

'He's trying to stop her coming to Go Outs, isn't he?' I ask. 'Like he did tonight?'

Betty sighs deeply. 'I've heard the rows.'

I lean in close. 'Do you think he would do anything to—'

'That's it, everyone,' calls Tim, 'break time is over. This will be final letting out, and there'll be plenty of drunken young university students thinking they can walk the three miles home to their student halls in high heels, so make sure to give them a pair of these.' He hands out carrier bags filled with plastic flip-flops. 'Why don't you and Betty head up a little way towards Royal Parade?' he says to me. 'But stay within eyeshot, and stay together.'

I'm relieved to be free of his oppressive energy.

Betty and I head east, towards Royal Parade and the ubiquitous Wetherspoons. We're just waiting for the lights to change when we hear the sound of anguished sobs. A greasy laneway runs out from behind a multi-storey car park and onto Union Street. Betty and I find ourselves walking towards that terrible sound, uncertain of what we'll find. It doesn't take us long to discover the source. A young woman, or girl – she's no older than eighteen – is sitting on the ground, her back against a blue plastic skip, legs splayed out in front of her in an inelegant V shape.

'Are you all right?' I ask.

'Get away from me!'

Her voice is wild, hysterical, and there is a fearful, desperate look in her eyes. I can feel the hairs on the back of my arms standing on end. Betty steps towards her.

'My name is Betty,' she says. Even though she is well past seventy, Betty is still able to crouch on the ground in front of her. 'I'm here to help.'

A passing car illuminates the scene, and now I can see that the young woman is wearing no underpants. In an act of discreet generosity, Betty reaches forward and gently pulls the young woman's skirt down past her thighs. I hear the sound of footsteps and see Tim approaching. He takes in the scene in a moment. Removing his rucksack, he takes a foil blanket from the front pocket and moving forward very slowly, he hands it to Betty.

'Are you all right, darling?' asks Betty. 'What happened to you?'

'*Mys boys friend,*' the girl slurs, and then making a feeble attempt to stand, collapses back onto the ground. 'Had a row, didn't we?' Fat teardrops spill from beneath her pasted-on eyelashes. She turns her face towards the light, and now I can see that she has been beaten. Her eye is blackened, and her right cheekbone is already starting to bruise. Blood trickles from one nostril, down her chin, and settles in the nook of her collarbone.

'Did he do this to you?'

The girl nods. 'Me mum and dad'll think I'm a twat for givn 'im another chance.' The hysterics have ceased, but I'm finding the girl's deep-seated despair far more distressing.

'No they won't, darling.' Betty gently lays the foil blanket across the girl's legs and pushes aside a strand of her sweat-soaked hair. 'You are loved, darling. They'll just be glad that you're safe.'

'Not so sur bout that,' she says, her voice heartbreaking and sweet. She hands Betty her mobile phone. 'Can you call my dad, pleeze? Hess name is Rob.' The tears have started again; the young woman's shoulders are shaking fiercely.

'Of course, darling.' Reaching forward, Betty gently dabs a drop of blood from the girl's chin.

'You shouldn't touch her,' I say gently. Betty looks up at me in surprise. 'You'll contaminate the evidence.'

I call the police, give the details and our location. Within minutes, two squad cars are on site, a couple of guys I know from my days with Alex.

'Be gentle with her,' I say, and indicating to Betty I add, 'be gentle with both of them.'

I'm finding it difficult to breathe. The smell of vomit, perspiration and urine, and the sight of that poor ruined girl, not much older than Jodie, the flashing lights of cars as they drive past, honking their horns and yelling profanities out of open windows, is all too much. I find myself stumbling down the lane towards a bench opposite a small row of terraced council houses that sit in the shadow of an overhead pedestrian walkway. To my right is a concrete stairwell that leads to the multi-storey car park. The door is partially open, and from within I can hear the sound of thuds and grunts. Curiosity conquers, and I find myself pushing open the door. The stairwell is barely lit by a flickering blue bulb. Junkies can't see their veins in blue light. On the concrete landing above two figures are kicking the hell out of third who is helplessly curled into a foetal position on the floor. Both assailants are wearing dark clothing and balaclavas, just shadows in the darkness. With each well aimed boot, the man on the floor arches, and buckles in pain. All I can think of is Nicky White choking on his own blood before being thrown in the harbour.

'What the hell are you doing?' I scream. 'Stop it!' The larger of the two figures turns, pauses, and then suddenly rushes down the steps towards me. I brace myself for the full force of their attack as they smash into me and pin me against the wall. Their hand reaches for my throat. I try to lift my leg to knee them in the groin, but they're too close. My hands are pinned against their chest. I'm grasping, tearing at the smooth leather of their jacket. They squeeze harder.

'Please,' I whisper. My attacker steps back as if struck, and for a moment loosens their grip. I reach into my pocket. My hand is shaky, slick, and my pocketknife clatters to the ground. In the distance, I can hear someone calling my name. 'They're looking for me,' I whisper. My assailant stands before me, seemingly unafraid. Then suddenly, they turn and flee, their sidekick following close behind. I find myself stumbling out of the stairwell and back down the road.

'Grace?' Betty emerges from the throng of people caring for the girl. 'Where have you been? I've been calling you.' I try to speak, but my voice is strained. I reach for her, desperately trying to control my uneven breath. 'The stairwell. I think they've killed him!'

20

By the time the police make it to the stairwell, it's empty. At first, there's some suggestion that I over dramatised it all. *Yeah, those red marks around my neck are self-inflicted...* but then they discover blood on the landing, and a human tooth. *Probably a drug deal gone bad,* is the general consensus. With no assailant, no evidence aside from a bloody bicuspid tooth, and with the CCTV camera spray painted over, there's not really much they can do. The attending PC asks if I need to go to A&E, but I say I'll contact my doctor in the morning.

Tim and Ingrid drive me home, the car cloaked in silence.

'I'm really sorry,' I say, as we reach my drive. Tim does not speak as he walks me to my front door.

'Perhaps you should reconsider if our programme is right for you,' he says as I slip my key into the lock.

I feel the heat in my cheeks. 'All I did tonight was try and save someone's life. Isn't that what your programme is all about?'

'Not if it means putting yourself in danger.'

'I was fine,' I reply, hoping that the marks around my neck have started to fade. 'I should have come back to get support, I know that, but it was my natural instinct to try and help.'

Tim looks unconvinced. 'We want people with passion and commitment, Grace, but also common sense.'

His words sting. Without speaking, I unlock my door and step inside.

I'm tired, achy, and just want to get my head down. Marcus is due to arrive sometime after lunch, and I need at least a few hours' sleep so that I don't look like a complete disaster. I take a couple of painkillers, and as much as I just want to climb into bed, I recognise that a hot bath is a must. I strip off my waterproof, jeans and T-shirt, and throw them to the bathroom floor. Something clatters onto the tiles, and I watch as a small metal disc spins in a wobbly rotation before falling flat. I bend over to pick it up. It's a silver button. Too tired to wonder how it got there, I slip it back into my jacket pocket, then step into the bath.

I sleep fitfully, waking up every hour imagining a balaclava clad figure standing at the foot of my bed. I break my own rules and allow Bismarck onto the bed, his steady breathing and solid presence some comfort at least.

I wake up at ten, change the sheets, have a shower, and do my best to make myself look presentable. When just after two I hear the rumble of Marcus' Mercedes pulling into the drive, I feel an odd mixture of excitement and unease. We've never talked about being exclusive, but for me there always seemed to be a tacit understanding. Unburdening myself now by telling him about what happened with Alex recently not only feels selfish, but unkind, especially since it will never happen again. I have chosen to live with my guilt discreetly. *I only hope Alex will do the same.*

I wait by the front door as Marcus removes his overnight bag from the boot. He's tall like Alex, but broader, and with a surprising grace. As he approaches, I feel my heart soar. I'm five foot nine, but at well over six feet, he towers above me. He drops his bag by the door, and envelopes me in a hug. He's warm and solid, smelling of citrus and sandalwood. I find myself clinging to him.

'You miss me?' he jokes, clearly surprised by the intensity of my greeting.

We go inside, and all of a sudden I feel shy. 'Drink?' I ask, and turn towards the kitchen. I feel his hand in mine, and he pulls me to him.

'Later,' he whispers, and leads me upstairs.

The sex is rough yet tender, passionate, liberating. We lie together afterwards sweaty, spent, the sheets entangled between us. He takes a lock of my hair and twirls it around his finger.

'So, what's up?'

'I missed you.'

'That's all?'

'Just a lot on my mind.'

I run my hand down along his chest to his stomach. He moans softly as I go lower. He grips me by the hips and lifts me onto him.

'Well then, we'd better do something about that, hadn't we?'

When we wake it's nearly seven. I order a Deliveroo, we drink red wine and catch up on old episodes of *Line of Duty* on iPlayer.

'How was the street pastors thing last night?' he asks, finally.

I tell him about Ingrid, Tim, Betty, and the poor girl by the dumpster.

He runs his fingertip across my neck, just under my chin.

'And this?'

'It's nothing,' I reply.

'Nothing?'

'Well...' There's no point in trying to talk my way around it.

'Christ!' he says, when I'm finally finished.

'I know it was foolish,' I say. He doesn't concur, or rebuke me, just listens. 'But it was automatic, you know?'

He pulls me in close. 'I know, but you've got to look out for yourself,' he plants delicate kisses all along the red line on my neck, 'because I couldn't bear to lose you.'

I sleep the best I have in ages, and wake to the smell of bacon frying. I throw on a robe, wash my face and head downstairs to find Marcus frying eggs, one of my old aprons wrapped around him. I kiss him fiercely and point to the lettering written across the front of it – *Kiss the Chef*. 'Just doing what I'm told.'

Marcus and I spend the afternoon mooching through antiques shops and eating ice cream. We walk back to mine hand in hand, and talk about our plans for a holiday together in Jamaica where I can meet his gran. He's just packing his bag to leave when I hear Jodie's key in the front door. I kiss his cheek.

'Come down and say hello.'

At first Jodie was aloof with Marcus, huffing and scowling at his every attempt to engage with her. When he happened to mention that he had met Banksy when working on an art fraud case one day, her icy disposition did a complete about-face. They discussed whether or not street art was vandalism, the artist's political activism, and finally the influence of colonialism on the Bristol art scene. I sat and watched them, spellbound.

We're halfway down the stairs when the door opens and she strides in, mucky from her weekend camping on the moors.

'Hi, Mum, hi, Marcus,' she says, heading straight for the kitchen. 'What's to eat?'

'I'm sure her and Kieran must be related somehow,' laughs Marcus.

Then another figure steps through the open doorway. I feel the blood drain from my face.

'*Alex.*'

My lover stands behind me, my ex-husband in front. I feel my heart pounding. Alex looks at me, to Marcus, and then back again.

'Jodie's rucksack,' he says, dropping it on the floor. 'You must be Magnus,' he says, gazing past me. The pin drop silence might as well be a roar. The two men stare at each other like boxers before a fight, Alex's jaw muscles flexing, Marcus' left hand clenching into a fist.

'Is there any juice?' comes a tired voice from the kitchen, and the dangerous spell is broken.

'I'll be right there, honey,' I call, my voice shaky. I turn to Marcus.

'Why don't you go upstairs, and finish packing?'

His eyes are fixed on Alex.

'Only if–'

'I'll be fine.'

I wait until I hear the creak of the bedroom floorboards above before speaking.

'What the hell do you think you're doing?'

Alex lifts his chin. 'Just dropping Jodie off like we agreed.'

'You knew Marcus was staying this weekend.'

'I thought it was about time I was introduced to the guy,' he replies, 'especially if he's going to be in the same house as my daughter.'

'Well you've seen to it that she isn't going to stay in this house much longer, haven't you?'

'Nice one,' he replies. 'Did you change the sheets?' Glancing upstairs. 'After we slept together?'

I can hear Marcus moving around the bedroom. He must have finished packing by now.

'Alex, please go.'

'And not spend some time getting to know your knew *boyfriend?*' He says the final word with such derision that it's like a needle to my skin.

'Mum?' calls Jodie, from the kitchen. 'Are we out of mayo?'

I see my chance. 'Don't do this to *her,* Alex.'

'That's rich coming from you.'

'Hey, Dad?' Jodie comes down the hall, clutching a sandwich. 'You still here?'

'Didn't get my goodbye kiss, did I?' Alex leans past me to give Jodie a kiss, his hand brushing against mine. I watch in relief as he turns and leaves, not even glancing back. Air rushes back into my lungs, and I grab the banister for support. I hear footsteps on the stairs, and look up to see Marcus standing there, his face hidden in shadow.

Marcus leaves with an uneasy sense of finality, the conversation beforehand awkward and tense.

'I mean, if there's still anything between you two...'

'There's nothing.'

Liar, liar...

'You sure?' He searches my face. 'I mean, it looked heavy.'

'Everything's heavy when it comes to Alex,' I reply, but don't elaborate. The less I say, the less I give away.

21

On Monday morning I wake feeling anxious and groggy. Work is a slog with recalls, uncooperative clients, and endless paperwork. I'm just returning from a one-to-one when I notice the waiting area is empty. It's after 3pm, and I'm expecting Billy Vale for his weekly meeting. I ask at reception, but he hasn't checked in.

'Have you heard anything from Billy Vale?' I ask my assistant. 'He was supposed to be here for three.'

She points to the disorder that is my desk, and there, stuck to my drinks bottle is a pink Post-it note.

> *Called about an hour ago. Said he had D and V and*
> *won't be able to make it.*

I doubt very much that Billy Vale has diarrhoea or vomiting, but he's schooled enough in probation protocols to know that any hint of an infectious illness means an automatic forty-eight-hour reprieve from required meetings.

Jodie texts to say she's having tea at Jasmine's house, and that her mum will drop her home around nine. I get that she wants to spread her wings, become more independent, but it feels increasingly obvious that my daughter is trying to avoid me. I feel a headache starting, and reach into my bag for a paracetamol, discovering instead the leaflet Ingrid gave me about her counselling practice. I glance around to make sure no one is watching. There have been enough scandals about me in this place to last a lifetime. *Maybe it's about time to start looking for some practical support.* I also owe her an apology for wandering off the other night. I have no doubt she got it in the neck from Tim for inviting me out, and I really need to try and make amends.

I go home, walk the dog, grab something to eat, then make my way to Paradise Church. When I arrive, the car park is full. I go around to the front entrance. The lobby is bustling with people and purpose. Handwritten signs are stuck to the walls. They're directing visitors to meeting rooms for Bible study, Men's and Women's Groups, an AA meeting. There are smiles, hugs, and there's genuine support going on here. I can understand why Jodie feels so safe.

'Grace.' I feel a great surge of relief when I hear Ingrid's voice. 'What a pleasant surprise.'

'I was just in the area–'

'I'm so glad to see you. A few of our helpers are off with flu, and...' She holds her hands up and looks around.

'Can I do anything to help?'

'Your name upholds your nature, Grace.' She's smiling, but I can see the stress on her face. She leads me into a small room adjacent to the hall. 'The AA meeting starts in ten minutes, and I still have so much to do.' She hands me a plastic storage box filled with books and leaflets. 'If you could just place the literature on the table there, I'll set out the chairs.'

'Are you chairing the meeting?'

'Me? Oh no. I sometimes sit in to offer support and let

members know about my counselling sessions, but Tim leads the meeting. He's been in the fellowship for a number of years.'

So, Tim is a recovering alcoholic.

'When we took over Paradise Church three years ago, Tim decided to start our own chapter here.'

'Have you only been in Plymouth for three years?' I ask, laying a copy of the *Big Book* on the table. 'I thought it was longer.'

'Nearly four now,' she replies. 'We were further north before that.' Ingrid gazes around the room. 'Could you do me a favour please? It's all a bit chaotic at the moment, as you probably can tell. We normally have the fellowship meetings in the back room, but it's being decorated. I've left the AA banner with the twelve steps in there. Would you mind getting it for me? It should be in the corner near the door.'

'Yes, of course.'

I stand up and leave the room. Ahead of me there are two corridors, one leading to the communal kitchen, and one to the meeting rooms. Above the entrance to the church hall is a large sign: *Jesus Saves*.

I turn left. The narrow corridor is lined with faded carpet. Here and there, where the edges have frayed and turned up, someone has stuck them down with swatches of black electrical tape. I see an open door, light creeping into the corridor. At the end are two small communal toilets. There is a red *'occupied'* sign on one of them. I follow the scent of fresh paint, and find myself in a large meeting room. The floor is lined with dust sheets, and tins of paint are stacked in the corner. On the far wall someone has started painting a mural. It's clearly of a biblical passage. There are dark stone columns, and steps that lead to a shimmering pool of azure water. There are also pencil sketches of people, clearly works in progress, gathered around the pool. Something about the style seems familiar. I step into the room, to study them closer. I hear floorboards creak, and turn, expecting to see Ingrid or even Tim. It takes a few seconds for my brain to recognise the figure standing in front of me.

'Billy,' I say, the word feeling like acid on my tongue. 'What are you doing here?'

Billy Vale stares at me, then very slowly, the corners of his mouth turn upwards.

'I could ask you the same thing, Grace.' His grin widens, and I can see a small wad of chewing gum in the corner of his mouth. 'I didn't know you hung out at places like this.'

'I don't.' My response is automatic, defensive. The last thing I want is for him to know anything about my private life.

'And yet, here you are.'

'I was just getting something for Ing...' I stop myself. Now that the initial shock has passed, I am able to assess the situation more clearly. Billy is wearing white overalls streaked with paint, and in his hand he holds a small bucket with paintbrushes. 'Is this where you're volunteering?'

'Sort of,' he says.

'You're going to have to be a bit more specific than that.'

'The pastor here runs the gardening project that I help out on.' He holds up his bucket. 'I just came to wash my brushes.'

'I thought you had D&V?'

'I thought so too, Grace,' he says smugly, 'but it might just have been something I ate.'

I'm finding Billy Vale increasingly annoying. 'You shouldn't be here.'

'What?'

'Do they know about your recent arrest, the situation with Nicole?'

His face goes very pink. 'It's none of their business.'

'I'm afraid it is.' I'm feeling irked about having to deal with a work issue in what I thought was a place of peace. 'You gave me the impression your voluntary work was outside, and not working with other people.'

'I said I just came in to wash my brushes, didn't I?'

I point to the splashes of azure paint on his overalls, then to the wall behind us. 'Remarkably similar don't you think?'

'Don't know what you're talking about.'

Don't play dumb with me.

'There's an AA meeting starting any minute.'

'What's that got to do with me?'

His look is one of anger mixed with confusion, and I berate myself for not discussing his volunteering more thoroughly in our first meeting. I know from experience that along with those emotions there will also be an acute sense of acrimony, which will do little to improve our increasingly fractious relationship. I know too that if Simon gets wind of this he will make a meal of it.

'Your licence conditions clearly state you are not allowed to be working or volunteering in an area where there are vulnerable women or under sixteens present.'

'I don't even see them!'

'They're just down the hall,' and glancing towards the door, I add, 'they must come this way to use the toilet all the time.'

'This is crazy, man!'

'It may seem crazy to you, but it's the law, and by contravening it you are in genuine danger of being recalled to prison.' His eyes are filled with a deep hatred. 'As your interim Probation Officer, I'm going to have to insist that you immediately leave the premises and have no further engagement with Paradise Church until we can review the situation more thoroughly.'

I have to cover my back. Sophie's, too.

'What? No!'

'You have outstanding charges, Billy. Charges linked to a

potentially serious offence. Your licence conditions are very clear.'

'You are not going to do this to me!'

I don't feel great about seeing Billy Vale lose his temper, but maybe at last he'll start to take things seriously.

He opens his mouth to speak, then thinks better of it. 'Now, Billy, I must ask you to leave the premises.'

'You're kidding me, right?'

'We can talk about this in more detail at our next meeting.'

'I can't believe this.'

I take a breath and force myself to remain calm.

'I'm trying to protect you, Billy.'

'Protect me, like fuck!'

'You've got your hearing in a few weeks. If the judge finds out you've been volunteering in a place where you've got direct access to vulnerable women, women like Nicole, they'll–'

'I never even thought about it!'

Did Sophie? Or was she so messed up...?

'*Billy.*' My frustration at finding him here, in my safe place, needs to be put aside. He may very well have not realised that his engagement with Paradise Church was contravening his licence conditions. It certainly wasn't in any of Sophie's notes. I need to remain calm, focused, and professional. 'What you are doing now goes directly against your licence conditions.'

'You've got it all wrong, Grace.' He runs his fingers through his paint flecked hair. 'The last thing I would want to do, after everything that has happened, is to hurt a woman.'

'That may be the case,' I say, choosing my words carefully, 'but as your PO, it's my duty to protect the public.' I pause to prepare for what I have to say next. 'I'm afraid, Billy, that at the moment, you are still considered a risk.'

'A risk! I've been volunteering here for the last six months.'

'We got it wrong, Billy, and now we've got to get it right.

The sooner we do that, the better it will be for everyone.' My eyes hold his. 'Do you understand?'

'You can't do this!'

This is definitely not going as smoothly as I had hoped. *Time to shut it down.* 'It's all about risk, Billy. Surely you know that by now?'

There is the sound of a door closing, and then an unexpected yet recognisable voice takes my breath away.

'Hey, Billy, did I leave my phone in here?'

I turn to see Jodie striding into the room, her smile fading in an instant.

'Mum?'

'Jodie.' After the cool professionalism of my exchange with Billy, my voice now sounds shaky. 'What are you doing here? I thought you were having tea at Jasmine's house.'

'I needed to work on my mural.' She points to the wall. 'It's for my GCSE art project.' She looks from Billy to me and back again, clearly sensing the tension between us. 'Do you two know each other?'

I pause to collect my thoughts. *I need to play this very carefully.*

'Billy is a client.'

'Of yours?'

I nod. Jodie looks to Billy. Billy clears his throat.

'We've all got history, man.'

'Recent history,' I say softly. I give Jodie what I hope is a reassuring look. Getting all probation officer about this situation may not be the best first move. 'So, the mural?'

Jodie looks at the mural, proudly. 'It's Jesus at the healing pool of Bethesda, though I have yet to draw the most important person.'

'I've seen your practice sketches,' says Billy, 'you should have no problem getting him down.'

'Thanks, Billy.'

'You're bloody good, Jode.' He winks at her, and I see my daughter blush.

I watch this exchange between my daughter and my high-risk client in silent disbelief. *He's flirting with her.* Billy Vale, a twenty-four-year-old convicted sex offender with a history of violence against women, is flirting with my fifteen-year-old daughter. I now understand how Sophie felt when she said about Nicky White, *'I'm glad the fucker's dead.'*

'I'm afraid Billy's going to have to leave now, Jodie.'

'What? Why?'

'He's not allowed to be here when there are other people around.'

'Is that one of your stupid instructions things?'

'Conditions, honey, and it's the law.'

I can see Jodie trying to work it out, trying to make sense of it all.

'But it's stupid. Billy's been helping me...' She stops mid-sentence, realising her gaff, and refuses to say more. There are red blotches on her neck, and her voice has taken on the slight sing-song tone that reminds me of when she was little and just about to cry.

'I'm sorry, Jodie, but I have no choice.'

'No choice!'

'Billy could get in serious trouble by being here.' I'm doing everything I can to try and stay in control. 'It's about protecting him as much as anyone else.'

'That's complete bullshit!' Jodie turns to Billy. 'Tell her! Tell her how hard I've been working. How you helped me sort out my problems with the perspective.'

Billy steps forward as if to try to comfort Jodie. I move between them.

'Billy has to leave now, and he won't be allowed to come back.'

Jodie glares at me, her face hard and unforgiving. 'Why do you always have to be such a bitch?'

'Hey, man,' says Billy, 'I'm pissed too you know, but that's no excuse to speak to your mum like that.'

'But she's being an idiot!'

'Just chill,' says Billy. His tone reminds me of the first day I met him, of how he charmed the young apprentice at Tamar House. 'Your mum's just doing her job.'

Before I can stop her, Jodie skirts past me towards Billy. For a horrifying moment I think she's going to rush into his arms, but I find myself absurdly grateful to see her only grabbing his hand. Billy gives me a look that can only be described as victorious. The red mist falls.

'Jodie, leave us alone please.'

'But, Mum–'

'Leave. Right. Now.'

'I don't want to!'

'I don't give a damn what you want.' My voice has a quiet intensity that silences her. 'This isn't about what you want. It is about this man here,' I point to Billy, 'and the fact that he knowingly engaged with you and other people at this location when he shouldn't have.'

'My conditions are for under sixteens.' He gives me a cocky grin then turns. 'You're sixteen aren't you, Jode?'

'Nearly,' she replies.

Billy's face blanches.

'I need you to leave right now, Jodie, or I'm going to call the police.'

'Mum, don't!'

By this point Ingrid has heard the commotion and appears in the doorway.

'Is everything all right in here?'

'Did you know about this? That this man has legal restrictions forbidding him from being anywhere near vulnerable adults and young people?'

Ingrid looks shocked, uncertain. She opens her mouth, but it seems to take forever before the words emerge. 'I've never seen this man before in my life.'

I'm debating what to do next. I could call the Police Protection Unit or the Managing Sexual Offenders and Violent Offenders team, and have Billy remanded in custody, but he could easily say that he had no clear guidance about wider restrictions at our most recent meetings. My main focus was on keeping him away from his ex and daughter, not exploring if his volunteering placement was a risk. I recall Sophie's notes and my interview with Billy last week. There has definitely been no mention of Paradise Church. *Boy did I get this wrong.* This needs to be tidied up, and fast. With the spotlight shining on probation services because of the recent murders, and Simon scrutinising my case files, this could be disastrous. *Even more importantly, just how involved is Billy Vale with my daughter?*

'Can you take Jodie to the office please, Ingrid?'

The pastor's wife looks at me, still clearly confused. Recognising that the situation is serious, she takes Jodie by the arm, and gently starts to lead her from the room.

'But I don't want to go!'

'Better do as your mum says.' Billy bends over and begins folding up the drop cloth. 'Being that I'm such a dangerous criminal and all.'

You are such a dangerous criminal!

'This is so unfair!'

'Just go, okay, Jode?'

There is a moment of intense silence as Billy and Jodie exchange looks. Finally, Jodie purses her lips in a typical teenage pout, and follows Ingrid out of the room. *Just how close is my daughter to this man?*

'Teenagers, eh?' says Billy, as if he and I are just another set of parents comparing notes at the school gates.

I find myself unable to speak. The room is silent except for my steady breathing as I try to regain my composure, and the sound of Billy snapping his chewing gum.

'I still don't know what all the fuss is about,' says Billy, as he continues to collect his kit. 'I was just helping out, doing my bit for the community.'

'If you have laid one finger on her—'

Billy has the temerity to look hard done by. 'What, Grace, you think I go for schoolgirls now?'

'Just get out.'

'I'm going,' he replies, deliberately taking his time to collect his tools.

This is becoming a lot harder than I'd expected. Finding Jodie here has rattled my thinking, but there is still one thing I need to ask. 'Did you not get a criminal record check to volunteer here?'

Billy's eyes narrow. 'I don't normally have anything to do with *people*. Usually, it's just me outside or in a back room somewhere, fixing things.'

'Yet Jodie said you were helping her with the mural?'

'*She* approached *me*.' His arrogance is revolting. 'Mooching around, asking for ladders and stuff. She just seemed like, you know, she needed help... like she was lonely.'

His words are a missile, straight to my gut.

'Is that what you do, Billy, look for the lonely ones?'

'Woah, fucking woah, mate,' says Billy. 'Don't be putting words in my mouth, or I'll be—'

'You'll be what?'

'I've got rights too, you know.' He moves closer, and even

though he is shorter than me, his wiry frame seems to fill the space. 'If you keep on harassing me like this I'll have to speak to my solicitor.'

'Harassing you?'

'Sophie said it was okay.'

He's taking a different angle now, playing the misunderstood innocent. I have to give him credit, he can change tack as quickly as a sailboat in the wind.

'Put your tools down, and leave.' As angry as I am, I still have a job to do, and I will do it right. 'I am trying to keep you out of prison, Billy!'

Even though it's the best place for you!

His gaze falters, as though he's having trouble reconciling the fact that someone might actually be on his side.

'So, what do I have to do?'

'You have to get out of here quick smart. Return home and don't come back. I'll speak to Tim to find out how this happened, and we'll try to resolve it as quickly as possible. The best thing for you to do at the moment is to keep clear of Paradise Church.'

'But I *will* be able to come back, won't I?'

The look on his face is almost hopeful.

'I don't know, Billy.' Privately, I feel relieved at the possibility that this man may well never be allowed to cross the threshold of Paradise Church again.

There's a very long pause.

'And Jodie?'

My brain has a moment of flux, a minor processing malfunction.

'What?'

'Can I still help her with the mural?'

'You're kidding me, right?' My response is immediate and unconsidered. The red mist has truly descended now. 'Do you actually think I will ever let you within five miles of my daughter again?' I step forward and square up to him. 'Because, I can assure you, that is never going to happen.'

'Not good enough?'

'I'm your probation officer. You're an ex-offender on licence for a serious offence. She's my fifteen-year-old daughter.' I give him a cutting look. 'You do the maths.'

'I'd never do anything to hurt her.'

The fact that he would even consider making such a statement chills me to the bone. I saw the photographs of Nicole's injuries.

'I'm scheduling an emergency meeting at Tamar House tomorrow morning at 9am, where we will discuss this further. Until then, I must insist that you stay clear of Paradise Church – and my daughter, from now on.'

Billy slides his hands into his pockets. 'I'm not sure I'm free tomorrow morning.'

'Then I'll send the MOSOVO team to pick you up, and remand you in custody. You'll be back in the nick before you know it. Do you understand what I'm telling you?'

'Yeah, yeah,' he replies caustically. 'Do as you're told, don't pass go, and go straight to jail. I get it.'

'It's time for you to leave, Billy.'

'Can I speak to Tim?'

'I'm afraid not.'

'I want to speak to Tim!' He stomps his foot like an angry child. 'I have a right to speak to him!'

My anger has found a new place. Somewhere deep, primal, yet still governed by logic and common sense.

'What makes you think that?'

'Who the fuck do you think you are?' he cries, his face pale with rage.

I hadn't intended to aggravate him, yet there's also no way

I'm going to give in. There's work to be done, protocols to follow. I reach into my handbag for my mobile phone, press the speed dial, and wait for it to ring. 'I'm calling the police. They'll ensure you get home safely.'

'Okay, okay,' he says, apparently compliant. 'Don't get your knickers in a twist. The last thing I want is the filth coming over here and stitching me up.'

I turn to him, my lips parted in surprise. 'Stitching you up for what?'

There's a moment, only brief, where Billy recognises it might be best if he shut up, take my advice and leave. But he's a man with a grudge, a lot of grudges in fact, and shutting up isn't really in his vocabulary.

'I read the newspapers. Two blokes murdered. Suddenly there's stop and search everywhere in Stonehouse. Easy to pin it on some ex-cons and close the case, eh?'

What the hell?

I take a moment to make certain my next words will come out sounding as neutral as possible.

'Do you know anything about the murders?'

Billy gives me his sweetest smile. 'Of course not,' and then so quietly that I almost can't hear, 'though if you really want answers I'd look a little closer to home if I were you.'

22

I force a protesting Jodie into a taxi, and ensure Billy has left the premises, before returning to Paradise Church to speak to Tim and Ingrid.

'I knew he had some history,' says Tim. He glances at his wife, who is seated opposite. Something furtive passes between them. 'But I had no idea–'

'You do background checks don't you, a DBS?'

'Well, yes,' says Tim, prickling slightly, 'but Billy was never supposed to be here, inside.' Another glance towards his wife. 'He's been working with us through a local charity that runs garden maintenance projects for ex-offenders.' He turns to Ingrid. 'What is it called?'

'Growing Your Future,' she whispers.

'I assumed they did all the safety checks for us.'

I can see where he's going with this, trying to deflect the blame, but I'm not the adoring parishioner or accommodating Ingrid.

'If he was on a garden maintenance project then what was he doing in here?' Tim and Ingrid are complicit in their silence. 'Billy Vale has a previous conviction for grievous bodily harm,' I continue, 'he was also recently arrested for contravening a restraining order. Did you know that?'

'What?' Tim shoots Ingrid a vicious look.

'Do you realise how much trouble you could be in for letting this man on your premises?'

There's a long pause.

'He seemed sound,' says Tim. 'He did a lot of work on repairing the roof, and we couldn't have built the pre-school sensory garden without his help.'

I say the next bit slowly, and very carefully. 'Billy Vale tied his ex-wife to a bed and burned her breast with a straightening iron.'

Ingrid covers her mouth with her hand. 'No!'

'He has legal restrictions that dictate he can't be near vulnerable women, or young people under sixteen.' I watch Tim's face turn ashen. 'He knows Jodie.' *No mercy, Grace.* 'He's been helping her with her mural.'

Tim has the audacity to look shocked. 'What?' He turns to his wife, his tone harsh, accusatory. 'How could you let this happen?'

I watch as Ingrid, normally so strong and upright, seems to slowly sink into herself.

'I'm afraid that's really not good enough is it, Tim?'

'I beg your pardon?'

'Taking for granted that everything was okay. Assuming that it was Ingrid's responsibility to vet *your* volunteers.' I can feel Ingrid's eyes boring into me, but I have Jodie to think about. 'According to the Paradise Church website you're the safeguarding officer, which means any responsibility for the safety of your parishioners rests with you.'

'Yes well,' replies Tim, 'we do our best you know, but it is a busy place. I'm certain Billy has never been working inside before tonight. Isn't that so, Ingrid?'

Ingrid's face is pale, her lips almost blue. 'I really wouldn't know.'

'What do you mean you wouldn't know?' Tim's voice is like thunder. 'To have a man like that in our midst, among our people.'

Ingrid trembles. 'I don't know!'

'Let's just calm down a bit, shall we?' I turn to Ingrid. 'I appreciate that you want to offer support to people. I really do.' This isn't the first time I've had a conversation with well-intentioned people, and probably wouldn't be the last. 'But this could have been a dangerous situation for you both.' Tim glares, but Ingrid refuses to meet his gaze. *Just how much can he try and blame her for this?* I clear my throat and wait until I have their full attention before continuing. 'It's clear that mistakes have been made, but the important thing is that we've discovered and addressed them before any serious damage was done.'

My supportive words betray my true emotions. Finding Jodie here with Billy has shaken me to the core. The last twelve months have made me feel like there was no safe place in life, work, family, or love. That everything I cared about was all balanced on the edge of a precipice waiting for that one false move or one bad choice, and no matter how hard I try the unruly world still manages to throw the stones of uncertainty at me, sending me hurtling into the abyss. Yet, for a brief moment here at Paradise Church with Ingrid, and even the self-important Tim, there was peace, security, family. There's nothing left now but to return to the safety and constancy of process.

'Billy has been safely removed from the premises, that's a good thing, but I must make it absolutely clear to both of you that he cannot return to Paradise Church or continue to engage with parishioners under any circumstances.'

'But what about Sunday Service?' asks Ingrid, then seeing my confused expression she explains, 'Should he wish to continue attending?'

'I thought you'd never seen him before?'

'I-I haven't.'

'So how would you know if he attends Sunday Service?'

'I don't.' She sneaks a glance at her husband who sits in stony silence. 'I just assumed.'

'Assumed,' I say, 'right.' A deep sadness creeps into me like smoke. Has Ingrid been lying to me? 'For the moment, I am going to recommend that Billy can only attend a service after a full safeguarding review from a specialist Sexual or Violent Offender Manager.' I look from husband to wife. 'I'll be making this absolutely clear when I speak to him tomorrow morning. Should he turn up on Sunday, you are to immediately ask him to leave. If he refuses to do so, you are to call the police. Is that clear?'

Ingrid opens her mouth to respond, but Tim holds his hand up to stop her. Reaching into his jacket pocket, he removes a small Bible. Soft black leather, simple white pages, gold embossed lettering on the front. Holding it between two hands, he hangs his head and begins to pray out loud.

'*But for the cowardly and unbelieving and abominable and murderers and immoral persons and sorcerers and idolaters and all liars, their part will be in the lake that burns with fire and brimstone, which is the second death.*'

Ingrid sits opposite with her eyes closed. *Is she praying, or is that a look of controlled hatred on her face?* Tim closes the book and returns it to his pocket. The steady drip of a nearby tap ticks off the seconds.

'You won't tell anyone will you?' asks Ingrid, her eyes pleading.

'I'll have to.' Seeing her terrified face, I feel conflicted. 'But I'll try and keep it as low-key as possible. These sorts of things aren't that unusual. Licence conditions can sometimes be confusing, and...' I stop myself from disclosing that Billy's recent change of PO may have had something to do with it, as I'm also sure that it'll be Billy's go-to line if he's ever pulled up about it. 'As long as everyone follows the rules to a T from now on, we should be all right.' Something about saying 'we' makes me feel as if I am colluding. 'That does mean you doing your part though.'

'What about his AA meetings?' asks Tim.

'What?'

'Billy attends the Wednesday night fellowship of Alcoholics Anonymous.'

I shake my head imagining the women at the meeting – susceptible, impressionable, vulnerable – and then the charming, manipulative Billy Vale sidling up to them during the coffee break. I'm really beginning to lose my patience with these two.

'What do *you* think, Tim?' Struck by something, I turn to Ingrid. 'Are you certain you've never seen Billy Vale before? If he was attending regular meetings...'

'I run the women's group on a Wednesday,' she says quickly. 'I have very little to do with the AA meeting aside from setting the room up.'

Something else strikes me. I turn to Tim. 'Did you know someone by the name of Michael Fellows? He might have been attending meetings here as well. Could he have met Billy?'

'Doesn't ring a bell,' replies Tim, 'though we have a number of Michaels who attend, most of whose surnames I don't know.'

'You don't know?'

'It's the nature of our fellowship to allow members a degree of anonymity.'

Is that the truth, or is Tim being duplicitous? I don't have the time, or frankly the interest, to try and unpick it all. I have a job to do. Once I've done my bit, I will be more than glad to step back, and straight out of Paradise Church forever.

'I'll arrange for Billy to find another meeting, and another sponsor.' Tim's lips tighten. He nods sullenly. 'I suggest you do a major overhaul of your safeguarding practices. I've got some contacts at the council who can help.' There's a hint of uncertainty, or defiance, on both their faces. 'Otherwise, I will have to take it further.' The last thing I need right now is to be in the middle of a safeguarding enquiry. I've gotten Billy out of here, advised Ingrid and Tim, and suggested a number of positive ways forward.

'You're right, Grace,' says Tim, unexpectedly repentant. 'We really both should have known about this. It is with faith and trust that we let these people cross our thresholds. "Put no trust in a neighbour; have no confidence in a friend; for a man's enemies are the men of his own house."'

When I get home, Jodie is standing in front of the refrigerator, drinking from an open carton of orange juice.

I throw my keys on the counter, turn on the kettle, and take a seat at the kitchen table. 'We need to talk.'

Jodie doesn't turn. 'You mean *you* need to talk, and I need to listen.'

'Come on, honey, you know enough about what I do to realise there's no way you can possibly be friends with Billy. It's not safe for you, and it's not safe for him.'

'Safe, safe, safe!' She thrusts the carton back in the fridge, slams the door shut and turns to me, her face a fury. 'That's all you think about, isn't it?'

'Unfortunately, a lot of the time, yes.'

'What about what I want?'

Hearing the click of the kettle, I get up and make us both cups of instant hot chocolate, placing them on the kitchen table. 'In this instance, being safe is more important than what you want.'

Jodie's posture is one of absolute defiance. 'I know what I want, and that's to be with Billy!'

I feel a sickness deep in the pit of my stomach and force myself to say the next few words carefully.

'*Have* you? Been with him?'

Jodie looks at me with such rancour, I momentarily lose the ability to breathe. 'He's never done anything, never even tried. We're just friends.'

'So, you met him before tonight?'

She stares at me, refusing to answer. In frustration, or perhaps desperation, I tell her something I shouldn't. 'He burned his ex-wife's body with her straightening irons.'

Jodie's eyes become huge. 'What? It's not true. You're lying!'

'I wish I were, Jodie, but Billy Vale has a conviction for grievous bodily harm, and was in prison for nearly four years.'

'No!' she screams. Stumbling her way out of the kitchen she knocks against the table, sending the mugs tumbling to the floor. There's a loud smash, flying earthenware, and a dark tide of liquid sloshes across the floor and over the cream-coloured skirting boards. Bismarck, watching from his bed, begins to whine.

'Jodie, wait!' I follow her out of the kitchen and up the stairs. I make it to the landing, breathless. 'Jodie, please.'

My daughter's face is tight, constrained, terrified. Seeing that broken, tortured look on her face makes me falter, and my anger dissipates. Now all I want is to find some sort of resolution, some sort of peace.

'Jodie, please, we have to talk about this calmly.'

'Calmly!' she sobs. Her face is mottled pink, mascara pooling on her cheeks like that poor girl in the alley. 'When have you ever done anything calmly? When have you ever done anything but for you, your job, and your fucked-up sense of justice?' She steps forward, and for a terrifying moment I think she's going to push me down the stairs. 'You just couldn't leave it, could you? Find a quieter time, a better place? Speak to me alone, afterwards, explain. I'm not stupid, Mum, or naïve. I get risk. I get danger, but you just had to have your big scene, didn't you? *I'm a probation officer,*' she snarls, '*I have to protect the entire fucking universe!*'

'Jodie, stop it!'

'You humiliated me!' She runs a hand across her sweaty forehead. 'And God knows what you said to Tim and Ingrid! I've finally found someplace where I feel happy and comfortable, where I can be myself, and like everything else in my life you have to go and ruin it!'

I stand open-mouthed, mute at my daughter's outburst. 'I don't understand how you can say that,' I whisper, finally finding my voice. 'All I've ever tried to do is help you.'

Jodie flings open her bedroom door and turns to me. 'If you really want to help me then the best thing you can do is just stay out of my fucking life!' She slams the door shut behind her. I resist the urge to bang on the door, threaten, cajole, insist Jodie speaks to me. That would be all too familiar, and all too futile.

23

Tuesday morning, 9am. As I step into reception to collect Billy Vale, I'm acutely aware of my overwhelming feelings of anger. I would even go so far as to say hatred. This morning, I found Jodie trying to text him. In a regretful moment, I confiscated her phone, and threw the SIM card into the toilet. Glowering with anger, she retreated to her room telling me again just how much she hated me, and that she couldn't wait to go and live with her father. Unable to let things lie, I took the few minutes to yell at her through her closed bedroom door saying that if I found out she had been in further contact with Billy, I would tell her father everything. Not much more is necessary. She knows what Alex can do. As much as it breaks my heart, I will not hesitate to sacrifice my relationship with my daughter to protect her.

'This way please,' I say, curtly. There are curious looks from my colleagues from behind the glass. Billy takes his time getting up and walking across the room. I knew this was going to be a difficult interview, but I had hoped after putting him in his place last night that he would be receptive. From the look on his face, and his hostile body language – balled fists in pockets, chest thrust forward – this is clearly not going to be the case.

It's one of the things that makes me good at my job. Every lie, falsehood, those not quite finished sentences, the bits that remain unsaid – I stop, explore, and neutralise, all to ensure that when my guys are out there, the world is safe. I can sense tension, anxiety, or a dangerous altering of mood as easily as a change in room temperature. It's a skill I never used to doubt, but discovering Billy at Paradise Church last night has changed all that. His connection with Jodie, whatever that may be, has penetrated my defences.

I lead Billy into one of the smaller interview rooms down the corridor. There are the usual reinforced glass walls that look out onto the grey mile, panic alarms, and hallway CCTV.

'Thank you for coming today.' I try to keep my voice light, professional, but the words sound false. 'I realise this isn't our normal appointment time, but considering what occurred last night, I felt it was important we discuss the situation as soon as possible.'

'Yeah, right,' he replies, resentment seeping from every pore. 'Let's *discuss* the situation.'

'You made it home safely, I take it?' He just glares. 'Why don't we begin by talking about Paradise Church?' He rolls his eyes. I've dealt with hundreds of men like Billy Vale. They rarely get the better of me, and this will be no exception. 'As I clarified to you, Tim and Ingrid last night, while you are allowed to engage in voluntary work as part of your agreed conditions, you are aware that you are not allowed to be in direct contact with under sixteens and vulnerable adults.' Try as I might, I can't restrain myself from sounding disdainful. 'Surely you must have been aware that your voluntary work at Paradise Church was not appropriate or acceptable regarding these conditions?'

He gives what sounds like a low growl, like a cornered

predator preparing for an attack... but instead of an expected onslaught, I only receive an invented look of uncertainty.

'It was all a bit sketchy, the conditions and restrictions. I clearly just got confused. Sophie was a bit all over the place to be honest. I'm sure she was doing her best, but it seemed a bit chaotic, and with her now on long term sick leave... maybe she just wasn't up to it.' He rubs his chin thoughtfully. 'Maybe that's something I should be speaking to my solicitor about.' He looks at me. 'What do you think?'

I resist the urge to bite back.

'How did you know Sophie is on sick leave?' I wrack my brain trying to remember if I mentioned it in any of our past meetings.

'Picked it up somewhere, I guess.'

I turn away, not wishing him to see the impact of his words. Jodie would have known about Sophie being signed off. I mentioned it enough times.

'Tim mentioned you attend AA meetings at Paradise Church?'

'Have done.'

'There's no indication of that in your case file.'

'Like I said, Sophie was all over the place.'

I will not be beaten. 'But there *were* vulnerable women there. At the meeting.'

'Don't know.'

'It's your job to know, Billy. We can't be everywhere with you.'

'Shame that.'

I decide to take the smirk off his face.

'How long have you been in contact with my daughter?'

'Yeah, what a coincidence, eh? I was just using the facilities, and she approached me asking for a stepladder.' He grins, displaying a small gold cap on his upper tooth. 'She told me she had gotten behind on her Art coursework and was working late.' He shakes his head and repeats the words that almost drove me to punching him last night. 'Teenagers, eh?' He gives me a questioning look. 'Did you even know that she was designing a mural as part of her coursework?'

I try not to let my countenance change. I had no idea that Jodie was doing anything of the sort.

'Can we please just stick to the issue at hand? Prior to last night have you ever had any previous engagement with my daughter?'

'Of course not.' He nods. I feel a sharp stab of fear, recognising from recent training that the use of non-congruent gestures – saying no, but nodding yes – is a good sign he's lying. 'And before you say anything else,' he continues, 'I am fully aware of my licence conditions as agreed with my previous probation officer and yourself, and have never knowingly contravened them.' His voice is rhythmic yet monotone, as if he is reciting his times tables. 'I have never knowingly had direct, unsupervised contact with anyone in the church hall. When I attend services, which isn't every Sunday I must admit, I am always supervised. When I attend AA meetings on a Wednesday night, I meet my sponsor Tim outside, and he supervises me from the moment we enter the church to when the meeting finishes at 9pm.' It sounds to me as if Billy has been coached. 'But you know,' he drawls, 'not to help someone in need, when they ask for something as simple as a stepladder, well that's just rude. My foster carers always raised me to be polite.' With his good looks and persuasive manner, I can understand how Jodie would be drawn to him. I, however, only see him as a predator, a shark. 'So, I got a stepladder from the shed and set it up for her. Yeah, we had a bit of a chit chat. She told me a bit about her project, asked me if I knew anything about perspective. I gave her a few suggestions on mixing colours, but that was it.' He puts his palms together, fingers facing upwards. 'Swear. To. God.'

'And you never met her before that?' I try to keep my tone light so that he doesn't get a sense of how worried I really am.

'Before last night I'd never met her in my life. Shame you lost your temper the way you did, or I would have explained.'

'I don't recall being the one who lost their temper,' I snap, and realise at once that I'm being played. Clearly, my worries about Jodie have left me open to a very skilful manipulator.

'I mean, I can understand your frustration if you didn't know about the mural, about Jodie's coursework. Teenagers can be so secretive, can't they?' This isn't the first time in our limited engagement that I find myself resenting him for speaking to me in such a familiar manner. 'You should speak to her about it. She's a very talented young woman.'

I force myself not to look away. That would allow him to think that he has gained the advantage. I'm not going to let that happen.

'Let's just stick to the relevant information, shall we?'

'Of course,' he says, raising his shoulders in an impression of innocence. 'It's just that you asked.' His tongue briefly touches his upper lip. 'She is a lovely girl, though.'

I imagine lifting my right arm, fist raised, and propelling it straight towards Billy's perfectly shaped nose. I'm acutely aware that he is trying to unnerve me, trying to shift the power in his favour. Even though I'm rattled by Jodie's involvement, I've been doing this job a long time, and have experienced just about every head game an offender can throw at me. *Time to shut things down.*

'I must insist that for reasons of confidentiality and appropriate boundaries, you do not make any further references to my daughter in any of our exchanges, now or in the future.' I'm pressing my thumbnail into my forefinger so forcefully, it's beginning to sting. 'I could also easily suggest to the court that these restrictions be changed and extended.' I don't even bother to hide my contempt. 'Do you understand what I'm telling you?' My voice is hard, lifeless, and I realise just how far I've come from my normal place of professional integrity and compassion. It doesn't stop me from carrying on, though. I will do whatever it takes to protect Jodie. 'The number one issue for yourself and a presiding judge, when I disclose to him or her at your upcoming hearing, will be that by being at Paradise Church last night, knowingly or not, you were clearly violating your licence conditions.' I pick up my phone, scroll down, and begin reading.

'A determinate sentenced prisoner released on licence must be released on a licence containing the six standard licence conditions set out below. To keep in touch with your supervising officer in accordance with any instruction you may be given. If required, to receive visits from your supervising officer at your home/place of residence. Permanently to reside at an address approved by your supervising officer and notify him/her in advance of any proposed change to address or any proposed stay away from that approved address. Undertake only such work (including voluntary work) approved by your supervising officer and notify him or her in advance of any proposed change. Not to travel outside the United Kingdom unless otherwise directed by your supervising officer or for complying with immigration/deportation. To be well behaved, not to commit any offence and not to do anything which could undermine the purpose of your supervision, which is to protect the public, prevent you from re-offending, and help you to settle successfully back into the community.'

'According to my reckoning you violated conditions one and six, and I'm not even including the threats you made to a National Probation Officer.'

I watch his eyes narrow and note how tightly his fists are clenched. 'This is a travesty of justice,' he growls. 'I am not a threat to young women.'

'No of course not,' I reply, 'just the young woman you were living with.'

'Careful now,' Billy sneers. 'I wouldn't want you to get into any trouble with your boss, would I?'

'What are you talking about?'

'I've already put a call in to my brief about the way you treated me last night.'

'The way *I* treated *you*?'

'It was harassment, Grace. Humiliating me like that.'

Have he and Jodie been comparing notes?

'That was standard procedure, Billy. I will be very happy to explain what transpired last night to your brief in full – including the threats made by you against me, and the fact that you were found unsupervised with a juvenile.' *God, I feel like screaming.* 'Do you know how lucky you are not to be in custody right now?'

Billy gives a grunt of perverse pleasure, as if our verbal battle gives him some sort of thrill. 'Just to reiterate,' he says, his arrogance mounting, 'I gave Sophie all the details about my volunteering, including the Growing Futures work with Paradise Church. It's all in my case file, isn't it?'

Of course it isn't, and you damn well know that!

I'm losing patience. All I want is to draw a line under the incident, and make sure he never goes anywhere near Jodie again. I lean forward.

'Let's make things clear, shall we? You are not in control here.' I glance up quickly to make sure no one in the office opposite is watching. 'I am not your ex-girlfriend, sister, mother, or any of the other potential number of women you have abused or assaulted in your shitty little life. I am a probation officer in the National Probation Service, a professional with a duty of care to any member of the public who might be at risk in your presence.'

'I am not a risk!'

'You burned your wife's breasts with straightening irons. You spent four years in prison for it.' The stress and uncertainty of the last few days has become overwhelming, and I realise that I don't have the internal resources left to deal with it. 'You are such a fucking risk!' My voice sounds loud, shrill, and I realise at once that I have made a mistake. There is a moment of intense silence as Billy scrutinises me, stares me down.

'You should take it easy, Grace.' He's clearly enjoying my agitation, even feeding off it. 'Or you might do yourself an injury.' His eyes sparkle with delight at my discomfort. 'We wouldn't want that happening, would we? You getting injured, I mean.'

I think of Sophie, and the burning rags being forced through her letter box.

'Are you threatening me?'

'Of course not.'

'Because if I sensed that you were...'

'I was just trying to offer you some support.'

'I don't think that's necessary.'

He frowns in an imitation of concern. 'I'm actually quite worried about you.' He turns and makes a show of looking towards the open-plan office. 'Maybe we should call someone. Simon, perhaps?'

'I beg your pardon?'

'Your boss Simon Ellison. He's the senior PO around here, isn't he?'

Just how much has Jodie told you?

'And how do you know that?'

'I do my research.'

I take the bait before I can stop myself. 'And what else do you know?'

'Loads, absolutely loads.' He waits a few seconds before continuing. 'Firstly, that you've got a dead kid on your conscience. Katie Cross, that was her name, wasn't it?'

My stomach constricts. 'What do you know about Katie Cross?'

'Just that you sent that letter.'

I force myself to remain calm. The situation with the letter was widely reported at the time of Katie's murder, but there had been no direct suggestion in the press that it had been sent by anyone from Probation Services. There were several agencies involved in supporting Sue Cross' attempts to extend the restraining order against her ex-husband, but none had been named specifically. As Alex had said to me many times before, the letter could have come from any one of them. *How could Billy possibly know that the letter may have come from me?* Even Jodie didn't know about that. I force myself to remain calm, but when I speak my voice sounds shaky.

'What makes you think the letter came from me?'

Billy taps his forefinger against the side of his nose.

There's a pause between us that lasts nearly a minute. Then Billy says something completely unexpected.

'What sign are you?'

'I'm sorry?'

'Zodiac sign, I mean.'

'I'm not sure this is–'

'I'm a Leo,' he continues. 'Loyal, honest, passionate.'

Has he seriously lost the plot?

'What are you on about?'

'Just looking for some common ground, Grace, like you said on the first day we met.' He grins, his gold tooth glinting. 'Jodie's a Sagittarius, isn't she?'

I feel my toes curl. 'How do you know that? You said you only had a five-minute conversation while you were setting up the stepladder for her.'

He gives a little chuckle. 'It's amazing what you can find out in five minutes.' Once again, I can feel the interview sliding out of my control. 'Did you know she's planning to go to art college?' A jolt of adrenaline rushes through my already frazzled nerves. 'In Bristol. My hometown.' Seeing my shocked face, he feigns concern. 'Oh, I guess not.'

I have lost control of the situation.

'We're done here, Billy.' I pick up my notebook, trying my best to control my shaking hands. 'I'll get one of the PPU officers to escort you off the premises. I also think it may be best if I get you assigned to a new probation officer.'

'Grace, wait,' says Billy, contrite once more. 'I'm not sure what you want me to say.'

'It's what I don't want you to say that matters.'

'And what's that?'

'I don't want you to talk about my daughter with me or anyone else, and I definitely don't want you going anywhere near her ever again.'

'I would never do anything to hurt Jodie. You know that.'

'I don't know anything about you, Billy, except that you restrained and tortured your ex-partner while your daughter slept in the next room. I also think that you deliberately misled Tim about your licence conditions and took advantage of his trust. I know that you knowingly engaged with people you shouldn't have and are now trying to make untenable excuses to try and explain that.' I'm desperately trying to hold on to some vestige of control, but it's slipping through my fingers fast. 'I also don't give a damn how honest or loyal you think you might be. You are not to go near my daughter, speak to or engage with her in any way, including any form of mobile communication or social media.' I glance at the CCTV camera in the hallway to make sure it's not pointing directly at us. I throw my notebook back on the table, where it lands with a sharp slap. 'Because if I find out that you have, I will personally make sure that you go back inside.'

'You can't–'

'I can make it happen, Billy. Very easily, and very fast. Do you understand what I am telling you?'

Billy's expression transforms from one of injured innocence to ferocious rage. His eyes narrow, and his lips curl back. He lurches forward, pushing himself from his seat. I reach for the panic button. His eyes shift to my fingertips sliding under the desk. In an instant, his disposition changes. He sits down and leans back in his chair, the creak of plastic putting my teeth on edge.

'Jodie turns sixteen in a few months, doesn't she? Then she can do whatever she wants, be with whoever she wants.'

My world goes red. Even though I haven't been running regularly for a few months, my calves are still strong, so when I put my foot on the front edge of his seat and push, he goes over hard. His chair tips backwards, and crashes to the floor, his head just narrowly missing a large plug socket that would probably have done considerable damage to the back of his skull. There's an enormous crash as his chair hits the wall behind him. For a second there is silence, then all hell breaks loose.

'I'm going to fucking kill you!' Billy yells, trying to scramble up from behind the desk, but I've already hit the alarm.

24

I'm sitting in one of the staff meeting rooms, staring at the untouched cup of water in front of me. After pressing the panic button, I fled into the hallway screaming for help. Within seconds two PPU officers had arrived and neutralised an incandescent Billy. Now, nearly six hours later, I await Simon's review of my statement. I hear a door handle turning and look up in surprise to see Alex entering the room.

'What are you doing here?'

He pulls up a chair from the other side of the desk, places it next to mine, and sits down.

'Simon called me,' he says. 'What the hell happened?'

'I lost it.' I dare to glance his way. 'Did he tell you?' Alex nods. 'Billy Vale knows Jodie.' The words come out in a frantic jumble. 'They were together the other night at Paradise Church.'

'What?'

'He's been doing volunteer work there, attends AA meetings on the same night Jodie helps out with the youth club.' I begin to sob. 'She says she wants to be with him.'

Alex inhales sharply. 'Why didn't you tell me this?'

'I only found out last night. That's why I lost it with him this morning.'

He stands up as if to leave. 'I'm going to fucking kill him!'

I grab his hand and pull him back down beside me. 'That's what I'm afraid of.'

Alex rubs his forehead. 'How could this happen?'

'I don't know. He must have slipped through the net.'

'Your net, my net, or Paradise Church's net?'

'All of them.' I reach for my cup of water then decide against it. 'Where is Billy now?'

'He's still being questioned.'

'Still?'

Alex stares out of the grimy window.

'There's something else going on that I'm not party too,' he says bitterly. 'I'm not sure what, but it's clearly connected to Billy Vale.'

'What do you mean?'

'Some bigwigs involved, way above my station.'

I don't like the sound of this. 'Bigwigs? Who? Why!'

There's a knock on the door, and Simon enters, worry etched across his face.

'How are you doing, Grace?'

'I've had better days.'

'We all have.'

I unclench my hands and lay them on the table in front of me. 'What the hell is going on?'

'The Regional SPO's just arrived,' he says, then turns to Alex. 'You're going to have to leave.'

Alex bristles. 'Grace's going to need representation.'

'And she'll have it,' says Simon. 'That's why I'm here.'

Simon leads me to another office down the hall. There's a tray with a flask of tea and biscuits. I stare at it in astonishment. This could be the last day of my career, and they put out a plate of custard creams? He puts a reassuring hand on my shoulder, then goes through the motions of pouring the tea, sliding a mug my way.

'Have a drink, Grace,' he says kindly. I know we're not the closest of friends, but I've never been so grateful for his presence in my life.

I sit, waiting. I weigh up all the possibilities.

1st – a warning, which would involve a minimum five-day suspension, then numerous reintegration training sessions on managing stress, personal boundaries, and personal protection. That's a possibility, though quite a long shot.

2nd – suspension awaiting formal tribunal, a process which could take weeks, even months. A definite potential career kiss of death. I would have to sell up, downsize, move on. There are plenty of reasonably priced new builds on the outskirts of town. *Maybe Jodie and I could leave town... if she still wants to live with me, that is.*

3rd – the big push. Suspension awaiting formal dismissal. I had only seen that once, a few years ago when a fellow female PO had gotten involved in an inappropriate relationship with one of her male ex-offenders.

There's a knock on the door interrupting my train of thought, and the Senior Regional Probation Officer Frances Grandage enters the room.

She's followed closely by Simon. I note with some interest that there are no scribes present, no notebooks or recording devices. Frances takes a seat opposite me, then looks to Simon.

'If you would be kind enough to locate a paracetamol or two please, Simon, that would be much appreciated.' She makes a show of rubbing the bridge of her nose. 'This warm weather really sets off my sinuses.' Simon gives a small nod, and hurries from the room.

'So, Grace?' Frances gives me a fierce look. 'You're one of

the best POs I've ever trained. How the hell could you get yourself into so much shit?'

'Crossed the boundaries,' I reply, and it's in that moment I realise just how far I have fallen. There's no point in delaying the inevitable.

'Is it going to be a warning, tribunal, or a sacking?'

Frances glances up from my report. 'Well, considering what I've read, there is the possibility of a recall.' The thought of Billy being forced back inside fills me with unexpected hope. 'But,' she adds, 'that may not be possible.'

'But he threatened me!'

Frances gives me a look. 'Was that before or after you deliberately pushed his chair over?'

'I don't know what you're talking about.'

She purses her lips. 'I had a long conversation with Mr Vale.'

'And what did he say?'

'He says he fell over.' I try to disguise my look of surprise. 'Says he was leaning back on his chair and fell over.' I stare at her in confusion. 'You are damned lucky, Grace.' Frances takes off her spectacles, and places them on the table in front of her. 'However, he's not stupid, and he's made it quite clear that there will be conversations with his solicitor.'

'Blackmail.'

'Depends how you look at it. If the magistrate won't sanction a recall, and he chooses not to take this further, we can reassign him to a new PO, even consider relocation.' I look at Frances hopefully. 'I said *consider* relocation. This situation at the church, and with Jodie.' She gives a little tut. 'Honestly, how did things get so messy?'

I shake my head. The last few weeks have been unbearable, almost surreal. I've watched with horror as everything that matters to me – my family, my career, my friends – seems to be slowly slipping away. If I try to explain that to Frances now, especially in the state I'm in, I would probably end up like Sophie, on long term sick with little hope of returning.

There's a knock on the door.

What now?

'Come,' says Frances, and the door slowly opens. A young woman dressed in an expensive business suit enters, followed by a broad male figure who almost fills the doorway.

'Marcus?' My words sound strangled. 'What are you doing here?'

'I had a call from the National Crime Agency,' says Frances, pouring me another cup of water from a jug on the table. 'Marcus suggested that considering your relationship, and your involvement with Mr Vale, it might be beneficial if he came and spoke to you in person.'

I've been staring at my lap for the last five minutes, unable to speak. Marcus sits opposite, his large hands crossed on the table in front of me. Simon enters the room and places two tablets on the desk in front of Frances, then he pulls up a chair and sits down next to me.

'Grace,' says Marcus. 'Look at me.' I raise my eyes to meet his. Dark, deep, with disgustingly thick eyelashes that I used to tease him about. 'The reason I'm here is that we're investigating Billy Vale in connection with a number of serious Prevent activities.'

'Jesus,' mutters Simon, 'we've got a major inspection in a few months.'

I can barely speak. 'Counterterrorism?'

'I'm afraid I can't tell you more.'

'What *can* you tell me?' I feel betrayed, furious. 'Were you investigating him before I mentioned to you that he was one of my clients, or after?'

Marcus clears his throat. 'Billy Vale has connections to far-right extremist groups across the southwest. We're also investigating a clear connection to a number of high-level organised crime groups in Bristol.'

'And you didn't think to tell me this when we spoke on the phone less than a week ago?'

'It's business, *Grace*.'

I look at him with growing understanding.

'So you did know.' I think back to our conversation and how he pressed me for more information about Billy. I shake my head. 'Is that the only reason you were interested in me, for the intel?'

His colleague looks away, uncomfortable with what is clearly becoming a personal conversation.

Marcus bristles at my questioning. If I've embarrassed him I don't care. He took advantage of my situation, my knowledge, and most of all my feelings for him.

'Like I said, business.'

I open my mouth to say more, but Frances interrupts.

'I know this is difficult for you, Grace,' she says, 'but this supersedes personal issues. This investigation,' she waves a hand in Marcus' direction, 'is probing illegal activity across the southwest of England, much of which may have a direct impact on the safety of the public. Mr Vale may have his hands in some very dangerous pies.'

I turn to Simon. 'That's another good reason for recalling him, isn't it?' I see a last glimmer of hope that Billy might be kept well away from Jodie.

'We're still investigating,' says Marcus. 'We need more concrete evidence, and more information about the key players.'

It all suddenly becomes clear, like sunlight breaking through cloud.

'You're going to let him go, aren't you?' My pulse is racing. 'You're going to let him go so that you can see what he's up to and track him to the big players.' I turn to Frances. 'Are you really going to allow this to happen?'

'It's out of our hands,' she replies, glancing at Simon. Then more forcefully, she adds, 'but may I remind you that by letting Billy go we not only offer the NCA an opportunity to take apart some major extremist and organised crime groups, protect the public, put Billy Vale in prison, but also save your career.'

'Do you think I care about that?' My career is the last thing on my mind. 'I just want him kept away from Jodie!'

'If you let Marcus and his team do their job, I suspect Billy Vale will be kept away from Jodie for a very long time.'

'I'm not sure.'

Marcus leans forward, so close I can smell his cologne. Jo Malone Wood Sage and Sea Salt. I bought it for him for Christmas.

'I'm sorry, Grace, but you don't have a choice.'

'For goodness' sake Marcus,' says Frances, and then bending low, whispers softly in my ear. 'This is a chance to save your daughter *and* your career, so don't blow it. At the moment we're looking at a review and a five-day compulsory leave of absence, followed by the usual mandatory training. Then it's back to work as normal.'

'I just don't–'

'Take Jodie away for the weekend. Get some space.'

I'm not sure Jodie would want to go anywhere with me right now.

Simon takes a sip of tea, his hand shaking slightly. There's an image on the side of his mug, a hand making an 'okay' sign. Next to that in flowing letters are the words, *Everything's going to be all right*. If I had the energy to laugh, I would. Instead, I take a deep breath, and stare at the wall in front of me.

'Can I go now?'

Frances touches her fingertips to my wrist.

'There are still a few things to sort out. Billy will be given clear instructions on what he can and can't do, and we'll ensure the PPU and MOSOVO units are updated. If there is any suggestion of him attempting to contact Jodie or yourself, he will be immediately arrested and placed in custody.' She glances at Marcus. 'I gather he will be under surveillance so, if anything, you and Jodie will be safer than you've ever been.'

'Except that because of his association with Jodie there's a good chance Billy knows where I live.'

'He knows he's walking a very tight line,' says Frances. 'In light of this new information from the NCA, there's a good chance he'll end up in prison anyway. If you can just hold fire until then.'

My throat aches, my head throbs, and I just want to get out of the stuffy room and into the fresh air. I still can't believe Marcus used the information I told him to reopen an investigation without telling me. I thought we trusted each other.

'I'll just pop out and get the paperwork,' says Frances. 'The sooner we get that done, the better. Simon, with me please.'

Simon gets up, leans over, and squeezes my hand. 'Everything will be all right, Grace,' he whispers, 'I promise.'

'Chloe,' says Marcus to his colleague. 'Could you give us a moment please?'

'Yes, boss.'

I wait until I hear the click of the door shutting before I look up.

'I can't believe you did this.' I'm not angry anymore, only sad.

'He's a dangerous man, Grace,' replies Marcus, 'with even more dangerous associates.'

'You should have told me.'

'You know I couldn't.'

'You used me.' He reaches across the table for my hand, but I pull away.

'You know the score, Grace, always have.'

'You could have at least warned me.'

'It wouldn't necessarily have–'

'I would have looked at his record more closely. Kept him away from Jodie.' Even as I say this, I know there's nothing I could have done differently.

'And possibly let him know he was under our eye?'

I look at the stranger before me. 'This is my *daughter* we're talking about. Are you honestly telling me your investigation is more important than her safety?'

'We had no idea she was part of the picture.'

'But you do now, and you still want him out there!' I try to steady my erratic breathing. 'You could put him inside in a heartbeat,' there's a long pause as I try to contain my growing anger, 'but you won't.'

'We need intel, Grace. This is bigger than you, Jodie, and even me.'

I say the next few words with an unmistakeable finality. 'Bigger than us, you mean.'

There's a knock and Chloe pokes her head around the door. 'Call for you, boss.'

'I just need another–'

'It's urgent.'

Marcus sighs, nods, and stands up to leave. 'I'll catch up with you later, yeah?'

'Yeah.'

Frances returns just as he's leaving, and we spend the next hour completing the paperwork for my mandatory leave, registering me for some retraining courses on managing violence in the workplace, and sorting out some more sessions with the in-house counsellor.

'Everything will be fine,' she says, squeezing my hand. 'Go home and get some rest.' I finally stand to leave. 'Oh and, Grace,' she adds, her tone softening further. 'I'm going to need your staff ID card.'

25

I arrive home to see Alex's car parked outside the house, and the sound of yelling coming from within. As I race my way up the path to the front door, I hear Jodie.

'You can't tell me what to do!'

Then Alex. 'I bloody well can, and will!'

I open the door and shut it quickly behind me, hoping the neighbours won't hear any more than they have to. As I make my way into the lounge, I discover Alex in the doorway, blocking Jodie's exit. She stands opposite staring at him with wild, furious eyes.

'What's going on?' I ask, though I don't really need to.

'You told him, didn't you?' she screams. 'Why did you tell him?'

'Shut it, Jodie!' says Alex, with such ferocity that both Jodie and I freeze. 'And stop trying to blame everyone else for your own stupid mistakes!'

'I didn't do anything wrong,' she screams. 'I was just talking to him!'

This is not how I want it to go. 'Can we please just–'

'Do you know your mother is in big trouble because of Billy

206

Vale?' shouts Alex, ignoring me completely. 'She could lose her job because of him!'

Jodie looks from me to her father, and then back again. 'Is that true?'

'It's sorted now,' I say, desperately trying to impose some sense of calm on the chaos around me.

'But not without a price,' says Alex. 'What was it, Grace? Suspension, tribunal?'

'Will you please calm down?'

'I will not calm down,' he barks. 'Not until she understands just what kind of people she's been associating with.'

'What kind of people do you mean, Dad?!' screams Jodie. 'Ones who don't screw around on their wives?'

Alex opens his mouth to reply, then closes it again. His expression, no longer angry, is one of almost unbearable hurt.

I watch from a few steps away, distant, separate, numb.

After finally calming Alex and Jodie down, I make us a supper of scrambled eggs on toast, and the three of us sit at the kitchen table barely speaking.

At least we're not screaming at each other.

Afterwards, I walk Alex to his car.

'What happened at your interview?' I watch as his eyes travel up to the soft glow of Jodie's bedroom window. After dinner, we all agreed a shaky truce – *we'll talk again later when we're all in a better state of mind* – and Jodie escaped to the sanctuary of her room.

'Like we said,' I reply. 'Gardening leave for a week, then a return to professional training.' I shrug. 'You know.'

'And did you find out what the big secret was?'

'Secret?'

'What weren't they telling us?'

I can't bear to confess the truth about Marcus, how he used me to forward his own investigation.

'It was something way above me too,' I lie.

'If it has anything to do with Billy Vale I'll find out soon enough.'

'What do you mean?'

'Let's just say I've got people keeping an eye on him.'

'What people?'

'Nobody you should concern yourself with.'

'You'd better not be doing what I think you are.'

'Best you keep out of it,' say Alex. 'You're in enough trouble already. Just know this. If Billy Vale comes anywhere near you or Jodie again, I'll make sure he goes down and never gets up again.'

'*Alex.*'

'But you didn't hear that.' He rubs his eyes, and sighs. 'I also think Jodie should come to stay with me as soon as possible.'

'What? She has exams!'

'She needs supervision.'

'And you don't think I'm capable of doing that?'

'Of course you are.' Jodie's bedroom window is open, so he drops his voice to a whisper. 'It's what *she's* capable of that worries me. That whole thing with the church, not telling us, and God knows how long she's been involved with that psycho Vale.' He spits out the last few words. 'I've put in for some leave from next week, and then asked to be put on desk duties. I should be able to keep a close eye on her for the next month or so. By then Billy Vale will either be in prison, or...' He looks away, his sentence unfinished.

Or what?

'I *can* look after her, Alex.'

He looks at me, but says nothing.

Just how ugly does this have to get?

I'm too tired, frightened, and messed up right now to argue. Jodie, Alex, Marcus, Billy, Sophie. I feel haunted. I need to get things straight in my head before I can be of use to anyone.

'A few weeks with you might be a good thing,' I say, finally. I hate acquiescing, but have no choice. If Alex decided to get the family solicitors in I wouldn't stand a chance. I also don't mention how I dread trying to talk to Jodie at the moment: the silence, contempt, and abject abhorrence like tiny daggers to my heart. We agree she'll move in with him next week.

'If you need any help with getting her to...'

I shake my head. 'She won't argue.'

After Alex leaves, I spend most of the evening avoiding Jodie while at the same time trying to monitor her every move. Once or twice, I notice some unfamiliar cars parked across the street, and wonder if it's NCA. I also go over and over in my head how I could have got it all so wrong. Any attempt to broach the subject with my daughter has been met with a cold stare and stony silence. At least there have been no signs of her trying to get in touch with Billy.

I fill the next few days with mindless errands: cleaning out the cutlery drawer, sorting out old clothes for the charity shop, and staring out of the kitchen window with a cup of coffee in my hand that's gone cold fifteen minutes before. What I'm waiting for can't be rushed.

Thursday evening, at twenty to five, I walk the two miles to Tamar House. I wait another half hour until the staff parking spaces are empty, before crossing the street to probation services. I need the office to still be open, but with no probation staff on site. When I handed in my staff ID to Frances, I managed to pocket my swipe card, which should still grant me access to the main building, but not the interior office. I know that using it will mean the date and time of my entry will be logged on the security record, but it's not like the records are checked that often. With CCTV limited to stairwells and other public access areas, I could probably enter the building with little consequence, even if it was recorded. If questioned I could simply say I popped by to collect a few personal items.

I've got it all planned out.

As I steal my way up the flight of stairs to main reception, I'm beginning to feel more and more like one of my guys. I hold my breath as I swipe the door into probation services. At first, it's unyielding, but giving it a firm push I feel it give and then open. *Thank God for that.* In a few minutes, I know the entire building will be secured for the night, with absolutely no chance of me getting in. I press three numbers and a letter into the keypad of the door leading to the grey mile, and wait for the familiar click. Nothing. I try again. The door remains firmly locked. *Has Simon disabled my access code? Breathe, Grace, breathe.* I take a few deep breaths, forcing my rattled brain to stay calm, logical. I check my watch, desperately hoping I've got my timings right. I glance through the narrow strip of glass that offers a tiny vista into the corridor. I wait another few minutes, but the grey mile remains empty.

Shit.

I catch a movement at the far end of the corridor. Joan, the night cleaner. Someone I get on with really well. I give a tiny gasp of relief. *I've got my timings right.* I watch as Joan finishes polishing one of the frosted glass dividers before starting to hoover the long stretch of carpet. I wipe away the dots of perspiration on my forehead, and gently knock on the window.

She can't hear me over the noise of the hoover. I watch as Joan pauses, turns off the hoover, and places a hand on her lower back. I knock again, this time much harder. Joan gives a start, and peers my way. I force a smile and wave.

Come on, come on!

Joan's look of uncertainty fades, as she recognises me and then waves in return.

As a teenager I spent two summers at Brittany Ferries cleaning the passenger cabins. I know how hard the job is, how as a cleaner you are often either disregarded or scorned, how inconsiderate and just plain filthy people are. Now, if I'm ever working late and happen to cross paths with Joan or the other cleaners, I always stop to chat, say hello, ask after their families. It's a small consideration, nothing really, but I still remember what it feels like to be ignored. I watch with growing anticipation, as Joan pushes aside the hoover and makes her way down the corridor towards me.

'Thanks, Joan,' I say, as she opens the door into the grey mile. 'I'm sorry to disturb you, but my code doesn't seem to be working.'

'Don't you lot ever go home?' Joan smiles. She steps back to let me pass.

'No rest for the wicked, eh?' I reply, with slightly too much enthusiasm. 'How are the grandchildren?'

'Fine,' replies Joan, 'the youngest starts school this September.'

'Doesn't time fly?' I reply, making my way down the corridor. The door into the open-plan office is being held open by a small wooden wedge, clearly to facilitate the hoovering.

Thank you, Joan!

I pass the rows of empty desks, and carry on to the far end of the room where the Police Protection Unit is based. On a desk in the corner is a nondescript office PC. Black and freshly dusted, it looks exactly like the dozens of other PCs that populate the room. I glance around, hoping to position myself slightly out of view of the CCTV camera that covers the corridor leading to the interview rooms. The one that almost caught me kicking over Billy's chair. I know that my entrance into the office may be recorded on CCTV, but if there's no incident associated with my arrival, there will be no need for anyone to review the footage. I also know that the footage is wiped every week if there are no security incidents. I can only hope for the best. If not, and that is a distinct possibility, then it could mark the end of my career. It might even potentially put me in prison. I try to shake the thought, and wonder once again why I'm doing this – putting my career, my personal safety and even my family at risk. Then I think of Michael lying in the abandoned boatyard, barely conscious while someone stuffed condoms in his mouth so that he slowly suffocated, and Nicky beaten to the point of helplessness and dumped into the water.

I run my fingertips across the computer keyboard, then to the top right button, and press. It takes a few seconds for the screen to flash into life. There are three icons on the homepage. I click on the one that reads ViSOR (Violent and Sex Offenders Register). Conscious that I don't want my name on the log-in register while under enforced leave, I do the unthinkable. I type in Simon's name and passcode, which I know is written on a Post-it-note under his leather desk mat. I drum my finger on the desk, waiting for the database to load. *Finally.* As I scroll through the information on Nicky White, I feel a growing sense of disappointment. There's not really anything that hasn't been listed in his probation services case file. The same is true of Michael Fellows, and I wonder in sudden horror if I have potentially risked my career for nothing. I close the database, my fingertips hovering over the mouse, make one more click, and open the Police National Computer. I wait for it to load, feeling a growing sense of separation from myself. It's almost as if someone else is doing this, a stranger I'm watching from behind a pane of reinforced glass. Conscious probation services only have limited access to the PNC, I type in Alex's name and add in the password Argyle1996, referring to the year Plymouth Argyle Football Club played at Wembley Stadium. I watch anxiously as the database glows into life.

'I'm glad you're a creature of habit, Alex,' I whisper. I check my watch. Joan will be finishing up soon, and it is imperative I leave the building with her. I enter Robert Lawson's name, one of the first assault victims, and scroll through his long list of offences. Nothing seems out of order. The dates and times are consistent and as far as I can tell, the list of victims and witnesses doesn't seem to be unusual or suspicious. I log out and type in another name: Darren Green.

He was the assault victim who had been partially blinded by an attack in March. His record is much the same as Lawson's, with a long history of petty crime, assault, domestic violence, and drugs.

I'm just about to log off when in the bottom right-hand corner I notice a tab. OIC – Officer in Charge. I click on it. I tap in Nicky White's name. Like most of the others, his arrest sheet runs to over a page. As I scan the flickering screen I feel a sudden surge of adrenaline rush through my body. I close Nicky's file, then open Michael Fellow's. *Please, please*, I mouth silently. By now, my heart is thumping allegro. I click on the OIC tab again, and immediately feel my stomach clench. I decide to look closer, to see if there were any other repeat patterns. I click on each name: Lawson, Murphy, White, Fellows, again and again, scrolling through the custody information on dates, times, offences, who the officer in charge was, arresting and attending officers, all the time feeling more and more alarmed. With shaking fingers, I close the database, turn off the computer, and hurry back down the hallway just in time to see Joan packing up.

'You all right, love?' she says. 'You're looking a bit peaky.'

'I'm fine,' I reply, barely able to speak. 'Thanks again for letting me in.' I race out of the building, into the cool evening. I stumble along a narrow alleyway, my knuckles scraping against the brickwork as I try to steady myself. Resting against a wall, I take in deep gasps of air, trying to clear the sense of panic that is flooding my brain. The arresting officer for at least two of Nicky White's previous offences and one of Darren Green's, was Detective Alex Treglann. He was also one of the key investigating officers in the Michael Fellows rape case. The attending officer in previous arrests for Darren Murphy and Robert Lawson was none other than Police Protection Unit Officer Ryan Denzies. I have to force myself to breathe. How is it that the same two police officers were directly connected to all the beaten and murdered men? Is that just too much of a coincidence? I think back to what Tel said when I visited him in prison, how someone from within the police service was leaking confidential information about sex offenders to the vigilante group *Justice South*. Could Alex or Ryan be that someone?

26

I arrive home feeling more unnerved than ever. Could it just be coincidence that Alex has been directly connected to three of the murdered men? It isn't beyond the realm of possibility, after all, they lived in his patch and were prolific offenders, all his area of specialism. What about Ryan, the less than PC, PC? I mull over the possibilities as I boil an egg and make some toast. I can hear music thumping from Jodie's room. From the remnants of a Happy Meal on the countertop, it's clear that my daughter has already eaten.

'How far is it to the bin?' I mutter to myself as I tidy away her rubbish. I've tried to broker a few awkward conversations with her since the incident with Billy and the scene with her father on Tuesday night, particularly as she'll be moving in with him in a few days, but it feels like I'm tiptoeing through a minefield. My greatest fear is that our relationship may be irreparable. The thought is excruciating, but I feel it might be a terrifying possibility. I slice open the top of the egg, and watch as the uncooked white slithers onto the plate. I push it aside and nibble on my toast, wondering why Alex has never mentioned his connection to the murdered men before.

Aside from calling Nicky White a 'little scrote', of course.

I very briefly think of ringing Marcus, but that would probably only get Alex on his radar, just as my mentioning Billy Vale had. I'm also not quite sure how to overcome my recent radio silence. I sent him a straightforward four-word text on Tuesday:

> I need some space.

To be honest, after discovering his betrayal, that space may be permanent. His response was typically compassionate:

> I'm here for you, Grace, whenever you're ready.

I make my way upstairs, stopping outside Jodie's door. *If there is any chance of forging a truce, I'm going to have to be the one to do it.* I knock, and then knock again.

'Jodie, honey,' I say, slowly opening the door. She's sitting on the bed notating some of the sketches she had made for the church mural. I cautiously move into the room. 'Can I see?'

Jodie looks up, hesitant. She shifts over slightly so there is room on the bed next to her. *Maybe we're just both exhausted of being angry with each other.*

'I'm using a colour palette similar to the one used in *The Last Supper*,' she says. Next to her sketches she has cut out and pasted images from the Da Vinci masterpiece. There are notes about the symbolic meaning of the rich blue, green, and red colours.

'Your sketches are amazing,' I say. 'And what you've done so far at the church looks fantastic.' I still have a lot of concerns about Jodie going to Paradise Church, and I wish she wouldn't, but a voice message from Ingrid today telling me that they have already started working with the local safeguarding officer has given me a modicum of peace. Trying to impose any more restrictions on my strong-willed daughter will surely backfire. Sitting next to Jodie like this has also made me realise just how far we have strayed from each other. 'Why didn't you tell me you were doing a mural?'

Jodie shrugs. 'I wanted to see if it was going to work before showing you.'

'But I could have helped.'

'You're not allowed to help, Mum; it's GCSEs. And before you say anything, *he* wasn't helping me either, okay?'

The mention of Billy Vale is like a blockade, separating us from each other, pushing us apart. I decide to change the subject.

'Is it true that you're thinking of going to art college?'

'Who told you that?'

I realise that I should have approached this differently, suggesting it might be something Jodie could consider, rather than indicating it was something I already knew about.

'What I meant was, *have* you ever thought about going to art college?'

'Thinking about it,' she says, relaxing slightly.

Then I ask her something I shouldn't. Something that has been troubling me since I found her and Billy together. 'You know when you go to Paradise Church for Sunday Service?' Jodie inhales deeply as if preparing for a retort. 'Is there any chance that you might have seen Billy one of those times?'

She looks away, will not respond.

'So, you *have* met before.'

She gives a notable huff, heavy with the sense of personal injustice.

'Don't say you're trying to protect me!' she yells, 'because your idea of protection feels a lot more like control.' She jumps up, sending her box of colouring pencils hurtling to the floor, rolling in every direction.

'Let me help you.' I get down on my hands and knees.

'I don't want your help!'

As she turns away, I can see the narrow ridges of her shoulder blades poking through the thin material of her T-shirt. I am consumed by an overwhelming desire to protect her.

'Jodie, *please*.'

'I'll be sixteen in a few months.' There's a sharp edge to her voice. 'I can leave home without your permission,' she looks up at me through heavily mascara-ed eyelashes, 'do other things without your permission.'

I feel as if the air has been sucked from my lungs. I never would have imagined my daughter could be this cruel. Not for the first time, I wonder if I have driven her to it.

27

Trailing someone, simply following them, is a fine art. First, you have to establish their routine. This requires highly planned and oft repeated observations – home to office, office to the gym, where you aren't allowed into the private car park – office to their home, which requires a little more discretion. School runs, Sainsbury's... or Lidl, depending on how close it is to payday. Starbucks, doctor, dentist, hairdresser, therapist. It can be hard work, frustrating, and risky, but with a little determination and a bit of planning you can track them to their home. That's the prize. Once there, the rewards are rich: glimpses of a face as they close the bedroom curtains, the curve of a silhouette through the frosted glass of a bathroom window, a nightdress-clad figure letting the dog out to do its business. *Magic.* You feel like you know them, you *do* know them.

Sometimes that isn't enough, though. Sometimes you go through their rubbish, collecting and categorising the detritus of their lives: make-up encrusted face wipes, old razors with the pale leg hair fluff still trapped beneath the metal blades, used tubes of semi-permanent hair dye, price tags from Primark and M&S, perhaps once or twice a discarded tampon. There are empty packets of miso soup, clumps of uneaten porridge, soggy herbal teabags and half-torn sachets of artificial sweetener. You can always know when they're on a diet, or on the rag. On warm evenings the open veranda doors provide a soundtrack to their lives. Is it Neil Young, Northern soul, Taylor Swift, or someone else you don't recognise? Is it *Downtown Abbey* or *Doctor Who*? *Strictly Come Dancing* or *Gogglebox*? You can often tell more about them from their listening preferences than from a ten-minute conversation.

You grin to yourself as you stand in the shadows. You've heard the soft clunk of the front door deadlock enough times to know it's Yale, which is easy, but the jangle of a safety chain means another entry point may be required. You've thought about the windows, but that could be too obvious from the street, and they're double locked. The last thing you want are nosy neighbours, lace curtains twitching, calling the police. The back garden is a bit trickier. No decent vantage points because of the high fence, and a back alley overlooked by flats. That flimsy back gate latch is a joke though. Might as well leave it wide open. Then there's the dog. A little dosed mince should do it, quick acting but with few aftereffects. You would never hurt an innocent animal. Still, caution is everything. Caution and stealth. If you're discovered by someone reporting a figure lurking in the dark, or by a police patrol on the rare occasion there is one, then it will all be over. You've worked too hard for that; you still have too much to do. Getting inside is the prize, after all. That's where you'll have your say. It's a bit of a challenge, but all worth it, because once you know how they live, you know everything.

28

After another sleepless night I wake early and take Bismarck for a walk. I follow our usual route, through the park then past the newsagents and pubs, many with chalkboards advertising karaoke and curry nights still left out from the night before. I stop at the Italian café Alex and I ate at last week, order a takeaway espresso, and sip it outside. My brain is filled with the dark possibilities about what Jodie said to me last night, almost echoing Billy's words from a few days before.

'Jodie turns sixteen in a few months, doesn't she? Then she can do whatever she wants, be with whoever she wants.'

Have they spoken about this, been planning? I still can't understand why Billy isn't in custody. Is Marcus' case really so important that he is willing to risk my daughter's safety? I decide that the only way to deflect my increasing apprehension is to try and focus my attention on something else. I force myself to return to what Michael's girlfriend said to me a few days ago, and then to what Tel said to me during my visit to Dartmoor Prison, as well as my discovery on the Police National Computer. Could it be possible that someone from within the police is leaking confidential information about sex offenders to

Justice South, and could that be Alex? Is that anything to do with what the NCA is looking into, and why Marcus can't tell me anything, because my ex-husband may be involved?

'Questions, questions, questions,' I mutter. The previous night, I scrolled through the Justice South Facebook page, growing increasingly uneasy. There were posts about convictions of sex offenders, domestic abusers and even fraudsters, as well as details about recently released ex-offenders – including photographs, and details of their current known whereabouts. There were polls about bringing back the death penalty, and comments like, 'Rapists should be castrated.' I'm shocked to discover a three-month-old post about Michael Fellows, with a particularly vitriolic comment from someone using the pseudonym *The Beacon*, ending with 'He should rot in hell for what he did.' I'd closed the page feeling disillusioned, and dirty. What was the point of all the hard work police and probation services were doing, if these have-a-go-investigators decided to take the law into their own hands anyway? That thought leads me to somewhere even more uncomfortable; the question of Alex's involvement with both Michael Fellows and the Chantal Atkins rape case. I know it's out there, maybe to the point of paranoia, but could it be possible that, frustrated Michael had been granted early release due to good behaviour, Alex leaked information about him to members of Justice South? Could he have done the same with Nicky White? This seems too far-fetched to even consider, but what about Ryan Denzies and his connection to the other two assaulted men, Darren Murphy, and Robert Lawson? *Could he and Alex have been working together, alongside the Facebook group, to deliver their own version of justice and retribution?* I shake my head, forcing aside these thoughts. Yes, there's a link, but it's a tenuous one that could easily be explained away as coincidence. More importantly, do I really believe Alex could be capable of such a thing? He's always approached his job with professionalism and integrity, yet his recent comments referring to Nicky, and the more disturbing one about Billy, 'I'll make sure he goes down and never gets up again,' have planted a seed of uncertainty that is ferociously propagating in my brain.

I need more information before I can even think of going to that dark and scary place. I recall Tel's words from less than forty-eight hours before, 'You a detective now, Grace?' *Maybe I am.*

I deposit my empty cup into a recycling bin, and watch as an elderly man in a grey cardigan places a sandwich board out in front of a small hardware store across the street. I glance at the board with little interest, but then something strikes me. Bismarck, in tune as ever to my moods, pricks up his ears. I give a decisive nod, and quickly head home. *There's something I have to do, and it needs to be done quickly.*

I arrive home, and go upstairs. Treading softly, I creep into Jodie's room. She is fast asleep, her body star-fished across the bed. I study my daughter's face. In sleep it is serene and beautiful, the forehead free of worried frowns, the lips parted as she softly snores. What I am about to do is an absolute betrayal of her trust. If Jodie finds out it could change our relationship forever. *Is my compulsion to find out the truth worth it?* I bend down for Jodie's handbag. It's a knock-off Louis Vuitton that she picked up on a school trip to London. I carefully undo the zip, then reach inside, scrabbling around for what I'm looking for, all the while keeping one eye on Jodie's face. Finally, I grip something round and furry, something that softly jangles when I remove it from the bag. It is a fluffy pink keyring, shaped like a pom-pom. A stocking stuffer from Christmas. I slip it into the back pocket of my jeans.

On the bedside table next to Jodie is her mobile, now with a new SIM card. The urge to check if there are any recent texts displayed, or even to try and crack her passcode, is hugely tempting. Resisting the urge, I head downstairs, and check the clock above the stove. Seven fifteen. Jodie's alarm is set for eight, but there's usually a good ten minutes of snoozing, then as always, a desperate dash to school. *I'll have to move fast.*

I race from the house, a surprised Bismarck running alongside me, and make it to the corner shop in less than five minutes. Unexpectedly for this early in the day, there's a small queue.

'Slate with a blue tit on the left-hand corner,' says an elderly woman ordering a bespoke home address plaque. 'No, maybe grey tit, or *should* it be blue?' I find myself stifling a scream. Then there's a chap who is debating the best type of screw for his new decking.

'I was thinking about Robinson's,' he says to the shopkeeper, 'but there's always the danger of the wood splintering. I was wondering if a Hex or a Phillips might be best.'

Finally, it's my turn. I slip the key off the pink pom-pom, and hand it to the shopkeeper.

'Can you make a copy? As quickly as possible please.'

When I get back, Jodie is in the shower. I sneak my way into her bedroom and slip the keyring back into her bag. I'm just tiptoeing back downstairs, when I hear the bathroom door open. I hurry on down to the kitchen.

She comes down with less than a half hour to spare until registration. Another typical dash to school, but this isn't the time for castigations.

'I'm sorry about last night, honey,' I say.

I hand her a foil wrapped buttie.

'Breakfast on the go.'

She smiles briefly, then grows serious.

'Do you think Dad's still mad at me about...?' She clamps her lips shut, unwilling or unable to say Billy's name.

I tuck a loose strand of hair behind her ear. 'It will be fine. He just needs a little time to cool down. You still going to the cinema with him tonight?'

'As long as he doesn't try and slip an ankle tag on me.'

I hand her a juice carton. 'He worries about...' I stop myself, and quickly change the subject. I glance at my watch. 'Would you like me to walk you to school?'

Jodie raises an eyebrow.

'You my personal bodyguard now?'

'I just meant for the company,' then I add, 'for me more than you, now that I'm not working and all.'

'I think I can manage on my own, Mum,' she says, a hint of kindness in her voice.

29

I wave Jodie goodbye, then go back inside. I know that Alex's shift starts at ten, so I spend the next hour trawling the internet for any further information about Nicky, Michael, and Billy. I can only access the PNC database via the secure PC in Tamar House, so there's no chance of investigating Alex's link to the trio any further.

I shower and change into something as innocuous as possible – jeans and a T-shirt – pull my hair into a ponytail, and pop on one of Alex's old baseball caps that I find in the back of the wardrobe. I place the key I had cut into the change section of my purse, and head out.

I debate whether to take Bismarck with me, but decide I will. That way if I come across anyone I know, or am questioned about why I'm wandering around condos in Sutton Harbour, I can just say I'm walking the dog.

I make my way past the Theatre Royal and down Notte Street, crossing to avoid Tamar House and any colleagues coming out of Probation Services. Simon has tried to ring me a number of times, but still feeling the humiliating sting of the mandatory break, I have let his calls go to voicemail. I listened to the last one only this morning. Something about wanting to get together, how maybe he's been too hard on me, how he wants to make sure I have all the support I need, all of which is very nice of him of course. At some point I will have to face him, but not today. At this very moment I am only interested in one thing.

I hurry my way to Sutton Harbour, only a stone's throw away from where Nicky White's body was found, turn right, and walk the short distance to an apartment building that borders the marina. I have no idea what the keycode is to let me in, so stand outside the front entrance until I see the lift doors begin to open, and a woman emerges into the foyer. I open my handbag and pretend to be looking through it just as she pulls open the door.

'Dammit,' I mutter, giving the woman an embarrassed look. 'I know my keys are in here somewhere. The poor dog is desperate for a drink.'

'At least come inside where it's cooler,' she says, holding open the door.

'Thanks.'

As I pass into the foyer, the woman turns. Her eyes narrow.

'I thought there were no pets allowed in this building?'

I force myself to look calm. 'Oh, he's not mine,' I reply casually, 'he's my mum's. She just can't manage the walks anymore. I'm just popping upstairs to give him a drink and get my wetsuit. I thought we'd go to the Hoe for a swim.'

The woman gives a slight nod of understanding. 'Water's still way too cold for me. I don't even think about wild swimming until at least the end of June.'

'I'll probably regret it,' I say, 'it's murder on my hair, but the dog loves it.' She starts to offer me some advice about hair products, but I'm already making my way towards the lift. 'Thanks again.'

I wait until the lift doors have shut before allowing myself to breathe.

I get out at the third floor and follow the hallway to the last flat on the right, all the while crossing my fingers that no one will emerge and see me. Arriving at apartment 3F, I slip on a pair of blue latex gloves and with shaking fingers, slip the key I had cut this morning into the lock. I turn the handle and enter Alex's flat.

Shutting the door behind me, I allow myself a few seconds to catch my breath. I have only been here once before since Alex moved in. Normally, he collects and drops Jodie off at home, a situation I never question as the thought of having to see the place where he and Denise cohabited was simply too painful.

The short corridor expands into a large open-plan kitchen, dining and living area. The gentle scent of vanilla wafts from a reed diffuser next to the hob. On the counter next to the refrigerator is a small rectangular wicker basket that holds post and advertising flyers.

'In for a penny,' I whisper, and begin looking through the opened post in the basket. There's nothing unusual: just bills, bank statements and a copy of POLICE magazine. The countertops are pristine. There's a matching chrome toaster and kettle, Nespresso coffee maker, and a glass jar half filled with individual sachets of herbal tea.

I move into the living area with its designer sofa and oriental rug. On a side table sits a framed photograph of Alex and Jodie at Harry Potter World last year. I run a finger across the top of the picture frame, an odd sort of caress, before carrying on down the corridor to the bedrooms. The smaller of the two, once painted soft pink, has been redecorated in what can only be described as Scandi style with white and duck egg blue walls, and furnished in an orgy of Ikea. There is a princess bed, and a built-in desk unit with shelves that stretch to the ceiling. On the opposite wall, next to a flat screen telly, is one of Jodie's artworks. It's a landscape of the moors which has been professionally mounted and framed. I feel a pang of sadness. *This is one of my favourite pieces; why isn't it hanging on our wall at home?* I sit on the bed and go through the bedside table. Just a few bits of make-up, a dog-eared old paperback, and a spare phone charger. The dresser holds some underwear and night clothes, nothing more. I move on to Alex's bedroom, feeling even more like a voyeur. *How would I feel if this was my house, and Alex was going through my private space?* I thrust the thought aside and carry on. The bedroom is a masculine enclave, all modular storage, dark leather, and wood. As with Jodie's room, I start with his bedside table: a Kindle, tape measure, torch, old epaulettes from when he was a police constable – and at the very back, a box of condoms, half full, which immediately makes me think of Michael. Maybe since his break-up with Denise he's been doing the one-night stand thing? After our divorce I had one or two indiscretions, but only when I was away, or on a training course. I never brought strangers into our home.

I slip my hand along the back of the drawer to check for any hidden recesses. Nothing. I make sure the items are expertly replaced, close the drawer, get up and carefully straighten the bedsheets. Bismarck, sitting quietly on the carpet next to me, gives a low, disapproving growl.

'I know, Bizzy, I know.'

I look around, trying to determine where a hiding place would be. The wall adjacent to the bed is made up of a built-in mirrored wardrobe with sliding doors. God knows what carefully archived in there, and how long it would take me to search it. I slide open one of the doors. Inside, the closet looks like a Sharp's catalogue, with multi-levelled hanging spaces, and wood effect drawers with glass fronts that promise a catalogue of perfectly rolled-up socks and underpants.

'Bloody hell, Alex,' I mutter, as I ease open a drawer containing identical black T-shirts. I investigate the hanging rail, carefully pushing aside work shirts, suits and an expensive looking jacket that still has the price tag on it. I can't resist sneaking a peak, raising an eyebrow at my ex-husband's profligacy. A second tag, one that reads *Real Leather,* breaks free from the thin plastic ring that attaches it to the zip, flutters to the bottom of the wardrobe, and adheres itself to a glass fronted drawer.

'Shit,' I mutter, kneeling on the carpet to retrieve it. As I peel the tiny leather tag off the glass, I catch a flash of white tucked in amongst carefully folded jumpers in one of the drawers in the bottom of the wardrobe. I slide open the drawer, and find myself removing a long, narrow envelope. I turn it over and stare in disbelief, my brain struggling to process what I have just seen, then I begin to retch. Bismarck whimpers. I place a hand over my gaping mouth and force myself to look again. On the front of the envelope, in the top right-hand corner, is a franking mark. It includes a date, the postage cost, and a licence number. The date is a year ago last Saturday. The licence number XP371094 is that of Tamar House. Just above the franking mark, written in pencil, are the words *First Class.* This is my handwriting. This is the envelope I sent to Anton Cross just over a year ago, the envelope that may have mistakenly contained the report with Susan and Katie Cross' confidential safehouse address, the envelope no one could find when they were investigating how Anton got the information that led him to locate and murder his nine-year-old daughter. I rush to the toilet, and vomit. I kneel with my cheek pressed against the wooden toilet seat, acutely aware that my world is falling apart.

I feel something warm and wet on my cheek.

'Bizzy,' I whisper. I nestle my face in his soft neck. I sob. After a few minutes, he growls softly and pulls away. I rub his soggy neck. 'Sorry, boy.' I flush the toilet, then get up and wash my hands and face. My reflection is so pale, it's almost translucent. Maybe I'm dead. *Maybe I should be.* I open the bathroom cabinet, in the hope of finding some toothpaste or mouthwash to freshen my rancid breath. The cabinet is as orderly as the rest of the flat. Razors, aftershave, dental floss, caffeine shampoo; *is Alex losing his hair?*

I return to the bedroom, the envelope still sitting on the floor. I kneel down, pick it up, hold it close. That is *my* handwriting. It is *the* date. I feel like I might be sick again, but force back the bile.

'What are you doing here?' I yell at the paper in my hand. Bismarck barks, but I don't care. I don't care if I'm discovered, arrested, condemned. Alex has secreted away the one piece of evidence that could have proven my innocence or my absolute guilt. 'How could he do this?' I whisper, now too tired to cry. I stare at that seemingly innocuous piece of paper for what feels like hours.

It's a good fifteen minutes before I can collect myself and stand up again. I briefly consider returning the envelope to its hiding place, or tearing it into pieces and flushing it down the toilet, but that won't tell me why Alex has it, and where he found it. That's the question I've been tormenting myself with for over a year. If Alex has the answer, I can wait a little bit longer, but the envelope is mine.

I sit on Alex's bed for a long while, staring at the Jack Vettriano print on the wall opposite, wondering what to do. In the end, Bismarck's impatience forces me to my senses. I return the bedroom and bathroom to their previous pristine states, then Bizzy and I sneak out of the flat, down the corridor, and out of the back entrance. I walk in a daze, stumbling over my feet and crossing roads without looking.

I arrive home feeling shaky and sick, the white envelope clenched between my fingers. I stare at the pale piece of paper, at my handwritten instructions – *First Class* – a true testament to my guilt. *How long has Alex had it? Why would he hide it?*

You wanted answers, Grace.

I briefly consider performing some sort of fire ritual in the wood burner, but instead slip it into my portfolio case alongside my undergraduate degree certificate, and my letter from the Deputy Director clearing me of any culpability in sending the damn thing in the first place. I hide it in the filing cabinet in the spare room, and lock it back into the darkness. Then I go to my bedroom, to the cardboard filing box I keep under my bed. I sit by the window, the sun dappling my face, and begin going through the countless documents and records I have been collecting since the murder of Katie Cross. There are newspaper reports, confidential internal memos, and even an excerpt from a police report questioning my culpability, which Simon surreptitiously slipped my way. The details are almost too painful to revisit, but I force myself to carry on. Six separate agencies had copies of the report I commented on, but did any of them happen to also be posting a document to the perpetrator that same day, just as I did? There have been countless reassurances from senior managers, colleagues, and friends that it wasn't me, yet still my ex-husband, one of the detectives involved in the investigation, was hiding the envelope in the bottom drawer of his wardrobe. Why?

I feel my mobile phone buzz in my pocket. It's St Benedict's.

'Hello?'

'Grace, it's Carrie. I just heard about Michael.'

I really don't feel like speaking to her, or to anyone in fact, but I owe her the courtesy. Wider support services get as invested in client well-being as much as we do. Carrie certainly does.

'I'm still in shock,' I reply. *Shock from his murder, and shock that there's a possibility my ex-husband may be involved in some way.*

'He seemed so positive about it all,' she says. 'He even stopped by later that afternoon to sign up for The Better Me programme.' She gives a tearful sigh. 'And even though he hadn't yet started that, he was just so enthusiastic that I put him on the waiting list for the free counselling straight away.' She sniffs softly. She talks a bit longer about how beneficial the clients have found the programme and counselling services, and refers to it all as 'life changing.' Then she tells me something that makes my jaw drop. I ask her to repeat it, and then grill her for ten minutes for the wider details, unable to believe what I have just heard. After which, I catch my breath and call Jenna at Dartmoor Prison.

30

I t's late afternoon, and raining, when I pull on my waterproof and follow the familiar route to Paradise Church. Knowing what may ensue I leave Bismarck at home with a Bonio and Classic FM on the radio.

Unexpectedly, the door to the hall is locked. I peek through the small window into the office, but the room is empty. I make my way around to the front of the building, hoping I might find Ingrid inside, welcoming parishioners for afternoon Bible study. Instead, I find a darkened doorway, and a sign that reads:

> *Due to unexpected circumstances, Paradise Church*
> *will be closed today, and all clubs and meetings cancelled.*
> *Church services will take place on Sunday as usual.*
> *Apologies for any inconvenience.*
> *Pastor Tim Anderson*

I stare at the notice in disbelief. As far as I was aware, Tim and Ingrid almost never close the church. Almost every day and evening there are groups and meetings, and every weekend, church services and Bible classes. I reach for my mobile, and dial Ingrid's number. It goes to voicemail. I consider leaving a message, but worry that after the debacle with Billy the other night Tim might be screening her calls. I'm about to give up and go home when I hear the crunch of gravel behind me. I spin around.

'Grace,' says Ingrid. 'What are you doing here?'

'I know I should have called.' I point to the sign. 'Is everything all right?' Ingrid closes her eyes, shakes her head. 'What's happened?'

'After Monday night,' she replies, 'Tim decided we need a rethink.'

'A rethink?'

'He wants me to cut a significant number of my meetings.'

'But you've worked so hard.'

'He says we've opened ourselves up to too much scrutiny,' she means me of course, 'and made too many mistakes.'

Ingrid looks fierce, almost brutal. 'Tim can have his moment of censure,' she says, 'but I will have my meetings back up and running by the end of the month.' I've never seen her this determined. 'But to you,' she's suddenly serene again, 'you needed to see me?' I stare at her, uncertain of what to say. 'Grace,' she says finally, 'I won't withhold good to others when it's in my power to do so.'

More silence.

'Why don't you come over for a cup of tea?' I nod, even though over the last week I've had enough tea to fill a swimming pool. She leads me across the street to a small, terraced house directly opposite the church. 'A parish house normally comes with the posting,' she explains. 'We've lived in many over the years, all over the country.'

I follow her into a tiny but tidy kitchen.

'Was it the thing with Billy,' I choose my words carefully, 'that caused the rethink?'

'The truth is, Grace,' she confesses finally, 'I *have* met him. It was when he was doing work on the roof.'

This comes as no surprise. 'So why did you lie about it?'

She shakes her head in self-recrimination. 'I sensed that he had some history, but I didn't question him, or ask for a criminal records check. I was just so grateful for the help. When you brought it to light that other night, I was terrified of...'

'What Tim would say?' She nods, clearly ashamed. 'But he's the safeguarding officer, Ingrid. He's the one who let Billy in the church in the first place. He's the one who should have done those checks.' The kettle's high-pitched whistle halts our conversation. I wait before continuing. 'Billy Vale is a skilled manipulator, who's been playing everyone off against each other, including you and Tim.'

'I always have such high hopes for them,' sighs Ingrid.

My professional landscape involves having high hopes for people, referring them to counselling, addiction support, getting them into work or their first flat after years inside. Sometimes it works – I've been sent countless thank you cards – sometimes it doesn't. The ones that don't work stick with you though. The promising men and women with the potential to change their lives, who foolishly decide they can manage that one last hit or extra shot, who lose their rag and throw that fatal punch. Once that ball is in play it inevitably leads to a spectacular and often irreversible downfall: violence, criminality and custody. It's a modern-day morality play, now fully documented on social media.

'Are you all right, Grace?'

I look at her in surprise. 'It's you we should be concerned about, not me.'

'But you look so... lost.'

'I'm fine.' I long to confide in her about what I found in Alex's flat, and to ask her about what both Carrie and Jenna have just confirmed. 'I just sometimes wonder if it's all worth it all, that's all.'

'Of course it's worth it. Do you remember what I told you that first time you attended Sunday Service with us? The Bible says, "Let each of us look not only to his own interests, but also to the interests of others." She pours the tea and hands me a mug. 'Come on, let's go and sit down. This house used to belong to one of the parishioners,' Ingrid explains as I follow her into the sitting room. 'When she passed away a few years ago, she bequeathed it to the church for the acting pastor and his family to live in.'

The room is plain and functional. The settee has seen better days, and the armchair has a noticeable bottom shaped indentation in the cushion. There is a bookshelf filled with Bibles, and hardcover books on religious themes. There is no television, but on a small table by the window is a battered laptop open to the church's webpage, where even from this distance I can see a large notice cancelling an upcoming Community Hub meeting.

To my right is a teak dresser covered with framed photographs. I go over to examine them more closely. There is a small, framed photo of what must have been Ingrid and Tim's wedding day. She is dressed in a simple white gown with a sweetheart neckline; he's in a dark suit and tie. Both gaze at the camera hesitantly. Next to that are numerous photos of the couple with children of all ages and ethnicities.

'Our foster children,' she says proudly.

At the back, behind the others, is a framed photograph of what appears to be a teenage Ingrid holding a small bundle wrapped in pink.

'You look about twelve. Is she your little sister?'

'Not my sister,' says Ingrid. I feel her arm against mine as she comes to stand beside me. 'My daughter.'

'Your daughter?' I say in surprise. 'But you look—'

'Fourteen. I was fourteen, living in Durham with my parents and three brothers.' She rests her hand on the dresser as if needing the support. 'Lily was the product of teenage rebellion and poor judgement.' She shifts the frame slightly, so that it is angled towards the light. 'But she was a beautiful baby.' I wait for her to continue. 'I was far too young to manage on my own, and my parents wanted nothing to do with the situation.'

'You gave her up?'

'To say "gave up" suggests an element of choice on my part.' Ingrid can't disguise the bitterness in her voice. 'She found me though, discovered some papers in a drawer.' She sighs. 'When she was eighteen she signed up for the adoption contact register and found me.' She reaches into her pocket, removes a tissue, and wipes her nose. 'Secrets never die, Grace; they only live on to consume us.'

I can't imagine what it would have felt like for Ingrid to give up her daughter and then rediscover her eighteen years later. I notice another photo, larger, and in a modern frame. It's of Ingrid standing by the Tyne Bridge arm in arm with a beautiful young woman. I lean forward to study it more closely. Blonde, blue-eyed, with the same full lips and high cheekbones, the resemblance is remarkable.

'It must have been amazing, seeing her again.'

'It was wonderful,' says Ingrid, 'a miracle. At first her adoptive parents were reluctant, she was still a teenager after all, but Lily was determined. Eventually I was able to have regular contact with her.'

Though it's really none of my business, I have to ask. 'And Tim? How did he take it, finding out about Lily, I mean?'

There's a long pause. 'They never met.' I wait in dreadful anticipation for what she's going to say next. 'Lily passed away when she was nineteen.' She turns and makes her way back to the settee. 'Tim and I met a few years later.'

Her matter-of-fact explanation is blunt, yet devastating.

'I'm so sorry. I didn't mean to–'

'You asked a natural question,' says Ingrid. 'Lily is gone, but not forgotten. I remember her every day.'

We stand in uncomfortable silence. I want to ask her about Lily, about what it was like to be fourteen and pregnant, about her parents forcing her to give up her baby. *How was it, coping with the loss of a child she never had the opportunity to raise?* It seems to put my issues with Jodie in humbling perspective. The sound of a car pulling up rouses us from our torpor.

'Is that Tim?' Ingrid jumps up and hurries towards the window. 'He said he wouldn't be home until later.' I can hear her shallow breathing from across the room.

All the pieces of the puzzle seem to fall into place. A controlling husband, a wife with a tragic secret, and a marriage based on desperation and fear. It's a pattern I have seen many times before. *Past history, guilt, isolation, controlling and coercive behaviour.*

'Ingrid?' I ask softly. 'Has Tim ever pressured you to do things against your better judgement?' I watch as the tissue she's holding flutters to the floor.

'What on earth do you mean?'

Be brave, Grace, be brave.

'I was speaking to someone at St Benedict's Drop-in Centre today.' Ingrid's eyelids flutter, and she looks away. 'She told me both you and Tim have been volunteer counsellors there for over a year.'

She opens her mouth to reply, then pauses. I've worked with a lot of people skilled in withholding the truth. After a while you notice the patterns, the tells. Gestures, actions, tone of voice. There may be subtle shifts or changes, action or inaction, chatter, or silence. Right now Ingrid, eyes downcast, body turned away, barely speaking, is displaying three of these.

'You both had a caseload of those in active addiction as well as ex-offenders.' I pause to settle my uneven breath. 'Sex offenders.' Ingrid now turns away completely. 'According to staff at St Benedict's, Tim taught two men on one of their personal development courses, Darren Murphy and Robert Lawson, at the beginning of the year.'

Ingrid turns. 'Who?'

I carry on undaunted. 'And he'd seen another, Nicky White, a number of times for compulsory addiction counselling as part of his probation conditions.'

Ingrid smiles benignly. 'I wouldn't know,' she replies. 'Tim and I respect the confidentiality of each and every client.'

Sadness floods through me.

'That's not quite the case, is it, Ingrid? A staff member at St Benedict's told me that you and Tim often read each other's case notes.'

Her lips tighten. 'It's not unusual for counsellors to seek each other's advice. All part of regular supervision.'

I don't have the time for this continuous evasion. I just want the truth.

'You spoke to Michael Fellows on Tuesday afternoon, didn't you? When he came in to sign up for the Better You programme.'

'I spoke briefly to someone about the programme, yes.'

'Did you tell Tim about it?'

Her expression freezes.

Bingo.

'But Tim knew him already, didn't he?' This is beginning to feel like an interrogation, and I hate myself for it. 'Because as part of his outreach work with St Benedict's he also did prison visits.'

'What exactly are you suggesting?' Ingrid is beginning to sound defensive, almost testy.

'I'm not suggesting anything.' Even I recognise the leap between Tim's connection with the four men, and their subsequent assaults and murders is a big one, but it's a connection nonetheless. 'It just seems quite a coincidence that four men in Plymouth who were brutally beaten, two of them to death, all had some sort of connection with Tim.' I reach into my pocket and take out a printout with a screenshot of the *Justice South* Facebook Page, of the hateful post about Michael from someone calling themselves *The Beacon,* and place it on the dresser in front of her. 'Tim posted that, didn't he?' Ingrid looks stunned, or is affronted, and for a moment my resolve falters. I point to the laptop. 'Shall we check?' Her eyes slice into mine. 'Someone was threatening Michael with exposing his personal details online, including where he was going to live, and with whom.'

'And you think Tim divulged this?!'

I don't blame her for being angry, but I've come too far to back down now.

'Michael Fellows was subjected to a sustained and brutal attack by someone who clearly had a grudge.'

'You've got this all wrong, Grace.' Ingrid's tone is self-assured, almost arrogant.

'Has Tim got you involved in all this?' I demand. 'Are you protecting him?'

Ingrid begins to laugh, a deep chuckle full of scorn.

'Tim wouldn't be able to organise his way out of a wet paper bag. I don't look to him for strength, or for guidance. I don't look to God for that either.'

'What exactly are you trying to say, Ingrid?'

'The truth.' She reaches forward for my hand, and I find myself taking hers. 'Lily was walking home from a friend's student digs one evening.' Her voice is soft, trancelike. 'She was in her first year at university, and there had been a party.' This unexpected disclosure has an eerie sense of inevitability. 'I got a phone call at two in the morning from her adoptive parents. They asked if she was staying over with me. I remember feeling confused at the time, because while she visited regularly, she never stayed.' Sickness is forming in the pit of my stomach. 'I got a call a few hours later from her parents, asking me to meet them at the police station.' There's a long pause. 'They told me someone took her as she was walking home, took her and raped her.' I open my mouth, but no words come. Her face is pale, impassive, *The Veiled Lady*. 'They found the man who did it. He had some previous history, but, you know, was given another chance.'

And the next chance was Lily.

'There was an investigation of course.' Ingrid's voice is a dreadful monotone. 'Lily was subjected to the most invasive processes physically, mentally and emotionally, then the trial, which was like a second assault.'

'And the outcome?'

'Oh, he was convicted,' says Ingrid, 'but the damage was done.' She gently runs her fingertips across her daughter's photo. 'Six months later, Lily took her own life.'

God almighty.

'And you lost your faith?' Ingrid nods. I look around me at the Bible, the simple wooden cross on the wall. 'But all this?'

'One sometimes makes concessions.'

'But you're living a lie.'

She looks at me in astonishment.

'Aren't we all?' There's a moment of silence between us, even calmness. 'I struggled for a long time after Lily's death. I was consumed with anger, with the *unfairness* of it all. When I met others who had suffered such injustice, such loss, it seemed natural for us to try and do something about it.' She picks up the paper with the screenshot on it. 'Some of the members of my victim support group decided more needed to be done to protect the worthy, so I started the Facebook group. I managed the content, including posting that message.' *She looks at me in disappointment, or is it disdain?* 'I once hoped you would consider joining us.'

Now I see the reason for all her attention. *She wanted to recruit me to her terrible mission. How useful would a probation officer be, with access to confidential offender records?*

I feel my face contort in disgust. 'By protecting, you mean disclosing their crimes, posting their home addresses, setting up stings, putting them at risk.'

Ingrid's voice becomes imperious. 'The Lord instructs us to rescue the weak and the needy, and deliver them from the hands of the wicked.'

'What a load of bullshit!' I've lost my patience with her attempts at justification. 'That's just some lame excuse to defend entrapping people who have been tried, convicted, and served their time.' Something strikes me, and I feel my skin grow cold. 'Do you know Callum Atkins? Chantal's brother? Have you been involved in the protests at Balliol House?' She gives me a sly *Mona Lisa* smile. A darker thought invades my consciousness. 'Do you know anything about what happened to Michael Fellows?'

'I have absolutely no idea what you're talking about,' she replies smugly.

The shock of this transmutes into an anger so profound I almost can't speak – almost, but not quite.

'You are a liar, Ingrid. A liar, a hypocrite, and no better than the people you vilify! I'm going to report you to the police, your church members, the newspapers.' I'm going full pelt now. 'You'll never be allowed to work with vulnerable people again.

I'm also going to tell the police to investigate both you and Tim in connection with the assaults on Darren Murphy and Robert Lawson, as well as the murders of Nicky White and Michael Fellows.' My anger has reached a place so deep that I feel numb. I grab the piece of paper from her hand. 'You're finished!'

For a moment there is silence, stillness, then suddenly she comes at me. Her hand grips my throat, and I am reminded of that night on the stairwell. This time though, I am prepared, and while we are about the same height and build, I don't expect Ingrid has had personal safety training like I have. I grab one of the fingers that is squeezing my carotid artery, and bend it back until I hear a satisfying snap followed by a scream of pain. I twist away sharply, fully breaking her grip, and then I run.

I race down Paradise Road, not daring to look back. I pass a trio of council flats with laundry drying on the balconies, cross the slip road for the Torpoint Ferry, then run alongside the ten-foot-high stone wall that borders the Royal Naval dockyard. My legs ache, I have a stitch in my side, and it starts to rain, but I push on. Before long, I find myself on a narrow road on a tract of scrubland and rubble adjacent to the dockyard, which had once been a concrete works and is now in the process of being converted into an industrial incinerator. The indigo hues of dusk cut through the evening sky, and the rain falls harder. I hear the rev of a car engine and turn to see a BMW with blacked-out windows pulling up beside me. Thinking the driver is trying to overtake, I slow down, but the vehicle starts to weave, speeding up and then dropping back, forcing me to jump onto the grassy verge, and nearly sending me tumbling down a bank. My body bristles with adrenaline. The passenger window slides open.

'Stupid bitch!' the driver yells, and then speeds up and away, vicious laughter trailing behind him.

Exhausted, I stop by an abandoned petrol station. *I need to call the police, Marcus, someone. I need to make sure Jodie is at home safe, or with Alex.* I reach into my back pocket for my mobile phone, but it's not there. Sometime in the last hour, either at Ingrid's or during my frantic escape from her house to here, wherever the hell I am, I have lost it.

'Shit!'

I'm alone, cold, wet, lost, and it's getting dark.

I take a few breaths, pull myself together, and walk on. It's only a few minutes before I return to the dubious safety of suburbia, and a mercifully familiar neighbourhood. I walk for ten minutes to a tidy semi-detached house on a suburban estate. I knock on the petrol blue door praying someone is at home.

31

I hear the gentle grind of a key in the lock, and then see a familiar face. 'Simon!' I fling myself into his arms. For a moment his body stiffens, and then I feel him relax and his arms encircle me. I have never been so grateful for a hug in my life.

'Jesus, Grace. What the hell is going on?' I try to speak, but all that comes out is one great blabbering sob. Marcus, Alex, Ingrid, Jodie, I feel as if I have no one to trust. Normally Simon would be the last on my list for support, but maybe his focus on process and protocol is just what I need right now. Plus, his house was close by.

He leads me to the lounge, sits me down and pours me a shot of whisky. 'Just try and calm down, okay?' I nod and take a sip, my face screwing up in distaste. He sits down beside me. 'What's happened? Is it Jodie, Alex?'

I shake my head and wait for the burning in my throat to ease.

'I think I know who killed Nicky White and Michael Fellows.'

I tell him about Ingrid – about the counselling sessions at St B's, and her having spoken to Michael on the afternoon he was murdered. I also tell him about the Justice South Facebook page, and her vile contribution to it.

'She confessed,' I say, still struggling to believe it myself.

Simon can't hide his own disbelief.

'And do you really believe she was capable of killing those men?'

'No. She wouldn't have done it herself.' I race though the details of what she told me only a few hours before. 'She lied about not knowing Billy Vale. She told me she had met him months before, when he was fixing the church roof.'

'So?'

'Maybe she got *him* to do it.'

'Now hold on, Grace.' Simon looks at me in alarm. 'Just because you don't like the guy doesn't mean you can make that kind of accusation.' He downs his own shot of whisky and gives a small cough. 'Saying things like that will get you into even more trouble.'

'I'm not making this up.'

'I don't believe you are. I just think you've gone from A to Z in record time with very little to back it up.'

'But I–'

'Where's the evidence, Grace? Solid evidence.'

'INGRID TOLD ME!' He raises an eyebrow at my outburst, and I silently curse him for his irrefutable logic. All I have is a verbal confession, and if I'm lucky an IP address that might possibly link the church to the malicious Facebook posts about Michael. It's hardly conviction territory. 'But she knew every single one of those men!'

'So did a lot of people.' Simon is speaking in the soft tone we normally reserve for clients with mental health issues. 'You, me, and half the probation service – as well as MOSOVO and the PPU – would have worked with those guys.' I open my mouth to reply, but he isn't finished. 'There is also a long list of ex-

LOUISE SHARLAND

offenders on probation that more than likely would have had some dealings with Ingrid or Tim.'

Something in my brain sparks then merges, like teeth in a cogwheel.

'How do you know about Tim? I never mentioned Tim.'

'It's in the case notes,' he snaps. 'Christ Grace, you really are getting paranoid.'

And the real Simon is back in the room.

'I'm sorry, Simon, it's just that–'

'I'm worried about you.' It's not the first time this week that someone has said this to me. 'Your behaviour with Billy Vale, and now this?' He starts to get up from the table. 'Maybe I should call Alex.'

The sound of my ex-husband's name sends a shiver down my spine.

'No!' Simon steps back, startled, and I realise that I owe him the truth. 'You'd better sit down.'

I explain to him about sneaking into Alex's flat, about finding the envelope, and the undeniable knowledge that it was me who sent it.

'I don't know what to say,' he says, finally. 'Sneaking into your ex's flat like that.' He gives me a wry smile. 'Maybe you should stop working with convicted burglars?'

'You're not shocked?' I whisper. 'Disgusted with me?'

Simon reaches for my hand, then decides against it.

'Anyone could have sent that letter, Grace, anyone. It's time to let it go.'

'I wish I could.'

'Telling me is a start,' he says, kindly.

I find myself relaxing a little. I've been carrying the burden of that letter for over a year. Finding out the truth was devastating, something I don't think I'll ever get over, but sharing it with someone may well be a start.

'Have you had anything to eat this evening?' he asks. I shake my head. 'Why don't you just sit there for a bit. I'll make you a hot drink and some eggs or something?' The thought of eating food feels impossible right now, but a hot drink would be a godsend.

He heads down the hall to the kitchen, and I'm left alone on the settee. I feel my sodden jacket sticking to my skin, and I start to shiver. I get up and make my way to the front entrance, to the coat rack that's mounted above the radiator. Even though it's May the heating is on, and I press my icy hands against its gentle warmth. I take off my coat and give it a little shake. Something in the front pocket clangs against the radiator. As I reach forward to hang my coat up, I notice a leather jacket on one of the far hooks. One of the buttons is missing. I feel a tiny blip in my brain, like an old film being run backwards, then forwards again. I reach into the pocket of my waterproof and retrieve the button I found on the floor of the stairwell the night of the Go Out, the night I was attacked. The small silver disc is exactly the same as the others on Simon's jacket and fits perfectly into its missing spot. A slow prickling sensation spreads from my forehead, along my skull, and down my spine.

'Everything okay?'

Simon is standing by the kitchen door, a tea towel in his hand. My eyes are wide in understanding and disbelief. My hands begin to shake. I drop the button. It rolls along the hallway towards him, spinning on its axis before dying by his feet. Simon picks it up and holds it to the light. There is a moment of silence so acute I can almost hear the air moving around us.

'*Ah*,' he says, and smiles.

32

Adrenaline floods my body. I race to the front door. My fingers, still numb from cold, slip on the brass doorknob. I try again. It's locked. I hear a sound behind me and turn to see Simon dangling a set of house keys from his fingertips. To my right is the staircase to the second floor, to a bathroom where maybe I can lock myself in and buy some time.

I'm not even halfway up the stairs, when I feel someone grabbing my ankles and pulling me back down. I find myself in a heap on the floor, my cheek pressed against cold ceramic tiles.

'It was you in the stairwell,' I scream. 'You attacked me!'

I feel Simon's breath against my ear.

'Oh, Grace,' he whispers. 'I was hoping this moment would never come. I really tried my best to do everything to protect you.' I feel his hand on my collar, and I'm yanked roughly to my feet. It takes me a moment to right myself, to think. 'I planned everything so carefully,' he presses his face close to mine, 'and now you've gone and ruined it all.'

'What's this about, Simon?

As if I don't know.

I've got to find some way to distract him, to stall for time. 'If you're in some kind of trouble I can help.'

Simon begins to laugh.

'Oh, I appreciate the offer,' he says, 'but let's be honest, most of the time you can barely help yourself.'

'Speak to me,' I plead.

For a moment my invocation seems to strike a chord, and his expression softens, then just as quickly reverts to a dead-eyed stare. I look past him, down the hallway to the kitchen, to the French doors, open just a crack. *If I could just...*

He grabs me by the shoulder, and turns me around so that I'm facing the staircase. I feel his hand on the small of my back. 'Upstairs,' he growls, and gives me a push.

I find myself stumbling my way to the landing, another push and then I'm in the bedroom. Panic grips me.

'Simon, please, *no!*'

He looks at me in surprise.

'You don't you think that I?' he seems preposterously offended. 'No, no, Grace, I'm not like one of *them.*' By '*them*', I assume he means the rapists and abusers we deal with every day, and yet here I am, locked in his house, bruises on my cheek, and forced into his bedroom. *Exactly what kind of assumption am I supposed to make?* He points to the bed. 'Sit down.' I hesitate. 'SIT DOWN!'

The bed is a low four poster, dark oak with acorn shaped finials at each corner. It seems oddly old fashioned for Simon, yet the rest of the room is similarly furnished. A dark highboy and chest of drawers, and thick damask curtains that block out the light... the sound too, I imagine. Simon reaches into the bedside table and removes a set of disposable gloves. Then he pulls up a chair and sits opposite.

'What do you know about me, Grace?' I hear the snap of

plastic as he slips on the gloves. 'I mean, really know about me?' His voice is low and even, his face calm. We could be having this conversation over a cup of tea.

Is this a trick question?

I wrack my brain for any hostage related training, but the closest I can get is a 2020 NCA doc on *Prevention Tactics: Kidnapping and Hostage Taking,* I helped Marcus update it a few months ago.

Try to establish a personal relationship with your kidnapper.

'I know that we're friends.'

He sighs in clear disappointment.

'Friends are a liability, Grace.'

I try again.

'I know that you're a dedicated probation officer.'

'Oh please,' he says dismissively, 'and?'

'And that you're from Bristol?'

'Now we're getting somewhere,' he nods, 'where in Bristol?'

'I – I...'

'Do I have any siblings? Have you ever met my parents? Have I ever told you anything about my childhood?'

I stare at him. The truth is I've worked with Simon on and off for nearly fifteen years and know virtually nothing about him.

'I never felt comfortable asking.'

'Exactly how I wanted it.' He pulls his chair a little closer. 'Shall I tell you?' I nod, anything to stall for time. 'When I was twelve,' he begins, 'my father murdered my mother.' He says this as if he is telling me a football score. 'That was after years of abuse of course. It's actually one of the reasons I got into probation.' He takes off his spectacles, and polishes them with the edge of his jumper. 'I really wanted to become a police officer to deal with the bastards firsthand of course, but with my eyesight and all...'

'We can fix this, Simon. If you just–'

'Shut up!' he yells, and I find myself cowering back onto the bed. 'You wanted me to speak, so I am.'

Be reserved, but cooperative.

'I'm sorry. I didn't mean to interrupt.'

For a moment he relaxes.

'Then there were the foster homes,' he continues, 'plenty of them, and not very pleasant, but then just how *does* one deal with a massively fucked-up kid?'

'If you'd only let me help...'

He leans forward, his face nearly touching mine. 'I SAID SHUT UP.' I stay silent, waiting for him to continue. 'It was that sense of helplessness that stayed with me. The anger and absolute self-loathing that maybe I could have done something to stop it, to save her. You know how that feels don't you, Grace, wishing you could have saved someone?'

Of course I do.

'There were a few experiments in retribution when I was younger,' he continues. 'Sorting out a sixth form bully who was knocking his girlfriend about, the neighbour who beat his dog, that sort of thing. Nothing a balaclava and a cricket bat couldn't sort out.' I think of those men on the stairwell the night of the Go Out, of the lost button that proved his guilt. 'Once I went to uni it went pretty quiet,' he continues, 'and then being married kept me on the straight and narrow for a while. After we got divorced though...' He runs his fingers through his hair. 'It started again. That need for vengeance, to see them pay.'

'See who pay?' I whisper.

'Anyone who deserves it.' He laughs. 'I did a few trial runs during my stint with Avon and Somerset Probation Services. Just a bit of GBH on some of the nastier ex-offenders. Nothing a few weeks in hospital wouldn't sort out.' Seeing my shocked expression he scowls. 'Oh, come on, Grace, violent offenders are the worst kind of lowlifes.' I wonder if he's aware just how ironic his words are. 'And the thing is, I got away with it. After all, no one's really interested in finding out who beat the shit out of a serial rapist, are they?' I can't believe I'm hearing this. 'I'm not stupid though. I knew statistically that the longer I did it, the more chance there was of getting caught. What I needed was a bit of distance, the opportunity to regain some measure of self-control, so I requested a transfer back to Devon and Cornwall.' He leans forward, and the chair gives a loud creak. 'And the thing is that it might have worked. I went for months without the need to scratch that itch,' he sighs, 'months. It might even have been permanent if—'

'I can help you,' I whisper, grasping for a tiny chink of light, 'do whatever it takes.'

'You?' he says, in way that confirms he's never really held me in much esteem. 'I doubt it, and anyway it's too late now, especially after what you've told me about the letter.'

I know immediately what he means. I've always wondered if Simon blamed himself for the tragic chain of events that led to the murder of Katie Cross. He was busy that day too, and no matter what Sophie said, he probably didn't have the time to peer check my outgoing post like he was supposed to. Maybe he's always wondered whether, if he'd noticed my mistake, he might have been able to stop it.

'I don't blame you for not spotting that fact that I got the letters mixed up, Simon.' If nothing else, at least I can finally admit the truth. 'It's my fault that I sent Anton Cross the letter with Sally and Katie's address on it.'

His horrified look says more than any words could.

Maybe I deserve all this.

'Oh, Grace,' he whispers. 'If only that were the case.'

I stare at him in confusion. 'What are you talking about?'

He runs his fingertip across his upper lip, wiping away the thin film of perspiration that has settled there.

'I really, *really* wanted to be Senior Probation Officer. I wanted it *so* much. With access to all that secure data, and like-minded people on my side, I just knew I could do my best work. Really make a difference when it came to justice.' His eyes meet mine. 'But everyone knew you were guaranteed the role.'

I can't figure out where he's going with this.

'I don't think that was really the case, Simon, and anyway, what does that have to do with—'

'For fuck's sake, Grace!' he yells. 'I did it! I switched the letters!' His voice deepens. 'I knew that Anton Cross was a serial moaner who complained to every poor bastard who would listen about how unfairly he had been treated, how the system was skewed against fathers, how he had a right to see his daughter, blah, blah, blah. I thought if I switched the letters, if he got a mistakenly sent copy of a confidential child protection report with your recommendation for discontinuing supervised visits, he would make a complaint to the Senior PO, Regional Director, Director General, and maybe even go to the press.'

Everything I have ever known to be true has exploded, and all that is left is an actual truth so horrifying that it is almost unspeakable.

'And with our franking mark and my handwriting on the envelope,' my voice sounds shaky, but I carry on, 'I would get the blame, probably be given a disciplinary, maybe a suspension, and then be out of the picture for the promotion.'

'I never thought he would kill her.' Simon looks away. 'I mean, I know he had a history of domestic violence, but I never for a moment thought that he would kill his own daughter.' I think he may be crying, but I don't care.

React appropriately and proportionately.

'You fucking murdering bastard!' Spittle flies from my lips. 'You deliberately switched those letters for a job promotion?!'

'I didn't mean for it to happen,' he whines pathetically, 'I didn't!'

'And yet still, a nine-year-old girl was shot and killed in front of her own mother!' I stare at him for what seems like ages, my expression clouded with disgust. 'The murders of Nicky White and Michael Fellows,' I ask, 'did you mean for those to happen?'

'I...'

'Did you kill those men?'

'It was for Katie.'

His words are like a detonator to my barely contained fury.

Refrain from appearing hostile.

'For Katie!' I scream. 'How could you possibly think your acts of unspeakable violence and cruelty are in any way a tribute to that poor little girl?'

'Not a tribute,' he says, 'retribution.'

Now I truly know that I am dealing with a madman.

'You're out of your fucking mind!' I scream. 'You think killing more people will make up for what you did?' *I have to get out of here, to get help.* 'Nothing will ever make up for what you did! Your foolish, thoughtless, selfish actions caused an innocent child to die, and your attempts at justifying it are psychopathic.' He slumps forward slightly, and I realise that it's now or never. I jump up and push against his shoulders with all my might. His chair tips backwards and he crashes to the floor, echoing what happened between me and Billy just days before. *I only have seconds.*

Only try to escape if you are certain of your success.

'Help!' I scream, as I stumble past him towards the door. It's dark now, and even though it's only a few metres to the landing, the room feels like a labyrinth. I pull open the bedroom door for my final sprint, down the stairs and along the hallway to the open French doors. I charge forward, hit something hard and find myself stumbling backwards. Even though it's nearly pitch black I recognise the figure standing on the landing immediately.

'*Billy.*' My voice is barely a whisper. '*Help me.*' He steps into the light and looks at me in surprise, or is it loathing? I move to push past him, but the shock of seeing him standing there, blocking my escape has dulled my senses and slowed me down. I feel sedated. *Did Simon put something in my whisky?* Before I can decide what to do next, I feel myself being grabbed from behind and dragged back into the bedroom.

'No!' I scream. 'NO!'

'Stupid bitch!' Simon throws me onto the bed. My temple smashes against the wooden headboard, and the world around me begins to spin. *Stay conscious, Grace, stay conscious.* I hear a soft click, and the bedside light glows into life. I force my muddled brain to think, and try and reach for the glass paperweight on the bedside table. A hand grabs mine, and I cry out as Simon squeezes my fingers, forcing me to loosen my grip. It thuds to the floor. 'Have you got the tights?' I hear him mutter. There's some sort of exchange between the two men, and then one at a time Simon raises an arm above my head and wraps pairs of tights around each wrist, securing them to the bedposts. He does the same to my feet.

'Simon – please – no!' I struggle against the ligatures, but the knots only seem to grow tighter. 'You don't have to do this.

You can stop this right now.' I look to the figure standing in the doorway. 'Billy, do something!'

Simon begins to chuckle.

'Oh, he's going to do something all right.'

I think about Nicky White being dumped in the water, of the condoms shoved in Michael's mouth.

'Is that what you do, Billy? Finish them off?' My challenge is met with silence. 'And the vigilante group? Were you a part of that too, working with Ingrid to source Simon's next victims for him?'

'Ingrid is an amateur,' sniffs Simon. 'Offered me some leads – people of interest that she and Tim had counselled, or who had been attending meetings at the church. She put me onto Billy of course, which has been useful, but she doesn't really have what it takes to go all the way.'

'By "all the way" you mean murdering Nicky White and Michael Fellows.' I know I'm doing the hostage protocols all back to front, but I don't care. 'Did you murder them, Simon?'

He takes a deep breath.

'It's like I said, Grace. It's all about justice. Justice and revenge.'

Billy moves in closer, takes off his baseball cap, and rests it on the back of Simon's chair. 'What the fuck is going on here?'

'An unexpected but pleasant surprise,' Simon replies. 'It was only a matter of time before she discovered the truth anyway.' He leans in very close. 'A little Miss Marple, aren't we, Grace?'

'Don't do this, Simon,' I plead. 'I'll keep your secret. I promise.' That last desperate plea only makes him laugh. Brain whirring, I try another tack. 'Think about what this will do to Jodie.'

Next to him, I see Billy flinch.

'Maybe you should have thought about Jodie before sticking your nose in,' Simon hisses, 'before using my login for VISOR, then your ex-husband's to break into the PNC, before poking around Justice South.' Seeing the surprised look on my face, he begins to laugh. 'I checked the CCTV, Grace.'

'I just wanted the truth!'

'The truth is a burden nobody wants to bear,' Simon huffs. 'Think about that letter in Alex's bedroom, about Ingrid,' he glances at Billy, 'the fact that this guy has been fucking your underage daughter for weeks now.'

'I haven't been fucking her!' yells Billy. Simon jumps up to face him, and there is a feeling of imminent confrontation. I see a chink.

'What about these, Billy?' I tug at the bindings securing me to the bed. 'Do you think it's an accident that Simon used tights to tie me to the bed, the exact same modus you used when you attacked Nicole? That he got you to provide them?'

Billy's eyes flash in understanding. He turns to Simon.

'Are you setting me up?'

I tug at my restraints again.

'There's probably enough DNA on these already to convict you.' Billy's posture changes, and I begin to hope that I may stand a chance. 'Did you know that it's his fault Katie Cross was murdered, that he made sure her father had access to her safehouse address so that he was able to find and murder her?' The air around us seems to thicken. 'She lived only a few streets away from where your ex and daughter live right now.'

'I think I told you to shut up!' Simon clamps his hand over my nose and mouth. I writhe and twist, trying everything within my power to free myself from his grasp. It's not long before my efforts exhaust me. My lungs are screaming, lights sparkle. 'Sorry, Grace,' he whispers, 'but you're not going to make it this time. Your poor little daughter is just going to have to live without you.' He turns to Billy. 'Did you bring the plastic sheeting?'

I close my eyes and think of Jodie, her dimpled cheeks, of Alex on our wedding night, Bismarck's chin on my lap, lying in Marcus' arms, Betty's words to that poor girl in the alleyway, *"You are loved."* Tears streak my cheeks and settle in the recesses of my ears.

33

I hear a loud thud, and the suffocating hand slips from my face. I desperately gulp in mouthfuls of air and force my leaden eyelids to open. Billy is standing by the bed, the glass paperweight in his hand. Slumped on the floor next to him is Simon. It takes a moment for my heart rate to steady before I can speak.

'Is he dead?'

Billy places the paperweight back on the bedside table. Its glass exterior is stained with blood.

'I hope so.'

For a moment there is silence. I return to the beginning of the kidnapping document in my head.

Try to establish a personal relationship with your kidnapper.

'Did Simon coerce you into all this, Billy?'

'Did the devil make me do it?' He laughs. In the dim light his pupils are huge dark spheres. *Is he high?* 'Depends on what you mean by coerced,' he replies. 'It was Ingrid who first put me onto the Facebook group, and to Simon. Said he could do with someone with my level of commitment.'

'Commitment, what commitment?'

Billy gives a slow, wide grin.

'The commitment to protecting other women from people just like me.'

Billy's reply, like so much of his overall thinking, is horribly, horribly skewed.

Don't make any provoking statements that could aggravate your kidnapper.

'So, you killed them?'

'I never killed nobody!'

'But you beat them up? Nicky, Michael, Darren, and Robert?'

'Just meeting my obligations.' He pulls something out of his pocket. At first, I can't make out what it is, but the glint of light on metal soon reveals its secret. My pocketknife.

'It was *you* with Simon on the stairwell that night.'

'My normal partner wasn't available, so Simon stepped in. The little pussy normally doesn't like to get his hands dirty... until the very end of course.'

'You knew.' I'm finding it hard to form the words. 'You knew he was killing them.'

'Didn't at first,' says Billy matter of factly, 'but after the second one–'

'Michael,' I whisper. 'Michael Fellows.'

Billy shrugs. 'Whatever. It was just bad luck you showed up on the stairwell that night. Lucky you got away as lightly as you did.'

I watch as he slips opens the knife, the curved swayback design making it look like a wave. 'If only you didn't have to poke your nose into everyone's business things might have been different, but hey, I guess you were only doing your thing.'

Being my authentic self?

He rests the tip of the blade against my jugular. 'I could cut you right now, Grace. It would be over in a second. You wouldn't feel a thing.'

Fear is normal. Try to gain control of it as soon as possible.

'But you won't.'

He runs his forefinger and thumb along his chin.

'What makes you think that?'

I know I don't have many more chances, so I'd better get this right.

Show your offender you're a human being with a family and worries of your own.

'Wouldn't killing a helpless woman go against your commitment?' There's a

moment of pregnant silence as Billy considers this contradiction. He withdraws the blade a few centimetres. 'And wouldn't killing me break Jodie's heart?' I can feel the uncertainty coming off him in waves. 'Please, Billy, don't do this.'

His expression is impenetrable as granite. 'I'm not a good person, Grace.'

'You must be,' I whisper, 'or Jodie wouldn't care about you so much.'

34

I'm tied to the bed with a dead man at my feet, his killer at my side, and the sharp, cool edge of a knife blade against my neck.

'I was beginning to have a life again,' says Billy, 'before all this... a future!'

'I'm a part of that future, Billy. I can help you. If you only just–'

'Yeah right,' he snaps. 'A future where you report me to the police, give evidence, and show up at my sentencing to recommend no option for parole. That would keep me away from Jodie for a long time, wouldn't it?'

Do not make any statements that can be proven wrong.

'I won't.' I reply vehemently. 'Just untie me, and I'll let you go.'

'Let *me* go!' he says in amusement.

The truth is he's absolutely right. If Billy Vale frees me now, the first thing I will do is call the police and do everything I can to make sure he is incarcerated for a very long time. But that's for later. *All that matters now is getting out of here alive.*

'There's a spare back door key under a terracotta plant pot in my back garden. Car keys are hanging on a hook by the front door, the Citroen is parked right outside.' I try not to sound as desperate as I feel. 'My purse is on the kitchen table. There's fifty quid inside, and my bank card. The PIN code is Jodie's birthday.'

'That desperate to get rid of me, Grace?' he snarls. 'And where exactly will I go? Once you've spilled? The police, NCA and even Interpol will be after me.' Simon has clearly told Billy about Marcus' visit to probation services. *Is that how he knew to escape the NCA surveillance team and get here?* 'But if there are no witnesses.'

Do not challenge the offender.

I glance at the paperweight, then to his baseball cap, which must have fallen to the floor when he hit Simon. 'There'll be plenty of forensic evidence to connect you to the scene no matter what you do.'

'Not if it all goes up in flames.' He glances around the bedroom. 'Those curtains should spark up a treat.'

From somewhere nearby I hear the low hum of a mobile phone. Billy reaches into his jacket pocket and takes out a cheap pay as you go model. A name illuminates the screen.

Jodie.

'Fuck!'

'Please, Billy, let me go.'

He begins pacing the floor beside me, stepping over Simon's prostrate body, light glinting off the knife blade.

'I bloody hate you, Grace!' he yells, 'with your self-righteous saviour complex, and your never letting things go.' His face is tortured, tormented. 'I couldn't give a shit about whether you live or die,' he continues, 'but Jodie...'

His phone rings again.

'Answer it, Billy.' He shakes his head. 'If you do this to her, you'll have to live with it for the rest of your life.' I choke back a sob. 'It will destroy her.'

Billy steps forward, so close that I can smell his sweat. He presses the knife against my chest, the tip cutting through my T-shirt and piercing my flesh.

I'm out of time, aren't I?

I hear him sigh, and suddenly the blade is withdrawn. I turn to see Billy placing the mobile phone on the table. He presses the sole contact number and then the hands-free button. The phone begins to ring.

'Billy?'

'Jodie!' I cry. 'Is that you?'

'Mum?' My daughter sounds confused, frightened, and unsure.

'I'm in trouble, Jodie,' such is my relief at hearing her voice I can barely speak. 'I need your help.'

'What kind of trouble? Where's Billy?'

'I'm here, Jode.'

'Billy? What's going on?'

'You need to call the police, Jodie,' he says calmly, 'tell them to come to 44 Trellice Way. Tell them the French doors at the back are open.'

'What, why?'

'Just do what I say.'

'What have you done to my mum?!'

Billy folds the knife blade back into its spine and lays it on the bed beside me.

'Nothing.'

35

By the time the police arrive, Billy is long gone. There are flashing lights on the bedroom ceiling, and footsteps on the stairs. They check Simon– he's alive, just – and cut me free, looks of shock and pity on their faces. I tell them that Billy might have taken my car and my bank card. I tell them all about Simon. They hurry about making radio calls, bringing in reinforcements. The paramedics arrive, check my neck, my chest. They work on Simon, their voices low and serious. It all seems to be happening in slow motion. I am numb. Somewhere in the distance I can hear Jodie screaming, 'I want to see my mum!' Alex arrives, takes me in his arms, and holds me until I stop shaking. He leads me downstairs towards a waiting ambulance.

'*Mum!*' Jodie breaks free from a female officer, and runs towards me, into my arms.

I made it. I bloody well made it!

It's only then that I begin to cry.

I'm sitting in the back of an ambulance in paper overalls, with a foil blanket wrapped around my shoulders, watching as the suited and booted crime scene investigators make their way into Simon's house. They've already taken scrapings from under my fingernails, placed my clothing into evidence bags, and photographed my injuries, the ligature marks around my wrists, cut to my throat, and a small puncture wound above my left breast. The paramedics have blue lighted Simon to Derriford Hospital, a PC in tow, and my father has arrived to take Jodie home. There have been no sightings of Billy Vale.

'Grace.' Alex steps into the ambulance and sits down next to me.

'How's Jodie?'

'She's pretty shaken up, but your dad's looking after her.'

'You should go to her.'

'In a bit.' He takes my hand. 'How are you holding up?'

It takes a moment for me to answer. 'I haven't got a clue.'

'They've taken Ingrid in for questioning,' he says, 'but there's no sign of Billy. Your car and purse are still at home,' he shakes his head in disbelief, 'the key still under the plant pot.'

None of that surprises me.

'I'd like you both to stay at mine tonight,' he says, 'and before you ask, yes, we can sneak the dog in.' I don't reply. 'Speak to me, Grace.'

I've been dreading this moment. Seeing Alex's face as he came into the bedroom, the way he held me until the ambulance arrived, then talked me through the forensic examination. How he reassured Jodie. *I so want him to be the good guy.*

'I broke into your flat.'

'What?'

'I thought you were involved with Justice South, so I stole Jodie's keys and broke into your flat on Thursday.' I can't tell if

Alex is furious or distraught. 'I found the envelope you had hidden in your wardrobe.'

He gives a deep exhalation. 'Christ.'

'Why, Alex?'

He glances at me, then away.

'I was one of the first detectives on the scene at Anton's bedsit after Katie's murder.'

'And you found the envelope with the franking mark and my handwriting, and thought that I had sent it?' He nods. 'So, you tampered with evidence to protect me?' He nods again. 'Do you know how messed up that is?'

'You're a good person, Grace, a good PO. I just couldn't bear the thought of you torturing yourself because of some stupid error.'

'It was a little more than that.'

I tell him about Simon's confession, about how he deliberately swapped the envelopes in order to discredit me.

'Jesus.' He stares down at his clenched fists. 'I hope the bastard never wakes up.'

'Me too,' I reply with not a hint of guilt, but wonder where that leaves us now, *two supposedly dedicated professionals with decidedly unprofessional conduct?*

Police, forensic teams, and ambulance crews move around us, doing their jobs to faultlessly high standards, while Alex and I sit huddled together ruminating over our sins.

'Do you know?' I say, finally. 'Maybe it would be better if Jodie and I stayed with my dad for a few days. He's got plenty of space, and I wouldn't want you to get in trouble over the dog.'

I see the forlorn look on Alex's face.

'That's probably a good idea,' he says, his voice laced with sadness, 'I mean with the dog and all.'

'It's just all so... complicated.' I suddenly think of Ingrid's words from only hours before, *Secrets never die, Grace; they only live on to consume us.* I could easily allow myself to plummet into the abyss of anger that engulfed Simon, or the torrent of resentment that twisted Ingrid into the damaged person she became. Instead, I reach across, grip Alex's hand, and interlink my fingers through his.

'But you'll visit?'

His despondent expression eases into a smile.

'Only if you want me to.'

'I do,' I reply, and then let my head fall gently onto his shoulder.

THE END

ACKNOWLEDGEMENTS

Originally written as part of my Crime Writing MA at The University of East Anglia, this novel has taken on many iterations and experienced many redrafts. As ever, the real writing is in the rewriting, and I owe grateful thanks to so many writers, readers, editors, experts, family, and friends who supported me in the process of bringing *Vengeance Street* to life.

Firstly my family, husband Nick, children Danielle and Dominic, and mother-in-law Ce.

Also thanks to friends who offered sound advice, gentle guidance, or even just listened: Finn Clarke, Rob Jones, Caroline Maston, Denise Beardon, Judi Daykin, Wendy Turbin, Antony Dunford, Karen Taylor, Natalie Marlowe, Sue Ferry, Ann Pelletier-Topping, Teresa Gray, Amanda Lees, Tessa Webb, David and Valerie Horspool.

To my wonderful colleagues at Arts University Plymouth, Emily Watkins, Jenny Evans, Jonah Gardner, Karen Clark, Rachel Gipetti, Donna Gundry, Adam Levi, Leesa Westlake, Kelly Hewings, Tima Metcalf, and Professor Paul Fieldsend-Danks, and to Gabriel Van Ingen, Jon Blyth, Sam Rowe and Phil Trenerry for your input on the book cover, for which my fabulous publisher Bloodhound Books gave me so much freedom to make design suggestions.

To the experts, Tony Shaw, Charlotte Davies, and Lorna Markille, and to the wonderful team at Bloodhound Books, Betsy Reavley, Fred Freeman, Tara Lyons, and Lexi Curtis.

Last but not least, to my agent Lisa Moylett at CMM and her brilliant team, Zoe Apostolides, and Elena Langtry.

ABOUT THE AUTHOR

Originally from Montreal, Louise moved to the UK after falling in love with a British sailor.

She began her career writing short fiction, and in 2010 won the *Woman & Home Magazine* Short Story Competition. Her entry, *Black Rock,* was subsequently published as part of an anthology, *The Best Little Book Club in Town* (Orion 2011), alongside writers such as Ruth Rendell, Jodi Picoult and Lee Child. In 2019 she won *The Big Issue's* Crime Writing Competition and her psychological thrillers, *The Lake,* and *My Husband's Secrets,* were published by Avon Books (2020/2022).

Her current novel, *Vengeance Street,* the first in a series, delves into the world of the criminal justice system through the eyes of feisty probation officer Grace Midwinter. Louise's background working with people who have experienced homelessness, addiction, and mental health issues, gives her work a strong humanitarian and social justice theme. Above all, Louise wants to tell a story that is entertaining, thought provoking and well written.

A NOTE FROM THE PUBLISHER

Thank you for reading this book. If you enjoyed it please do consider leaving a review on Amazon to help others find it too.

We hate typos. All of our books have been rigorously edited and proofread, but sometimes mistakes do slip through. If you have spotted a typo, please do let us know and we can get it amended within hours.

info@bloodhoundbooks.com

Printed in Great Britain
by Amazon

43945594R00162